THE WRONG KIND

by
Austin S. Camacho

Copyright December 2019

ISBN: Paperback: 978-1940758978
ISBN: EPUB: 978-1940758985
ISBN: MOBI: 978-1733779302

Cover Design: GinnefineArt

Published by:
Intrigue Publishing, LLC
10200 Twisted Stalk Ct
Upper Marlboro, MD 20772

THE WRONG KIND

Chapter 1

Sunday

"Everyone deserves a safe place to stay."
Sophia remembered him saying that soon after he arrived, just before 9pm. He seemed like such a nice fellow, a gentle soul. He called himself a troubleshooter, so she thought he might be the man who could help her. And since she couldn't sleep, she thought she would just try to chat with him a bit.

As she eased the front door open he sprang from his chair out on the front porch. He was so handsome, thin and wiry, in his black suit, white shirt and tie. And he wore black driving gloves, even though it was still warm out. He reminded her of that Morgan fellow on the television show Criminal Minds. And now, without his sunglasses on she could see by the porch light that his eyes were blue, or maybe hazel. Unusual, she thought, a black man with hazel eyes.

"Mrs. Blanco! What are you doing up at this hour? It's after midnight."

"I just couldn't sleep, Mr. Jones," she replied, extending a steaming mug toward him like an offering. "And I remembered you work such a long shift. Not everyone volunteers for twenty-four hours at a time. If you're going to be out here all night I thought you might like a cup of coffee."

"That's very thoughtful, ma'am," he said, accepting the mug and inhaling its rich aroma. "And please, call me Hannibal."

"All right," Sophia said. It was a warm night for September, and she was comfortable in her long cotton bathrobe and mule slippers. "Would you mind if I sat with you for a while? The shelter is wonderful, But even after living here for six long months it still isn't home. Sometimes it can feel a little close."

"Happy to have the company," Hannibal said, pulling another wicker chair up beside his own. The wooden porch seemed like it didn't belong, as if it were stuck onto the front of this tall brick building just to try to make it look more like a home. He sat, sipped the coffee, and gave her a warm smile. "Thank you, this is great. So...Puerto Rico, am I right? You have the slightest bit of an accent."

Sophia blushed. If only he was a few years older. "You have a good ear, Mr., er, Hannibal."

"My girlfriend is from there, and her father's accent is stronger. So it's easy to..." He stopped and turned toward the street. A Ford Explorer rolled to a stop but the lights stayed on. Sophia's pulse quickened and she muttered a short prayer under her breath in Spanish.

"No no no," she said in a shaky voice. "That is not one of the escort vehicles they use. But no one is supposed to know where we are. No one is supposed to know what this place is."

"Stay calm," Hannibal said, tugging the edge of his gloves to tighten them on his hands. "I'll take care of it."

There were four men in the car but only one got out and started stalking toward the building. He was short but thick with a big barrel chest and the arms of a dock worker. His golf team shirt said "Chico" and anger clouded his face. When his heavy work boots hit the first porch step Hannibal rose and stepped in front of the door. He looked relaxed, neither smiling nor frowning.

"Can I help you?"

"Get out of my way," Chico growled, puffing up his barrel chest. "My wife's in there and I'm bringing her home. Can't believe she made me chase her all the way down to this God-forsaken place."

Hannibal smiled, but didn't move. "Trust me, God has not forsaken Hughesville. I don't know how you found this place but I don't think you understand what it is. The whole point of the Angel's Watch Shelter is to provide a place for women and children to get away from, you know, abusive assholes like you."

Chico balled his fists and squared his shoulders in the way that Sophia had seen so many times before. It was another way of saying get out of my way. "No, YOU don't understand. It took me damned near a month to find this place. And if you the fucking security, I'll go right the fuck through you."

Sophia was struck by the contrast, the menacing brute on one side, the picture of tranquility on the other. Hannibal held his hands low and open, but his tone was a little sharper this time when he spoke.

"Look, first of all, I'm not some rent-a-cop here to make a few extra bucks. I volunteer out here because these ladies deserve some peace. And the door's locked so you can't get in anyway. But after driving an hour to get down here from DC, I'm not about to let you disturb the residents by pounding on this door in the middle of the night."

"Think so, huh?" Chico turned and pointed to his car, waving his friends in. Sophia's breath caught in her throat when she saw Chico's outstretched hand curl into a fist. He was going to sucker punch Hannibal. She saw him spin, swinging his big right fist toward Hannibal's nose.

Hannibal easily side-stepped the punch and slammed his right into Chico's gut, doubling him over and backing him down the porch steps.

"There's a reason they protect the location and identities of the residents here," Hannibal said. "You must know we're going to protect their safety just as well. Last chance. Go home before somebody gets hurt."

"Bite me," Chico said.

A harvest moon watched Hannibal swing an uppercut that put Chico on his back. The three newcomers reached him, and helped him to his feet. Hannibal smiled and settled into a ready stance, fists raised the way Sophia had seen professional boxers do. The four men in the driveway, all wearing golf team shirts stood shoulder to shoulder and slowly stepped forward.

If the men brushed Hannibal aside this Chico could burst into the shelter, find his wife, and drag her out of there. Sophia knew she should run inside and raise the alarm but fear locked her in place.

As Chico's foot hit the first step he noticed Sophia for the first time. Just as his eyes met hers, Hannibal's right foot thumped into Chico's chest, slamming him back into the man whose jacket said he was Dave. Then Hannibal leaped from the porch, smashing his right fist across Billy's jaw. A side stamp dislocated Jimmy's right knee. Dave swung past Chico and clipped Hannibal's cheek. Sophia gasped at the flesh-on-flesh sound of the blow.

Hannibal blocked the follow-up punch and snapped two crisp jabs into Dave's face, staggering him into the tree growing up out of the sidewalk. Chico tried to slip past Hannibal, still driving for the door.

"Not tonight," Hannibal said through clenched teeth. Sophia didn't think Chico ever even saw the three punches, left-left-right that put him on his back, barely conscious.

With no standing attackers, Hannibal stepped back up onto the porch. "That was fun, but now I'm running out of patience with you boys." Hannibal reached inside his suit coat, under his right arm, and pulled out a pistol. He pointed its muzzle down at Chico's face.

"There is nothing lower than a man who beats his woman, although anybody helping him is mighty close. I'd beat your asses some more, just for fun, but I don't feel like answering questions at a hospital. Now, all y'all, drag your sorry asses out of here. And if I ever hear you came back here, or if you tell anybody where this shelter is, I will hunt you down and end you."

Chapter 2

For women and children facing domestic violence or homelessness, Angel's Watch Shelter in Charles County, Maryland, represents a safe haven and new beginnings. It's been that way in southern Maryland for many years. The 52-bed dormitory facility, outfitted with mobile home furniture and donated appliances, is neither luxurious nor expansive, but to its temporary residents like Sophia Blanco it is the difference between living out of a shopping cart and hanging onto a bit of dignity.

Hannibal Jones reminded himself of all that sitting in the visitor's lounge while Sophia Blanco fussed over him. She had prepared the ice pack he held against his cheek and the fresh coffee in front of him. The red plastic sofa and mismatched chairs told one story. The freshly painted cream-colored walls and scrupulously clean tile floor told another. The room smelled of baby powder and cheap perfume but in the silence of the wee hours it was a surprisingly comforting atmosphere.

"You volunteer to protect us," Sophia was saying. "I see you here at least one night every couple of weeks. And you are always polite to the girls, even the younger ones. You never try to get too close to them, even though I know how some of them look at you."

Hannibal smiled, then winced. "These girls are vulnerable. It wouldn't be right. Besides, I have a very fine lady already."

"So, what do you get out of doing this?"

"Volunteering is…" Hannibal paused to gather his thoughts. "This is how I give back. Some people give money or donate supplies. I share my time and my skills because they're needed here more than a few more dollars. I let my lady take care of the material stuff."

Hannibal flashed back to the day he first found the Angel's Watch shelter. Cindy Santiago had heard about the place from a business law client who supported the place. She decided to clean out her closet and donate the still like-new items to the shelter. When she finished sorting she had a trunkful to give, but no car. She could have used, of course, but how much better to fill the trunk of Hannibal's Volvo with her giveaway wardrobe. He called his 850 GLT Black Beauty. His car was his companion and part time office, not a pickup truck. But just as Hannibal steered the car with comfortable ease, Cindy steered Hannibal with little effort.

Then she'd made him stop at a drug store so she could fill his back seat with makeup, hair products and a collection of fragrances

"These women are down and out," Hannibal had said. "I'm sure there's stuff they need more than perfume and expensive shampoo."

Cindy just shook her head. "Shows what you know about women," she said. "I've been broke and I can tell you, this is the stuff that makes you feel whole, that makes you feel like you're worth something. The stuff you can't afford when you're buying diapers and nylons."

She was right, of course. They were welcomed with open arms and broad smiles when they arrived at the shelter. Cindy was everybody's best friend and it didn't take Hannibal long to realize this was where he needed to be helping out. They had a hard time finding guys who would serve as unpaid security, so he signed up.

Lost in that memory, Hannibal almost didn't notice that Sophia had slipped away. But he heard the shuffle of her mule slippers when she returned clutching a round cookie tin. She settled into her chair but kept the tin on her lap.

"You are a detective, right?" she asked after a short pause. "People hire you to find things?"

"Sometimes. Have you lost something, Mrs. Blanco?"

She nodded. "I've lost everything. All I have left, Mr. Hannibal, since my Robert's heart gave out and he passed away. My daughter, Concepcion. She is missing."

"Missing," he repeated, sipping his coffee and leaning back. "How old is your daughter?"

"She turned twenty-one last month." Sophia said. "I sent a birthday card. She had sent me a card for my birthday in June but when I sent her card...well, she never answered it. And I haven't heard from her. This card was the last I heard of her."

Sophia's speech became breathless as she spoke, her throat tightening. Hannibal didn't know if she was getting closer to tears but he could see the wrinkles deepening on her face and her lower lip started to quiver. She looked as if worry was pressing down on her and trying to drag her under like a coastal riptide. She popped the top off the tin and Hannibal saw it was not filled with cookies but instead it held layers of paper and a sewing kit. A young woman's photo lay on the top. Sophia lifted it, kissed it, and laid it on the table.

The picture held Hannibal's gaze. It was a younger version of Sophia, thinner, with hair streaked a variety of shades from blonde to auburn. He resisted picking it up. That would be like someone bringing a puppy to your door. If they get you to hold it, you know you're going to keep it. Instead he asked to see the card. Sophia smiled as she held it up for his inspection.

"She was always so considerate. And I was so proud when she got that job."

"She was working?" Hannibal asked. He slid the card out of its plain white envelope. The card bore a generic picture of painted flowers. Inside in a feminine script it said, "Happy birthday, Mama. I love you. Connie."

"Oh, yes! She was accepted to be a life guard down in Virginia Beach. She looked so sweet in that little red swimsuit I got her. When she wrote in July she said she loved it down there."

"I'm sure she does," Hannibal said. "Of course, it's pretty quiet down there off season." Which might have explained why the postcard was postmarked from Washington DC. "She signed the card Connie. Is that what she goes by?"

"I gave my girl a beautiful Spanish name," Sophia said. "Her father was not Spanish but he loved it too. But since Middle School she has wanted to be called Connie."

"And did you say your birthday was in June?"

"Yes," Sophia was looking down, intent on removing things from her tin. Or avoiding Hannibal's eyes. "It has been two months and four days since I heard from my baby. I worry, Mr. Hannibal. She is so young and so all alone."

"Yes ma'am. She is also a grown woman, and she has the right to go wherever…" Hannibal let his voice peter out because it was clear Sophia was not listening. She was very carefully laying bills out on the table. They had been pressed flat in the tin and while they were clearly old, well-used bills, they looked almost as if they had been ironed. There were six 20-dollar bills, stacked in such a way that it was easy to see their number. A separate stack held four 10-dollar bills and seven 5-dollar bills. When they were in place Sophia sat quietly staring at them for just a moment, as if saying goodbye. When she looked up her face seemed to expose her broken heart.

"Mr. Hannibal, will you find her for me? I don't mean for you to bring her home, or make her do anything. I just want to know she's safe and well. It is a dangerous world out there and I could not really prepare her for…"

Hannibal held his palm toward her. "Ma'am, you don't have to…"

"You work by the hour, yes?" Sophia asked. "That's the way it always works in the detective novels. How much time can you give me for this? It is all I have right now, but I can get more."

He could have been thinking about the actual value of his time. Sophia's entire fortune would barely cover a couple hours at his usual rate. Or, he could have been thinking about this nice woman whose world had crashed and his likely ability to pull it together for her in a couple of days by tracking down her daughter and telling her to call home. Or he might have focused on his ego, how it would make him a hero in the eyes of this woman and her friends if he did her this favor. But actually, his only thought in the moment was: what would Cindy Santiago say if he told this poor woman "no"?

"This may not even be an investigation, right?" Hannibal asked, offering a smile. "Maybe she's just too caught up in her own life to call her mama. That happens with young people sometimes. Do you have her last address?"

"Of course!" Sophia rummaged through her tin, triumphantly pulled out a slip of paper and placed it on top of her bills. "If you could just get her to call the shelter…" Her smile was a nice act, but he could see the worry in her eyes.

He laid his hand gently on top of the bills and looked into her deep brown eyes. "Ma'am, why don't you hold onto this for now? I'll see what I can find out in the next couple of days. I can't promise anything, of course, but if I do get her to call you, we can discuss my fee then, okay?"

Chapter 3

Monday

Virginia Beach in August is a bustling metropolis, a city so steeply tilted toward the Atlantic Ocean that it causes waves of barely-dressed sun worshippers to roll down its streets, across the blazing sand and into the rumbling surf. Hotels, restaurants and gift shops, three-blocks deep, are packed with loud, laughing vacationers who appear to wake up partying and continue until the next sunrise.

Driving into the city in mid-September, Hannibal could almost hear the whistled theme from "A Fistful of Dollars" and he half expected to see a tumbleweed roll across the street in front of him. Without the crowds it was too easy to see how the salt breeze wore the paint off walls and corroded fences and lamp posts.

After a bit more than four hours on the road Hannibal was happy to find himself on a series of one-way streets with almost no traffic to deal with. Finally he came to a set of two-story buildings, long rows of apartments called Shea Plaza. He parked in front of the rental office, stepped out of the black Volvo and looked around, absorbing the environment. The buildings wore brick on the first level, beige aluminum siding on the top. Grass was mown, hedges neatly trimmed. Children played on the simple jungle gym that stood in for an actual playground.

Hannibal judged it a quiet, wholesome place with a family feel. People here were blue collar, minimum wage families trying to keep it together and climb that ladder. They would weed out drug dealers and loud drinkers. A low-

11

income party girl wouldn't be welcome. A dull woman wouldn't choose this. A defeated girl of low self-esteem wouldn't be here unless she was living with, and on, a man. But it looked like a good place for a smart young lady to hide, reinvent herself, and plan her next move.

Hannibal started every case hoping that this time he would get lucky. He held onto that hope as he walked into the office. Maybe it would be this easy. He showed the woman behind the counter his credentials and explained his mission. Yes, they did have a record of a Concepción Babcock. She was able to tell him her apartment number and the date she moved out almost three months prior. She confirmed that Ms. Babcock was a quiet tenant, never caused trouble and always paid on time. However, she did not leave a forwarding address and no one had co-signed on the lease.

It was a hope, but Hannibal knew he had no right to expect it be that easy. He thanked the woman and left her his card in case for some reason Connie made contact. Outside he wandered among the buildings for a while until he figured out the system, then strolled over to the apartment that had been Connie's. Standing at the door gave him an easy line of sight to the nearest play area. It was a square, cordoned off by a wooden rail and covered with wood chips instead of grass. The simple wooden jungle gym included a yellow sliding board. A boy and a girl, both maybe five or six years old, were cycling around it: slide down, race back to the wooden ladder, repeat. The woman watching them wore a mother's proud smile. There were no chairs or benches nearby but she stood comfortably in cheap sneakers. She was thin, in jeans and a fuzzy pullover sweater, auburn hair and lipstick too bright for her coffee complexion.

Hannibal had nothing on which to judge his quarry except a photograph and a card. His read of this girl's smile, and the fact that she shortened her name to something common and very American, was that she was the type that would have wanted to make friends. The playground mom seemed a likely candidate. She didn't jump when Hannibal walked toward her, but her eyes were wary. He stopped six feet away and did not threaten by staring at her. Instead he watched the children.

"They're awfully cute."

She grinned. "Thank you. You're new here?"

"No, just visiting. Was looking for someone, but it looks like I missed her. Connie Babcock. Did you know her?"

"Connie?"

"Pretty Latina, twenty-one years old, hair streaked different colors."

When his companion hesitated Hannibal handed her his card. He noticed no ring on her hand when she took it. A woman alone with children was smart to be cautious. "Her mother sent me," he said. "She's a little worried."

She stared at the card, looked up at him, down at the card and up at him again. "This is you?"

He held out a gloved hand. "Hannibal Jones. Mrs..."

"Sorry. I'm Jennifer." She quickly reached out and shook his fingers. "And you are..."

"Like it says, I'm a troubleshooter. Connie's mom is afraid she might be in trouble."

The boy sprinted across the play area, slamming into Jennifer's legs, momentarily separating the adults further. "Mommy! Mommy!" He clung to her thighs as if momentarily afraid someone else might hold his mother's attention. She stroked his head in reassurance. Hannibal squatted down to be on the boy's eye level.

"Hello, little man. I'm Hannibal."

"Hannibo?" the boy said. "That's a funny name. I'm Brian."

Both adults chuckled and Hannibal asked, "Brian, what's your favorite cereal?"

"Froot Loops!"

"Froot Loops?" Hannibal asked. "Really? That's my favorite too." Then he stood to address Jennifer. "Did you know Connie? I think you were neighbors."

"Actually, we were pretty good friends. I hope she's not in trouble. I hated to see her go. She was always so nice to everyone. I cried the day they loaded her stuff out."

"Did she say where she was going?"

"I asked," Jennifer said, "but she wouldn't tell me. Just kind of dodged the question so I just let it go. Is somebody after her?"

"I don't think so," Hannibal said. "But you said they loaded her stuff out."

"Her boyfriend Danny helped her pack and move," Jennifer said. "Not that he was living there or anything. Nothing like that. But he did stuff for her, and like I said, he helped her move out."

The girl ran over next, capturing her mother's unoccupied leg. Brian told her, "This is Hannibo," and she looked up at him. "I'm Marcie."

"She likes Froot Loops too," Brian said.

"And you are a lovely young lady," he said, eliciting a bright giggle. "So Jennifer, did you happen to catch Danny's last name?"

"Sorry, no." Now she was beginning to look worried.

"It's all right. Any other friends or visitors?"

"Nobody I knew," Jennifer said. She shook the children loose and started to pace while the kids went back to sliding. "Could this have to do with the guy who was stabbed? Is that why she had to go?"

Now it was Hannibal's turn to look worried. "Someone was stabbed? In her apartment?"

"No, no. Danny brought him. I know because Connie came running to my house for bandages and antiseptic. We patched him up and I never asked how he got stabbed. Do you think whoever hurt him might be after Connie? Is that why she moved?"

14

Hannibal wanted to relax her, but the best he could do was "I don't know anything about that, but it could be her mother has reason to be worried. Tell you what, I will try to find out about it, and if I do I'll come back and let you know."

Chapter 4

"You don't just walk in here and say I want to be a lifeguard, you know," Vinnie said, poking a finger way too close to Hannibal's face. "You got to pass the running test, a mile under eight and a half minutes. Then there's the swim test, 500 meters under ten minutes. You got to know CPR and basic first aid. Then comes certification…"

It wasn't hard for Hannibal to find the man who hired Connie Babcock. He sat in a small second story office appointed with a gray metal desk and gray metal filing cabinets. No family pictures on the desk, just papers in disarray. The well-chewed cigar taking a break in its cheap ashtray had already filled the room with a bar room smell. Its owner, Vinnie, had the look of an athlete past his prime. It wasn't the thinning brown hair that gave him away. It was his beachball belly, stretching his golf shirt to its limits, and the arrogant half smile that told anyone entering that this was his domain, his court, and they had better recognize that. One look at Vinnie told Hannibal that he'd have to sit through a certain amount of defensive bluster before he could get down to the facts he came for. He settled into the plastic chair and sat patiently, waiting for Vinnie to run out of steam.

"I'm sure you're quite thorough," Hannibal said when Vinnie stopped for breath. "That's why, when Mrs. Babcock told me her daughter Connie was a lifeguard, I knew you would be able to help me with some of the details of her leaving."

"Well of course she worked for us," Vinnie bellowed. He was a barrel-chested man with huge hands that must have been handy for hauling people out of the ocean some years ago. "BLS is the biggest and oldest beach service in Virginia, with the biggest professional lifeguard staff. We protect more lives than any other beach service. Fifty stands, strategically placed and numbered to ensure maximum safety."

"Of course," Hannibal said, "And you had Connie Babcock serving at one of them. The question is, why did she leave?"

Vinnie paused a moment, as if Hannibal had touched a sensitive nerve. "Yeah, I get to know every one of these kids, and Babcock was one of the best. Driven, determined, you know? But the good ones tend to go. Turnover here is unbelievable."

"Glad you got to know her," Hannibal said. "Did she happen to mention where she was going when she left?"

"Afraid not. You know, she was one for keeping her business to herself. But it hurt when she quit. She and her partner Fox split within a week of each other."

"Partner?"

"Not like that," Vinnie said. "Babcock liked the boys all right. But Evelyn Fox was her, her bestie she called her. I usually had them at the same station on the beach."

Hannibal sighed. "I don't suppose she told you where she was heading when she left."

"Well, no…but I seen Evelyn from time to time." Behind his glasses Hannibal's eyes widened. He took a deep breath. Then, not wanting to signal that this could be valuable information, he responded in a very calm voice. "Really? I wonder if she's still in touch with Ms. Babcock. Where did you see this Evelyn Fox?"

"Sounds like you really want to find Babcock," Vinnie said, rubbing his palms together. "Maybe this lead is worth something to you."

Hannibal rose slowly to his feet, letting his jacket flare open in what would appear to be a careless gesture, so Vinnie could see the Sig Sauer hanging in the holster under his right arm. Then he leaned forward, resting his palms on the desk, and fixed Vinnie with an icy stare.

"It would be worth us keeping this a friendly conversation."

Vinnie pulled back from his desk. "Easy, man. I seen her at one of the local watering holes. She's tending bar down at Casey's Pub."

Casey's turned out to be one of those warm, hole-in-the-wall taverns that Hannibal would call a dive, but in an affectionate way. Like a lot of those places it was bigger inside than it looked from the outside. It had all the normal requirements: jukebox, several television screens, a dart board, a couple of pinball machines, bar top video games and a pool table in the back. What it didn't have was a big crowd inside, so it was quiet for a dive bar.

The mixed aroma of beer and grease told him all he needed to know about what was on the menu. Hannibal slid onto a bar stool. Not much more than a minute passed before the bleached blonde with a lifeguard's body sauntered over and planted her welcoming smile in front of him. This had to be Evelyn.

"What can I get you, hon?" Subtle makeup said she was proud of the features God gave her, and with good reason. She read as confident and relaxed and he immediately liked her.

"What have you got for Scotch?"

She turned to check the shelves. "What do you like?"

"Me, I drink Laphroaig but…"

Her chuckle was musical. "Yeah, that ain't happening. We got a couple colors of Johnny Walker, but you hit the wrong joint for a decent single malt. I'm afraid…wait. There is a bottle of Glenlivet back here."

She spun, displaying her discovery like Vanna White showing today's big prize. "Water? Rocks?"

"Straight up," Hannibal said, "and can I get something to eat?" The girl jerked a thumb at the rack of snacks behind her, something Hannibal didn't think he'd ever seen in a bar before. But chips and candy were not what he was looking for. "Something a little more substantial? Maybe some wings?"

"I can do that," she said, pouring a generous drink. Hannibal nodded thanks and took his glass to a table toward the back. He settled in with his back to the wall, pulled one of his business cards out and dropped it on the table. He spent the next ten minutes watching a local teen artfully hustle a tourist at the pool table.

Hannibal was expecting to be called to the bar when his order was ready, so it was a pleasant surprise to find the girl standing beside him with a plastic foam container overflowing with crisp chicken wings.

"Hope the food's as good as the service," Hannibal said, handing her a credit card. "And I could use another Scotch."

"It's quiet," she said, smiling. "Be right back."

On her trip back to the bar Hannibal registered taut legs and a firm behind that said she still worked out and probably swam every day. He was good at reading people, and her attitude said that this was not her final fate, just a break between real life gigs. Once she was behind the bar again he bit into his first piece of chicken. A little bland, he thought, but at least not dripping with sauce as was the local custom. He hadn't realized how hungry he was until he started. A little pile of bones was already growing on one side of the container when she returned with his drink.

"Thanks. Since it's so quiet tonight, any chance you could sit with me for a minute?" Hannibal saw her hesitation so before it could take root he added, "It's about Connie Babcock," and tapped his business card with a fingertip.

At that Evelyn glanced around, shrugged, and settled into the chair opposite Hannibal. "Connie? What's up with my girl?"

"That's what I'm trying to find out," Hannibal said. Her mom hasn't heard from her in a while. I understand that you two were friends."

"Besties, at least for a while. Then she just…" Evelyn flung her fingers out, turning Connie into a puff of smoke.

Hannibal pushed his plate aside and pulled a small notebook from his inside jacket pocket. "Maybe I can get a lead from someone else. I heard she had a steady boyfriend. Danny…"

"Hernandez," Evelyn said, filling in the blank. "Haven't seen him since Connie disappeared. Figured they might have took off together. Not like her not to tell her mom though. Seemed like they was tight."

"How well did you know Danny?"

Evelyn shrugged. "Not real well. Him and Greg, my ex, was best buds. We kinda double dated a lot, me and Greg, Connie and Danny." Hannibal's pen hovered over his notepad until she got it and said, "Howard. Greg Howard."

Hannibal jotted the name while he rearranged the puzzle pieces in his head. "Best buds," he said under his breath. Then looking up he asked, "So, was it Greg who got stabbed?"

"What? How did you know?"

Hannibal tapped his card. "I'm a detective. And right now I'm wondering if whoever was mad enough at Greg Howard to cut him might also have an issue with Connie."

"Oh no, she had nothing to do with that," Evelyn shaking her head hard enough to make her blond locks fall into her eyes. "That was a drug dealer. Purely Greg's business. Connie would never get mixed up in that stuff."

Hannibal sipped his drink and looked again at this obviously fitness-conscious girl. "You were dating a guy in the drug business?"

"Oh, hell no!" Evelyn fired indignation at Hannibal. "None of us was into that crap. Especially Greg. He was a fitness nut. If this guy hadn't pulled a knife Greg would have destroyed him."

Hannibal raised his palms in surrender. "Okay, okay. So what did Greg do to piss this fellow off so much?"

Evelyn glanced toward the door as a pair of men in biker jackets and boots stepped through the door. "Look, Greg used to be a fighter but now he's a fight promoter. Mixed martial arts. I think these drug guys were trying to get involved in his business and he wasn't having any. That's the deal. All Greg's issue."

She stood, but Hannibal held her forearm. "Greg's issue," he said. "But Danny was Greg's friend."

"Yeah," she said, leaning toward the bar.

"So he might have stepped up to help his friend."

"Well, sure," She took one step away.

"And if Connie was being a good girlfriend and supporting Danny…"

Evelyn looked at the two men now standing at the bar, then at Hannibal, then back at the bar before snatching Hannibal's card off the table.

"Look, I don't want nothing bad happening to my girl. I don't know nothing else, for reals, but if I think of anything at all I'll give you a call, okay?" She turned her smile on her new customers and quick-stepped toward them. But just as she got behind the bar she turned back to Hannibal and mouthed the words, "Find her, would you?"

Chapter 5

A full moon hung above by the time Hannibal pressed the doorbell back at Shea Plaza. Then he took a big step back to make sure the person on the other side of the door could make out his face clearly between the brown paper bags he carried, one in each arm. After a short pause he heard a chain unhooked, a lock bolt turned, and the door squeak open a few inches. Jennifer's face reflected more curiosity than concern.

"You wear them things at night?" she asked.

Hannibal squirmed one hand up to pull his sunglasses off. "May I come in? Just wanted to put these down somewhere."

He saw the slightest flush of embarrassment as she pulled the door wide. Hannibal moved straight to the Formica kitchen table and settled the bags in place. Jennifer stood in a fuzzy slippers and a terrycloth bathrobe that wrapped nearly twice around her slender frame. Her face was scrubbed clean revealing a flawless, creamy complexion. Hannibal guessed bedtime wasn't far off. She stood staring at the bags, probably reluctant to assume anything. He worked to keep the awkward out of his voice.

"Ma'am, you probably want to put this stuff away. I wasn't sure what was best so I went with some basics. Milk, bread, soup, peanut butter and jelly, some cheese, spaghetti and the sauce, and I figured…"

"Froot Loops!" Brian shouted, running into the room just as Hannibal pulled the box from the top of one of the bags.

"Figured I couldn't go wrong with cereal," Hannibal finished. Then he stepped away.

"Well, I…" Jennifer took a deep breath as Marcie joined them. Both kids jumped up and down, evidently celebrating the arrival of their favorite breakfast. Hannibal saw her face color again, but she looked him in the eye to say, "Thank you." Then to her kids, "Almost bed time but before you go in help me take care of this."

The apartment was small enough that Hannibal stood with his back against the door to get out of the way. Jennifer directed the kids to put the dry goods into the cupboard while she loaded the refrigerator. He stayed in place while she told the children to say goodnight to Mr. Jones and get to the bathroom. He saw it all in his mind's eye: teeth being brushed, faces wiped, pajamas pulled on, prayers said, small bodies tucked in with a kiss. Then a pause and he thought it was the sound of hair being brushed.

When she came back into view she stopped at the other end of the room. Her curly auburn locks were very neat, not tousled but businesslike. Her robe was cinched very tight around her waist. Her eyes were cast down, her arms crossed. Then, as if realizing the message of her body language she relaxed her arms so that one hand held her other wrist. Finally she raised her eyes to meet his and pulled a small smile from someplace under her pride.

If you asked Hannibal the most important skill a detective needed, he would say it was the ability to hear what people don't say. Here stood a good woman who loved her children and lived at the very edge of taking care of them the way she thought they deserved. And now a stranger had made all that easier, at least for this week.

"Right now you're wondering what the groceries cost," he said. "So let me be clear. This was a gift with no strings attached. You can say goodnight right now, I walk out this door, and you never see me again. But I'm hoping you'll think about another mother who's worried about her little girl and chat with me for just a few minutes about that girl you described as a pretty good friend."

A deep breath. A second. When the silence became too heavy she said, "Coffee? It's decaf but…"

"That would be nice."

She waved him to a chair while she prepared two cups, then joined him at the table. He sipped, hiding his disappointment. Well, at least it was hot.

"Thank you for the groceries," Jennifer said, daring to look into his eyes again, as if for the first time. "Are they blue?"

"Sometimes. Or green. I guess hazel is the official color."

She wrapped both hands around her cup and sipped slowly. When she looked up he could see he had transitioned from intruder to guest. "I'm not sure I know anything that will help you."

"You might be right," Hannibal said. "But I think you were a good friend to Connie. Very often people are reluctant to discuss a friend's business with someone they don't know too well. So I thought it might be worth five more minutes of talk to see if you remembered anything that might help me find Connie. she may be in danger."

Jennifer's eyes got bigger. "What? Why would Connie be in danger? She was a good girl."

"That rarely keeps people out of danger. And it looks like one of her friends got on the wrong side of some bad people. This guy that got stabbed, looks like he was a wrestler and he got on the wrong side of some gangsters."

Hannibal stopped because Jennifer's eyes went up and rolled to the side, as if she was trying to remember something.

"Something happen?"

"Not really," Jennifer said. "It's just that after she was gone, these guys came looking for her. Big guys. Spanish guys. One had that bulge on his waist like he had a gun but didn't care who knew it."

"So, you think the drug dealer's friends maybe? Gang types?"

Maybe," she said. "Or wrestlers. Either way they were scary." She paused, her eyes falling on the loaf of bread out on the counter. "Listen, I really want to…"

Hannibal raised a palm. "If you thank me one more time for the stuff I brought we're going to have an issue."

That earned him a small giggle. "Sorry. It's just… But anyway, those guys came looking for Connie, but that was after she left with Danny."

"And was Danny a wrestler?" Hannibal asked. "Did he work with Greg, the guy who got stabbed?"

Jennifer glanced around looking guilty. Then she stood, opened a cabinet, and stretched to the top shelf. Her eyes shined with an evil grin as she placed a package of Chips Ahoy cookies on the table.

"These are supposed to be for the kids," she said, "but I think you deserve a special treat. And no, Danny was too small to be a fighter. He handled the money end of the business."

Hannibal reached into the package for a cookie after Jennifer pulled one out for herself. He watched as she wrinkled her nose and dunked her cookie in her coffee, then pushed half of it into her mouth.

"So Danny and Greg were in business. And Danny was the money man. Ever mention any other members of their team?"

Jennifer chewed and swallowed the rest of her guilty pleasure before responding. "A guy named Juan. And Kenny I think. Big guys, fighter types, you know. They all hang out at the same gym I'm sure."

Hannibal washed down his second cookie with the last of his coffee, fighting to keep his excitement hidden. He wiped his mouth with a paper towel Jennifer handed him, then said, "This gym. Any idea where it is?"

Jennifer threw her hands up. "Of course. It's up in The District, right there in Northeast."

"There are several…"

"But the name sticks in my head." Jennifer said. "It's a Greek letter. RHO. Not like row your boat, but with an H in the middle, you know? Does that help?"

Chapter 6

Tuesday

From the outside, the RHO Martial Arts Academy was no more impressive than any other in the row of storefronts on this midtown building. As he approached the door Hannibal reflected on the thin thread he had followed to the location where he might get a lead to his quarry's location. If he had just asked the right questions when he met Jennifer he could have saved himself most of a day.

As it was, he was grateful that he was able to get home, get a good night's sleep, and get back at his current case the next morning. He wasn't sure what to expect inside, and there was no reason to wait to find out.

Stepping inside, Hannibal was reminded that there are health clubs, and then there are gyms. Inside The Beltway, the first designation means certified instructors who offer personalized workouts, newly developed workout techniques and cutting edge equipment. The other is a place to sweat, get back to basic exercises, punch a bag or lift a barbell.

RHO Martial Arts Academy looked, felt and smelled like a gym. Their signs made it clear that they specialized in training for real fighting. Thai kickboxing, Brazilian Jiu-Jitsu and mixed martial arts were not concerned with style or philosophy. These arts were about winning.

Trophy cases behind and beside the reception desk, and dozens of medals hanging from hooks, spoke of tournaments won. Standing in front of that desk, Hannibal could see three large rooms. From the mats he knew that two of them were training areas for classes. A boxing-style ring dominated the center of one room and plenty of gloves and other protective gear were neatly laid out for use. The third room had everything he would look for in a gym: the free weights, jump ropes, and both heavy bags and speed bags. Yeah, he would work out here. In fact, he felt odd being in such a place in a black suit and tie with dress shoes on.

Two people moved in that third room. A young Latin man was very focused on beating a heavy bag into submission with his fists, feet, knees and elbows. Hannibal figured him for a welter weight, five foot seven or eight, weighing less than 150 pounds with slicked-back hair and a fierce energy.

Across the floor a woman casually dropped into a split and stretched forward, her torso flat on the mat. She was thick and well-muscled with light brown hair wound into a bun at the nape of her neck. Hannibal imagined it would reach nearly to her waist if she let it down. Like the man, she was in her own world.

As reluctant as he was to break their concentration, Hannibal softly cleared his throat. The man spun, startled but showing no irritation. He waved to Hannibal, then pulled off his gloves and foot pads. These he hung neatly in their place with others along the wall. Then, still barefoot, he moved lightly across the room to the reception desk.

"Sorry about that," the fighter said. His enunciation was clear despite a South American accent. "It's usually quiet here during the day so I try to get my workout in early. Anyway, I'm Luis." He offered a hand which Hannibal took, offering his own name in return.

"Hannibal? That's not a name I'll forget. Are you looking for lessons?" Then he leaned back, assessing Hannibal the way a gambler might appraise a racehorse at the track. Curious, Hannibal held his smile.

"Kick boxer, yes?" Luis asked.

"Yes. Very good."

"You don't need lessons," Luis said, reaching for paperwork. "You're looking for a place to work out, practice, maybe spar with some of the regulars."

"Maybe another time," Hannibal said. "Today I'm trying to catch up with one of your coworkers. Danny Hernandez? He works for Greg Howard, right?"

Luis flashed a ready smile. "I guess you haven't talked to him in a while. Danny's the boss now. Took over not too long ago. Mr. Howard had some issues with the owners I guess, so Danny moved up."

Hannibal nodded. "Was this after Greg got stabbed?"

"Oh, so you know what went down," Luis said. "Yeah, it was right after that."

"Well now I really want to catch up with Danny."

Conversation stopped for a second when the girl walked over. Even in sweat pants and a tee shirt, with a towel hanging around her neck, she was an impressive package. Just a couple inches below Hannibal's six feet and probably a bit more than his 180 pounds with a café-au-lait complexion and light brown curls cascading halfway down her back.

Luis spoke first. "Marisol, this is Hannibal Jones. He knows Danny and is trying to catch up to him." Then to Hannibal he said, "Marisol's been with the Academy a bit longer than I have. In fact, she's the reason I'm here."

Subtle, but unnecessary. Hannibal knew from the nature of their eye contact that Luis and Marisol were more than coworkers. He smiled to himself. Luis was fast and fierce, but she looked like she could take him. Yet the look in her eyes said Luis was definitely in charge of whatever their relationship was.

"Yeah, Danny hasn't been around for a few days," she said. "No big, we run the place fine without him, but it's odd for the boss not to drop in to check things out, you know?"

"So, how about a phone number? Or you could just give me his address and I can run by."

The two exchanged glances and the atmosphere thickened. Hannibal guessed they were concerned about sharing more than the boss might want them to. Of course, they might not know how to contact him, which would make him wonder if the business was totally legitimate. Finally he saw a solution rise in Marisol's eyes.

"You should go see Nicky. Danny's dad might know where he is." And know whether or not Danny would want to see Hannibal, she didn't say. Hannibal nodded. He understood this kind of caution. And Marisol must know Danny pretty well to know his family.

While she wrote the address on an Academy brochure Hannibal said, "It's good that he trusts you to keep the place going. Must be tough, though, working without the money man."

"Oh, Greg wasn't hurt that bad," Luis said. "He's back in full swing."

"Greg," Hannibal said, accepting the brochure. "Now why did I think it was Danny?"

"Danny?" Marisol said with a smirk. "Wrong skill set. Greg Howard has always been the collector."

Chapter 7

The term "collector" carried interesting connotations in Hannibal's world and he was contemplating them as he knocked on the apartment door. Nicky Hernandez lived in a new building on M Street in the neighborhood now known as NoMa for its location, north of Massachusetts Avenue. When Hannibal moved to The District this area was just a collection of old industrial lots. Now it was a real neighborhood with modern developments fanning out north of Union Station which had practically become a shopping mall thinly disguised as a train station.

Hannibal had some nice memories of coming to the eastern side of this hood a couple of times with Cindy. They wandered the stalls and shops of Union Market. She looked for home décor, he grabbed Korean tacos. He smiled, thinking of how much fun they could have doing simple things.

Nicky's building still looked more like a factory than an apartment complex. The brick front spanned the entire block, but it showed more glass than brick, with small panes grouped into sets of fifteen. The ultramodern lobby featured a U-shaped table surrounded by orange leather chairs where, Hannibal imagined, new tenants signed away their lives for the privilege of living in such luxury. Maintaining the industrial feel there was also a fireplace that reminded Hannibal of a water tower. He assumed on purpose.

The elevator whisked Hannibal halfway up the thirteen-story building with such speed that he feared his ears would pop. The tiled hall was narrow but brightly lit. After one false start in the wrong direction Hannibal navigated to Nicky Hernandez's door.

Hannibal pressed the door buzzer and stepped back so he'd be easy to see through the tiny lens set into the door. He smiled and put on his non-threatening face. He waited.

Three doors down a Latin senior citizen stepped into the hall and looked both ways before closing and locking his door. He turned toward Hannibal, straightening his Hawaiian shirt. Hannibal stepped back against the wall. The bulky fellow moved with a slow, uncertain gait. He didn't speak until he came between Hannibal and Hernandez' door and when he did he kept his eyes straight ahead.

"He's not home, you know."

"Excuse me?"

He kept walking. "Nicky's not home. He's at the hospital."

"Thank you," Hannibal said. "Is he sick?"

The neighbor waved the idea away, never slowing his forward progress. "No no. He's down there visiting his son. Danny had a bad accident I hear."

The hospital turned out to be the one attached to George Washington University, and Hannibal rushed there, hoping Danny hadn't met up with whoever didn't like his friend Greg. So far Danny sounded like a right guy in a bad business, and if he had pulled Connie into that mess Hannibal might end up with bad news to deliver to Connie's mother.

The hospital was just off the vicious multi-lane traffic circle that tied K Street, Pennsylvania Avenue, New Hampshire Avenue and 23rd Street together. Hannibal wondered if it was a coincidence or good planning that placed an academic medical center so close to what any sane person would expect to be a continuous source of patients.

The lobby felt more like a busy delicatessen than a hospital to Hannibal. He waited in line to get to the reception desk where he told a stern-faced matron in a blue uniform who he wanted to visit. After signing a visitor's log book he received his wrist band indicating he was cleared to enter the building. Was this the reality of hospitals everywhere, or just a security oddity in the nation's capital?

After wandering the labyrinthine halls for twenty minutes Hannibal finally reached the right floor, the right ward and the right room. The door was open about two inches, which Hannibal took as an invitation, but as his hand touched the door handle, voices from inside made him freeze. It was a tense conversation between two men.

"This life, this life," the older man was saying, "It is going to kill you one day."

"Papa, I can't be you, all cautious and scared all the time." That had to be Danny, Hannibal thought.

"You can not get dead," Nicky responded. "You can ask for help. You can…"

"I can live my own life," Danny said. "And you can let me live it my own way."

There were a couple more mumbled words that Hannibal thought might be goodbyes, so he backed away from the door and turned away as if he was heading to another room. In his peripheral vision he watched Nicky almost stomp down the hall toward the elevators. As soon as he was out of sight, Hannibal turned back and slipped through Danny's door. It was a double room, but the bed closest to the door was empty.

The man in the bed sat upright, his eyes widening in alarm. An unruly mop of straight black hair flipped when he moved. His robust torso was wrapped in blankets and surgical tape. Yep, a wrestler, Hannibal thought. He closed the door behind himself but stayed there, not wanting the patient to raise an alarm.

"Danny Hernandez?"

The man nodded.

"Look, whoever you were expecting, I'm not them. My name is Hannibal Jones. I'm a detective and I just wanted to ask your help with a case I'm working on. May I come in?"

33

Danny nodded again and relaxed a little. "So, you're a cop?"

"Private investigator," Hannibal said, stepping closer. "You look like you were expecting trouble. What happened to you?"

Danny chuckled, then grimaced in pain. "Truth is, I had an accident while working on my plane."

"You're a pilot?"

"Yeah, stupid hobby, right? But one of those things I wanted since I was a kid and as soon as I had the money I got me one. Just a little Piper Cub, but I love getting in the air with her."

"So, nobody's after you?" Hannibal asked, dropping into the guest chair.

"I didn't say all that. What do you care, anyway?"

"I was hired to find your girlfriend, Connie," Hannibal said. He tried to hide his reaction to the smell of antiseptic and wondered what kind of airplane maintenance accident could have caved in Danny's ribs. "Or, is she still your girlfriend?"

Hannibal could see Danny's thoughts racing behind his eyes. His easy smile was a well-practiced mask. Hannibal waited for Danny to decide how much to share.

Danny said, "You're looking for Connie?" Hannibal heard, "Your investigation has nothing to do with me?"

Hannibal said, "That's my only mission. No reason to get into your personal business. I'd appreciate any help you can offer. Then I'll get out of your life for good."

Danny nodded, as if he saw the offer as a mutually agreeable compromise. "I got in a situation where I thought Connie might be involved in some stuff she shouldn't be in. She got in Ozzie's car and he got her away from here. Ozzie's my little brother. Does that help?"

"Well, it's a next step." Hannibal hated hospitals. The constant beeping of monitors and the antiseptic smell reminded him of how close death was always standing, even when you can't see him there, only his shadow. He wanted to move on, and this girl was leaving quite a twisted trail. But he smiled at Danny, pulling a notebook and pen from his inside jacket pocket. "Give me Ozzie's address and I'll be out of your hair for good."

Danny took the pad and wrote in a disjointed scrawl, saying, "He won't be home, you know. I haven't heard from him since he took off with Connie, and neither has Pop. He's not even answering his phone."

"Thanks," Hannibal said, accepting his notebook back. "I'm pretty good at finding people. After all, I found you here following some pretty thin threads. Now I'm following this one. Hey, er, get well soon."

"Don't worry. The doc says I'm out of here this afternoon."

Just as Hannibal stepped through the door, Danny called, "Hey man. Good luck finding Connie. And if you find Ozzie, tell him to give me a call, would you?"

Chapter 8

Red Robin was Hannibal's restaurant chain of choice when he was travelling alone. Aside from his love of a good burger, he found that a loud, happy place made it easier for him to sit isolated, as if the wall of sound created a protective barrier around him. So after a simple dinner and a chocolate shake he was ready to get back to work.

Dinner was at the Bowie Town Center, and Ozzie Hernandez lived in a small condo on a quiet street not far from there. Hannibal parked about a block away and strolled to the one-level place, thinking it was a fine choice for a bachelor. White vinyl siding with red window trim made it look pretty inviting, and it seemed a pretty quiet neighborhood. He saw no one outdoors on the narrow lane, which he figured to be the norm in the evening. The smell of fresh-cut grass and raked leaves told him there was pride of ownership. Maybe Ozzie, a Hispanic man with a mainstream name, was living the middle-class American dream.

No lights were visible through the front windows. No car parked in front. It seemed Danny was right. Ozzie was elsewhere. He might have to wait and pick up the trail tomorrow. Still, he rang the bell just to be sure. No response.

On an impulse Hannibal tried the door and found it unlocked. Even in the friendliest neighborhood that was unusual. Before proceeding Hannibal tightened his gloves and pulled out his mini-Maglite. Scratch marks around the lock and doorsill set off alarms in his head. This was pry bar work by a pro. Whoever broke into Ozzie's place, this was not their first or second time.

The flashlight beam slid past the door into the living room, revealing quiet chaos. Perp almost certainly gone.

Resident possibly injured. Hannibal pushed the door slowly open and called hello. Again, no response. And no choice, really. Hannibal stepped inside and flipped on the ceiling light.

The scene reminded him of photos he had seen of homes after a tornado touched down. Couch cushions upended, the contents of drawers dumped on the floor, closet doors standing open. Only amateurs and FBI agents searched this way. Professional burglars are much neater. This was evidence of someone in a hurry searching for something not someone. A plate on the kitchen table still held a half-eaten meal. Ozzie was surprised, then, and either ran off, or was taken away. Or…

Hannibal stepped carefully as he checked the two bedrooms and one bath for signs of life. He wasn't sure if he was disappointed or relieved to find no one in the place. He stood for a moment to absorb the one spot of order in the midst of chaos. The bed in the master room was still neatly made. One item lay atop the spread: a red, one piece swimsuit. The kind a lifeguard might wear.

Behind him a voice said, "Why'd you have to make such a mess?"

The hairs on the back of Hannibal's neck stood at attention as he spun, and he saw the gun's muzzle before seeing the man behind it.

Chapter 9

Hannibal held his hands low but out to his sides, palms facing forward. The gunman almost smiled as they took a moment to evaluate each other. The gunman, in chinos and a denim jacket, was tall and beefy with a wrestler's broad shoulders and deep chest. The Fu Manchu mustache and straight black hair made him the current model for badass Latino. The small pistol held close to his side marked him as a pro. Without turning his head he said, "Juan."

The man who stepped from behind him was shorter but similarly dressed and just as muscular. His nose had been broken so maybe he had a boxing career before switching to wrestling, or he could be a mixed martial artist. Hannibal tossed aside any thoughts of trying take them both on. Instead he slowly raised his right hand to pull his suit coat open, revealing his own automatic. Juan nodded, one professional recognizing another, and pulled the weapon from its holster. Then he stepped behind Hannibal and patted him down thoroughly.

The gunman asked, "You are?"

"Jones. Hannibal Jones. Private detective. And on balance you must be Kenny. I understand you and Juan here work with Danny, or maybe just Greg now."

Kenny nodded and his smile grew by ten percent. "If you know our work, you know not to be stupid."

"Mutual respect leads to fewer messes to clean up."

Kenny nodded as Juan returned to his side. "So, why are you here? And what's all this?" He waved the pistol to indicate the mess in the house.

"Looking for Ozzie Hernandez. He owes me money. He wasn't home, so I figured I'd take a look around to see if I might find enough to cover his debt. No luck." If these boys knew Connie, the truth could have been a wrong answer. Hannibal's lie would be safer and impossible to disprove.

"A private eye," Juan said. His accent was stronger than Kenny's. "Looking for Ozzie. Interesting coincidence, eh? You know, I think El Jefe would like to meet this boy."

Kenny nodded and stepped to one side. "You're coming with us. Do I need to handcuff you?"

"Are you going to hit me over the head, or shoot me in the leg or something?"

"Only if you make that necessary," Kenny said.

"Then no, you don't need to handcuff me. Show me respect, I'll respect you."

Once outside Hannibal took a deep breath of the crisp night air. Juan led him to a red F-150, directed Hannibal inside and got in beside him. Kenny followed and hopped into the driver's seat. In an oddly synchronized movement, Kenny holstered his pistol as Juan drew his and held it facing Hannibal. Well, at least there wasn't a bag over his head.

Hannibal had no idea where they were taking him or why, and he saw no point in speculating. He was in no danger. If they wanted to kill him it would have been much easier to leave his corpse in Ozzie's house. And he had been taken for enough rides to know the rules. No question, no sudden movements and no smart remarks.

It was a long ride with one amusing moment when they swung through the drive-through at McDonald's. Kenny asked Hannibal for his favorite flavor, and they were soon back on the road with three chocolate shakes. Not as good as Red Robin's of course, which are made with real ice cream instead of the mysterious paste the fast food places use.

In a little less than an hour the truck was pulling into the driveway of one of the stereotypical min-mansions clinging to the shores of the Potomac in Alexandria, Virginia. When they left the truck, all guns were put away. Juan led the way in while Kenny walked behind Hannibal. Once they were inside, Juan and Kenny stopped, apparently waiting to see how impressed Hannibal might be. Marble floors, chandeliers and a spiral staircase leading to the upper level put only one thought in Hannibal's mind: In a movie, this is where the master villain would live.

The two thugs escorted Hannibal through the professionally decorated house to an office that might have blinded him if he didn't have his Oakley sunglasses on. White walls rose out of the white marble floor. The room smelled of roses, although there were none in evidence. Dark cherry bookcases covered one curved wall, matching the desk that dominated the room. That desk was littered with office supplies.

Only then did Hannibal take in the man behind the desk. While Hannibal stood just inside the door between Kenny and Juan, his host remained seated.

"So this is Hannibal Jones. I thought you'd be bigger."

"I'm afraid you have me at a disadvantage," Hannibal said. "And you are…?"

"My name is Pablo Rodriguez. Perhaps you have heard of me."

Hannibal's eyes widened behind his dark glasses as Rodriguez opened a cigar box and selected one. His black hair was neatly styled, his black eyes sharp and penetrating, and his teeth perfect. He was broad in the shoulders and deep through the chest and a small scar near his left eye spoke of a near miss long ago. He was, unlike most men, everything Hannibal expected.

"I do know your name. As I understand it, you are the top of the MS-13 food chain hereabouts."

Rodriguez snipped the tip of the cigar with precision then lit it and filled his lungs. "You know who I am. You know who we are?" His words echoed slightly off the hard walls and floor. Hannibal guessed his origin to be Salvadoran, although his accent was well controlled. His skin was tanned leather despite his apparent youth. Hannibal wondered how a man could rise to this level before reaching thirty.

"I know that Mara Salvatrucha – am I pronouncing that right? I know MS-13 is a gang that's reached across the country from L.A. I know you're mostly Central American but other Latinos join in. I know you've stepped out of the ghetto and infiltrated suburbia. Friends tell me you've got a death grip on Fairfax County, which I suppose is why you live here. And I've heard you own PG County over in Maryland."

Rodriguez planted his elbows on his desk, pointed his cigar at Hannibal and laughed. "You do not disappoint. You know quite a bit about us."

"Yeah, but here's what I don't know." Hannibal broke rank with his escorts to step forward and settle into the comfortable visitor's chair. "Why am I here?"

Rodriguez puffed his cigar, his eyes boring into Hannibal. "You are here because my man Juan is a smart lieutenant. You are here because he knows you are hunting something that I want. That makes you valuable to me."

"Yeah, I told your boys I was chasing Ozzie Hernandez."

"As am I," Rodriguez said.

"Well, I kind of gave them a shorthand version of the truth," Hannibal said, turning to nod at his two escorts. "Actually, it's Connie Blanco I need to find."

"Yeah," Rodriguez said. "I understand Hernandez has been running with Blanco, and that makes her of interest too."

The smoke reached out like a wreath around Hannibal, chasing off the floral scent like a dark cloud descending on his night. "Well you know I haven't found him. And I don't have Connie Blanco. So again, why am I here?"

Rodriguez chuckled again. He laughed easily. "Because you are Hannibal Jones, the detective, finder of lost people. This is what you do." He pulled a desk drawer open, reached in, and dropped a stack of bills on his desk. "So here is what

I'll do. I'll give you twenty-five thousand dollars to bring me Connie Blanco." He placed a second tall stack of bills neatly beside the first. "I will pay fifty thousand dollars for Ozzie Hernandez."

"And just why do you want Ozzie so bad?"

Rodriguez's face darkened for a moment. "At these prices, Chico, you don't need to know any more details."

Hannibal nodded, realizing he had wandered into "offer you can't refuse" territory. He nodded and smiled. "Fair enough. But I don't have any good leads yet."

Rodriguez's smile returned as he leaned back. "This is where I can help you. My woman Isabella is one of those people that people talk to, you know? She tells me she heard that Connie is back in Virginia Beach, but without Ozzie. I think she may be able to point you to him."

Hannibal nodded. "So you know where she is. Why not just send some of your boys down to get her?"

"Virginia Beach is a big place, and my people don't specialize in finding lost girls," Rodriguez said, as if explaining something to a slow-witted child. "This is more in your skill set. So find the girl and let her point you to this Ozzie. If she won't you can bring her to me and my friends here will get her to point me to him. Either way, you get paid. So, we are in business, yes?"

Hannibal took a moment to consider his options, which had suddenly narrowed to one. Rodriguez knew that Virginia Beach didn't have the kind of Hispanic community that would give him muscle and influence there. He also seemed to be a canny business man striving to bring some class to a street gang and looking for respect, but there was no question he could make Hannibal disappear without a trace from his home on the Potomac. Hannibal stood.

"A temporary alliance then," Hannibal said. "Today, you are a client like any other. I'll need my gun back, and your friends here can give me a ride back to my car."

Chapter 10

Wednesday

"She looks underage," the bartender said.

"Just looks young for her age," Hannibal replied. "Look, I'm not trying to jam you up or anything, just want to know if she's been here."

The bartender was a swarthy man with hairy hands who nonetheless was able to mix cocktails with style while holding a conversation. He glanced at the photo one more time, pushed two colorful, fruity-looking drinks toward two girls at the bar and turned back toward Hannibal.

"That face doesn't ring any bells for me, pal. Sorry."

Hannibal nodded and smiled, nudging the two twenty-dollar bills forward and turned to go.

"But I will keep an eye out for her," the bartender said, sweeping up the two bills with the rest of his tips.

Hannibal stepped back out onto the boardwalk, turning his back to the ocean breeze. The last twenty-four hours had been nothing to cheer about and so far, this night had given him little to raise his spirits. The night before the two Latin gangsters who dropped him off at his car were treating him like a coworker, which irked him quite a bit. He had driven home for a late dinner of leftovers. He had gotten his woman, Cindy Santiago, on the phone, but it was late and she was tired from a long day in court, so he let her go after a basic recap of each other's day. He lay down, but sleep avoided him for a good hour. His mind tumbled over the events of the day, fitting together the pieces of how his missing person's case that started more as a favor than anything else

43

had somehow evolved into working for a major player in the gang world. He assigned his subconscious to finding a safe way out of that situation.

Morning had brought a bright ball of sunlight in through the big bay window of his front room. He got up and got into shorts and a tee shirt before his body had time to realize what was coming. He went out and did a strong three-mile run that took him up around the Capitol building and down through the neighborhood being totally rebuilt by ambitious young professionals before looping back to his place in Anacostia. Breathing deeply, he pushed himself up the six steps of his stoop and through his front door. His best friends lived upstairs but Hannibal had the first floor. The railroad apartment on his right was his office, but he turned left to his apartment. He followed a hot shower with bacon and an omelet for breakfast, with French press full of Blue Mountain coffee. Then he was ready to face his day.

Dressed in the black suit, white shirt and tie he always wore for work, he went next door to start his business day with a quick phone call to his only friend on the force, Detective Orson Rissik of the Fairfax County police. The receptionist recognized Hannibal's name and patched him right in.

"Got a busy start, Jones," Rissik said as soon as he picked up he phone. "No time for small talk."

"Okay. So Orson, you know Pablo Rodriguez?"

"Not personally. Wouldn't mind an introduction though."

"Okay, so you know who he is. But do you know where he hangs out?"

"He's got a three and a half million dollar crash pad in Alexandria, Right on the river. Technically not my jurisdiction since Alexandria's its own city and not really part of Fairfax County. Why? You looking for him?"

"No, but tell me this. If you know who he is, and you know where he is, and I can see he ain't what you'd call low profile, how come he's not locked up?"

"Because, smartass, he's like Teflon," Rissik said after a long sigh. "We've had him for drugs, prostitution, human trafficking, even a couple of murders. Nothing sticks to him. Are you mixed up with him? And if so, why?"

Hannibal took a long drink of coffee, thinking for a moment how much nicer Rodriguez's desk was than his own. "He picked me up because he wants me to do some work for him. Nothing illegal, a missing persons gig, but I don't think it's in the missing guy's best interest to be found. Of course, this Rodriguez guy can be pretty convincing."

In his mind's eye, Hannibal could see Rissik setting his own coffee down. After a brief pause, he said, "You watch your ass with this guy, Jones. These boys in MS-13, they don't screw around. This is not some local gang, my friend, this is an international franchise. On the West Coast they own Los Angeles and the San Francisco Bay area. We're dealing with them here, but they're also very strong in The District. It's worse in Maryland, in Montgomery and PG County. Boston. Long Island in New York. Charlotte. Houston. Even Toronto up in Canada."

"Okay, okay. They're SPECTRE and they're bent on world domination. I get it. You trying to scare me, Orson?"

"Just wanted to give you some perspective," Rissik said. "And look, I appreciate you giving me the call, I know you didn't have to. Keep me in the loop on this one, okay?"

The rest of the day had brought a series of disappointments as Hannibal walked through the basics. Phone calls in search of known associates. Calls to hospitals and Virginia Beach law enforcement. A quick check in with his real client, Mrs. Blanco, to be sure she hadn't heard from her daughter. A background check of Nicky, Danny and Ozzie Hernandez yielded one surprise: Those were all their real, given names. Finally he reached out to a friend on the DC force for a brush-up on the latest MS-13 intel. Just to be safe.

All of which led him to an early supper in Virginia Beach and the most used tool in any private detective's kit: shoe leather. Standing on the boardwalk he pulled out the list he had spent the afternoon compiling. Virginia Beach was a resort town, with more than 150 restaurants and even more bars and clubs. If Connie was in town she'd want to eat and drink, and would probably have favorite spots. Even fugitives hiding out often can't resist their favorite watering holes.

By nine pm Hannibal was getting a little hungry. He had started with the clubs most populated by singles in Connie's age group and was working his way up. His next stop was a beer bar, and he figured it was as good a place as any to grab some food.

The 1608 Crafthouse had a reputation for great beers. He stepped in out of the crisp night air into a warmer, more humid space that was full, but not yet crowded. A quick glance around made him smile. Despite the wall mounted televisions, the atmosphere was not sports bar. In fact, the place felt more family than frat house. It held a nice, warm beer smell, and the chatter was held to a comfortable level.

He managed to secure one of the small, dark wood tables against the wall not too far from a sign that read, "Beer takes me to my hoppy place." Just about as he got comfortable a waitress blew past, dropping off a menu. Good. He was in no mood to fight his way to the bar.

Inside of three minutes the girl returned. She couldn't have sneaked too far past 20. Her hair was up, but one long blond lock of it had worked its way out of its hair clip prison and hung across her right eye.

"What can I get you?"

Hannibal knew what he wanted, but would take care of business first. He offered her a twenty dollar bill, his card and a photo.

"Before I order, let me give you half your tip in advance," he said. She accepted the bill, but in a tentative way, as if she understood there were strings attached. She raised one eyebrow and waited.

"I just need to know if you've seen this girl," Hannibal said. "Connie Babcock."

"She looks Latin."

"Short for Concepción," he said.

"Can't say I recognize her. She in trouble?"

"Nope." He offered his most sincere smile. "Hunting her down to deliver her inheritance before it goes to somebody else."

She nodded and tucked the bill and his card inside her apron. "I'll keep an eye out for her. Was that it, or are you going to eat?"

Hannibal was tempted to order the Big Ass Soft Pretzel, just for the name, but settled on a safer choice: a bacon cheeseburger. For a beverage he asked the waitress to surprise him with a good stout. In a place with a good craft beer selection it was often a good idea to let the waitress choose.

The beer arrived fast and he was grateful that she brought the bottle along with his glass. The label implied some nationality confusion, but he had to admit that O'Connor Ibrik Imperial Turkish coffee stout just sounded good. He poured the almost black liquid into his glass, pleased with the low but dense head. Raised in Germany by his German mother while his father fought and died in the Vietnam War, Hannibal knew his beers. This one called to his nose with an aroma of flavored coffee and spices. His first sip brought a smile to his face. The beer actually had a bold, deep roasted flavor with just a little tang at the end. About halfway thru the impressive beer his burger arrived. He was surprised, but after one bite very well pleased. The burger was crusted with apple smoked bacon and instead of a slice of cheese holding the bun in place, the burger was stuffed with cheese. White American cheese at that. That beer and this burger combined to make a perfect meal as far as Hannibal was concerned.

Halfway thru the burger Hannibal looked up to see a tall, spindly white guy approaching his table. Normally cautious, Hannibal got no danger vibe off this smiling stranger with tousled brown hair and a pencil thin mustache. Maybe it was the Hawaiian shirt he wore beneath his distressed leather bomber jacket that made him seem harmless.

The man stood there smiling while Hannibal chewed and swallowed. When his mouth was empty Hannibal asked, "Can I help you?

"Quentin Sands," he said, offering a hand, which Hannibal shook. "And you're a private eye named Hannibal Jones."

"Have we met, Mr. Sands?"

"No sir, but I heard you're looking for Danny and Connie. Do you mind?" he asked, indicating the empty chair at Hannibal's two-seat table. Hannibal nodded. Quentin sat. The bar was too public for anyone to cause real trouble and Hannibal's curiosity was piqued.

"You here to check on me, Mr. Sands?" Hannibal asked. "You don't look like one of Rodiguez's usual boys."

Sands lowered his voice. "You mean Pablo Rodriguez? Hell no! These look like gang signs to you?"

Sands pointed to the patches on his jacket's shoulders. It occurred to Hannibal for the first time that the bomber jacket could be real military wear. Then he looked more closely.

"That says, 75th Ranger Regiment. Is that the first Battalion badge?"

"Roger," Sands said. "Jumped out of a lot of perfectly good airplanes, but now only do it for fun."

Hannibal nodded. "Yeah, I don't imagine any gangs recruit from the Army veteran population much."

"Nope. But I do know who Pablo Rodriguez is, and I heard he's looking for Danny and Connie too. That the word you got?"

"Well, yes and no," Hannibal said, taking another swallow of beer. "But either way, what makes you think I'm looking for them?"

Sands had the arrogant kind of smile that Hannibal wanted to smack off his face. "I know people. That's my talent, Mr. Jones. I had asked the waitress to let me know if anybody came looking for Danny or his wife. Actually I paid her to let me know. But you don't look like any gangster and she showed me your card so I wanted to know what the deal is."

"His wife?" Hannibal asked, wondering if Ozzie was out of the picture.

"Well yes, and pretty slick of you to only look for her, Mister. She's not really coming in to an inheritance, is she?"

"You caught me," Hannibal said. "I'm just trying to find her because her mom's worried about her."

"I figured it was something like that," Sands said, pointing with both index fingers. "Know why? You just look like a good guy to me. And I'm a pretty good judge of people. But yeah, I rented a place to them not long ago. That was cool, no problems, but then I learn from this reporter that Danny was one of the people she was digging into, on account of his connection with a gang called MS-13. You heard of them?"

"A little," Hannibal said, scanning the room to see if anyone was listening too closely. "A reporter? You heard from a reporter?"

"Like I said, I know people."

"So you wanted what? To get rid of Danny?"

Sands waved the idea away with a spastic hand. "No no, it's not like that. I was trying to help them. Danny's on the run from those guys. Honestly, I think he stole from them, and now the gangsters are on his trail."

"So you're helping them hide out," Hannibal said. "Is that it?"

"Well," Sands lowered his voice, forcing Hannibal to lean in. "I own a number of properties. Condos and small houses. I stashed them in one of them, a place where no gang banger is ever likely to go."

Hannibal concealed his own suspicions. Why was Sands trusting him with all this? He was being altogether too forthcoming, but Hannibal could not turn his back on a possible lead. "So you're talking to me because you're worried about Danny? He asked.

"Yeah, well…" Sands blushed just a little. "I don't really care about Danny, but I do want to help Connie."

"I see. Apparently her milkshake brings ALL the boys to the yard,"

"What?"

"Never mind," Hannibal said, dropping cash on the table to cover his bill and adding a twenty, wondering how much Sands had already paid the waitress. "Tell you what. Why don't you and me go see them, and I'll see if I can't get these two lovebirds out of trouble."

Chapter 11

It was a long drive north, following Sands' aging BMW up I-95. Why did Sands know that Hannibal was looking for Connie in Virginia Beach if he had the couple tucked away up in Colchester, just over the Occoquan River? Not that it really mattered. If Hannibal could just make eye contact with Connie he could close out his real case and get onto dealing with the Rodriguez situation. Danny might even know where Ozzie Hernandez was and the entire issue would solve itself.

After nearly three hours on the road and putting a couple hundred more miles on his Black Volvo 850 GLT, Hannibal stopped behind Sands who pulled to the side and parked in front of a small ranch-style place that was out of sight of any neighbors or streetlights. A long, gravel driveway led up to a single-car garage. They had parked on the street to avoid blocking the driveway. Small lights lined the driveway on both sides. Twin security lights illuminated the white front door, the narrow stoop in front of it, and the flower beds on either side. Hannibal imagined the real estate ad if Sands ever decided to sell: "ideal hideout, in a remote area of Fairfax County, Virginia. Perfect for avoiding the law or those annoying gang members."

Hannibal got out and went to Sands' car, assuming they'd enter together. When the window went down he knew better.

"Hey, listen," Sands began. "Me and Danny… things aren't really too good with us right now."

"Yeah, I can get that if he knows you want to screw his wife."

Sands screwed up his face. "Jesus, don't say it like that. But, yeah, I think your conversation about sending Connie anywhere will go better if I'm not standing there, know what I mean?"

"Yeah, I think I know what you mean," Hannibal said, shaking his head. "But he doesn't know me from Adam. Why would he let me in?"

"Just tell him you're lost or something," Sands says. "Once you're inside you can let him know the deal and gain his trust."

"Yeah. Or maybe I'll just be honest. You'd be surprised how often that works."

Sands shrugged, and Hannibal crunched up the gravel drive, followed by a loud cricket concert. He was struck by the well-kept lawn and flowers along the front of the house, hanging on late into the season. They spoke of a woman's touch, well-tended and laid out in neat rows. The flowers made him wonder how long the couple had been playing house here. Had Danny rushed here after being released from the hospital? Or was Ozzie standing in for his brother without telling the landlord?

Hearing no movement inside he rang the doorbell and waited, spotlighted by the bulb beside the door. He felt rather like a target there, and mentally measured the number of paces between him and the darkness he could hide in.

Thirty long seconds dragged past before he heard footsteps on the other side of the door. One, two, three locks were thrown and the doorknob turned. The door swung inward and the sparse moonlight glinted off the silvery finish of a revolver pointed at his navel.

The gun looked too big for the dainty hand holding it. The woman was compact and shorter than he expected. She was pretty in an aggressive way, her tan eyes daring you to take a chance. And her hair was still three inches past her shoulders and streaked a variety of shades from blonde to auburn. She had failed to do the first thing a person who is hiding should do: cut and dye her hair.

"Connie Babcock?" Hannibal asked. "We meet at last. Your mother is worried about you. May I come in?"

She nodded and paced backward, keeping the gun on Hannibal's center of mass. He moved forward, one step for each of hers, maintaining her comfortable distance.

The light from a single pole lamp behind a cheap love seat showed him a small living room, evidently furnished from a mobile home supplier. It showed an absence of the kind of clutter than homes usually gather if people stay there any length of time, unless they are the kind of people who are ready to move out at a moment's notice.

That lamp also revealed just enough of Connie's face to make her fear evident. Hannibal didn't like having a scared woman aiming a weapon at him. Guns in the hands of frightened people tended to go off. He held his hands out to his sides, palm forward. When she stopped, he stopped. It seemed she was waiting for him to speak, but he let the silence build between them until she felt its weight.

"Who are you?" she asked at last. "Are you alone? Where's Quentin? How do you know my name?"

"Well, those are the right questions," Hannibal said through a friendly smile. "My name is Hannibal Jones. I'm a private investigator. I'm alone. Quentin is outside in his car."

"What? Why?"

"Well, he says he and Danny don't get along too well."

"You saying Quentin brought you here? Why the hell would he…?"

Her eyes went to the front window, as if she could see through the closed blinds and drawn curtains. Hannibal shifted a little to his left. "Quentin found me because I was asking about you down in Virginia Beach."

"Again, why?" Connie held the gun at full arm's length now, as if that made her less likely to miss if she decided to fire. "Are you one of the MMA fighters? One of those gang boys Danny was dealing with?"

"Nothing like that," Hannibal said. "I'm here for your mother. She's worried about you."

"Mama?" the woman repeated. Some memory surfaced and for an instant she was looking into the past, not at the revolver's front sight. This was the moment.

Hannibal stretched and swung his left hand forward to grip the five-inch barrel. Connie gasped as he twisted the gun hard and snatched it out of her hand. She shuffled backward, her feet tangling each other, and her behind slammed down on the hardwood floor. She never stopped staring up at her visitor.

"Bad idea to point a gun at a brother unless you intend to use it."

The fear on her face changed to total horror. Between the rapid breathing and gaping eyes Hannibal feared she would pass out. Then he realized her eyes were not on his face but focused on the pistol he had just taken from here. He crouched to get closer to her and flipped the gun to the side. It skidded across the floor and disappeared under the couch.

"Now relax, girl," Hannibal said, "and tell me what you're so afraid of that you greet a stranger at the door with a gun."

She swallowed hard. "It's Danny. He's mixed up with some really bad people. I don't trust any of them. I don't know how he could want to get himself mixed up with that crowd. He's not one of those guys."

"Danny," Hannibal said with a derisive smirk. "Yeah. And Ozzie. Oh, and Greg. You do seem to get mixed up with guys who run with a dangerous crowd."

"What do you know? I'm just trying to make it," she said, and this time Hannibal saw a little fire beneath the fear.

"Look, I'm not trying to run your life," Hannibal said. "You're a grown ass woman and you're going to make your own choices, good or bad. I was just hired to find out what happened to you, to make sure you were still breathing and safe. I've done my job, but listen, if you take my advice you'll go back up to Charles County and look in on your mama. It might not matter to you but it will make her feel a lot better." He stood, leaned forward and offered a hand to help her to her feet.

And then the lights went out.

Hannibal spun in the sudden darkness, one hand snatching his Oakleys off his face while the other darted under his suit jacket reaching for his weapon. Before his fingers could manage to grip the gun his head exploded with pain.

The impact staggered him. The left rear corner of his head. With luck that might be enough of a clue. He whipped his left fist around and back. He hit nothing but air. Then an arm wrapped around his neck. Another arm went under his right arm and he felt the hand at the back of his head. He knew the hold, not a choke in the classic sense, but what television wrestlers called a sleeper hold, cutting off the blood flow in both his carotid artery and jugular vein. He could breathe fine but with no blood going to his brain it didn't matter. He felt a deeper darkness moving in and his balance deserted him. The arms suddenly came away. Something crashed into his knees. Most likely the floor. His arms were unresponsive, and it felt like he was falling forward. He took a deep breath because he knew the next part was really going to hurt.

Chapter 12

Cold. Just as dark as before but cold now. The smell was damp leaves. Moving his head set off flares behind his eyes. He had a Keith Moon drum solo going on under his skull and a taste like battery acid in the mouth.

As it turned out it wasn't as dark as before. Hannibal just hadn't forced his eyes open yet. The moon was up there, nearly full and too bright to look at directly. He was cold because the hardwood floor had been replaced by front lawn grass. He sat up without any negative consequence and checked his watch. It looked like he had been out for about five minutes, during which time his assailant must have dragged or carried him outside.

Next he felt around his body. The results were mixed. He still had his wallet, his phone and his keys, but his Sig Sauer P226 was gone. That prompted a flash of anger that only strengthened the pounding in his head. Getting blindsided was par for the course. He had been knocked out before, no disgrace there. But to let someone take his gun? That was simply not acceptable. All because he got lazy and forgot a cardinal rule. If a lead seems too good to be true, it almost always is.

Hannibal forced himself to his feet and looked around. His car was still parked in the same place. Quentin's was gone, of course. He let himself get played and now he was paying the consequences. But at least he wasn't stranded. He just needed to recover his firearm and...

Hannibal's eyes snapped to the door. His sunglasses were in there someplace. He marched back up the driveway thinking it would probably be good to look around in there anyway. But when he gripped the doorknob he knew it was not to be. The door was locked again. He could probably get in anyway but it had been a long day, it was pushing toward midnight, and he was beat. Screw it, he thought. He would pick it all up tomorrow.

Hannibal stumbled back to his Volvo, thinking that if he pushed it he could be in his own bed in half an hour or so. Once in the driver's seat he pressed the button bringing the engine to life and put the car in gear. Warning lights pulled his attention. Both passenger side tires were low. What the hell? With a tired sigh Hannibal stepped out of his car and walked around to the other side.

"Son of a bitch!" In the stark moonlight he saw both tires were completely flat. So whoever hit him over the head wasn't just vicious, he was a thief and an asshole. He pulled out his phone to call for roadside assistance when he realized that he didn't quite know where he was.

His head snapped around at the sound of a smooth-running engine. He looked up to see the headlights of a car rolling down the road toward him. He had no way to know what this might mean. It could be the person who knocked him out, coming back to finish the job. Or worse, it could be the gangster crowd looking for Danny and Connie. If that guess was right, his night could end poorly.

But when the navy blue Lexis pulled to a stop in front of him he was pretty sure none of that was true. The brunette rolling her window down was in her 50s or early 60s. Hard to tell with white women.

"Do you need some help, young man?" she asked. "Car trouble?" The kind of polite voice some Southerners uses toward their black brothers and sisters to show they're not bigots.

"No ma'am, I'm fine, so… no wait. There is one thing."

From the driver's side of the car came a gruff, "Mind your business Tina," to which the woman replied, "Shut it, Vic!" Then her smile returned and she looked hopefully at Hannibal, so eager to be of help.

"Look, my name is Hannibal Jones and I'm a private investigator," Hannibal said. "I came out here on a case and, well, as you can see I'm having a bit of car trouble. I was just going to call Triple A but I followed someone else out here and well, I'm not exactly sure where I am."

Her laugh was lilting, as if his request was truly hilarious. "Oh you poor man. We're not in the middle of nowhere, you know, it just looks that way. Tell them you're on Old Colchester Road, maybe a mile or two off Route One. They'll find you quickly enough."

"Can we go?" the driver asked in a deep, rough voice.

Hannibal winked at his new friend. "Please, don't let me hold you up. And thank you very much. Nice to meet a real lady out here." Almost as an afterthought he pulled a card out of his inside jacket pocket. "Here. And listen, if you're ever in a jam give me a call. I'm usually the one helping people out."

Tina accepted the card and nodded thank you. The Lexus pulled away and Hannibal made his call. The tow truck was only twenty minutes away and the service man confirmed that whoever wanted to delay Hannibal had just let the air out of the tires, rather than slash or puncture them. In a couple of minutes compressed air had Hannibal's car road worthy again. He checked the number on the door to put the address into his on board GPS. Then, that same GPS quickly got him onto Route One and in a couple of minutes onto I-95 heading north.

The car was like an extension of his body, and even in the wee hours the drive was effortless. His body relaxed into the seat even as his mind relaxed into the drive. But his spirit was restless. Anger, frustration and resentment wrestled for dominance. What had started as a simple case, a favor for a nice person, had become complex and dangerous, and he still had no idea where it was going. The guys Connie was mixed up with were seriously dangerous men, but did Connie know it? How was he going to deal with a gang boss expecting him to finger an enemy? And how was he going to get his gun back?

His apartment was on the other side of the Potomac but without thinking Hannibal turned off the Beltway onto Exit 177 into Alexandria. Before he was fully conscious of his detour he was rolling down North Fairfax Street toward a familiar townhouse. He parked on the street and considered calling to let her know he was there, then rejected the idea and just walked up to the door.

He checked his watch before pressing the bell. Yeah, this was wrong, and he would apologize. But he was tired, and she would accept that because she was who she was.

A minute passed. Then two. Then she was leaning against the door asking, "Who?"

"It's me."

"Thought so." Two locks clicked, and Cindy Santiago opened the door. She was tall and slender, her Cuban heritage showing in her high cheekbones and the dark eyes that told him he had awakened her from a solid sleep. Her beauty reached out to him like a tender kiss. Shoulder-length brown hair sagged around her lovely face, curling in just at the ends. The heavy terrycloth robe hid what Hannibal knew was a robust figure despite her narrow waist. Anger would have been an appropriate facial expression but what greeted him was curiosity and understanding.

"Hard day, lover?" she asked.

"Too much to tell. Set up. Knocked out. Lost the girl. Lost my gun."

Cindy leaned in to wrap her arms around him, then backed off in horror. "Oh my God! You are soaked! How long have you been in these wet clothes? Get in here and let me get you warm and dry."

She took his arm and guided him inside. There was only one person on earth he would allow to take care of him and he hadn't known that he needed taking care of until she opened the door. Silent, he walked inside and let her do what she did so well.

Chapter 13

Thursday

Stripes of sunlight nudged Hannibal awake. At that moment the world was warm and soft and comfortable. He stayed under the covers for a few minutes to savor the sweetness of last few hours.

Cindy had helped him strip and led him to her bed. He had snuggled against her beauty and fallen into a troubled sleep. Some time afterward she had awakened him in the darkness and administered a more personal kind of healing. After that release he had passed into a deeper sleep.

When he awoke Cindy was nowhere in sight but he was sure he knew where he would find her. Ten hours of solid rest made the world look better, but still not good. The rush of energy he felt when he rose was driven more by anger than dedication to any case or cause. He quickly showered, dressed in clothes he kept at her place, slipped a backup pair of sun glasses into his suit coat pocket and moved to the kitchen.

Cindy's little two-bedroom brick town house was definitely a woman's home, with lacy coverings on every table and shadow boxes filled with porcelain and crystal figurines. The kitchen was bright and open, all yellows and black appliances. He spotted the tray of fresh Danishes on the table and sat behind them. A mug of coffee magically appeared in front of him and he looked up to find his smiling woman in a tailored navy blue suit. He captured her hand to hold her attention.

"Sorry I woke you, last night. I know it was late."

"Don't apologize," she said. "You take care of me. I take care of you."

He nodded his agreement, then said, "And thank you for taking such good care of me. Thank you for everything."

"Oh, no, baby. Thank you!" She sat facing him and picked up a cherry Danish, breaking it in half. "I hate you getting knocked around but, you know, I think you're better when you've had a bad day. I like the way you channel your anger, good sir."

She was teasing him, but his mind was already wandering away from their good-natured banter. "Going into the office late?" he asked.

"Lawyers who expect to be up late researching a case are allowed to go in at noon," she said. "At least if they're partners they are. And I assume you are getting back on the trail. You have that look."

"I'm afraid so, lover. I don't like getting dumped on the lawn, and I need to track down whoever took my pistol before he does something stupid with it."

An hour later, Hannibal was wondering if he was too late. He had returned to the house Quentin said he rented to Danny and Connie. He pulled into the driveway this time, as if he belonged there because in his mind he did. This house owed him.

It was really quite a nice little cottage in daylight. White aluminum siding looked new. The well-kept lawn showed no evidence that he had been dragged out onto it the night before. In daylight he could see that the flowers across the front were bright yellow buttercups, well-tended except for a patch that had been chopped away, perhaps by a careless lawn mower. Still, those that remained seemed to be smiling at him. But when he tried the door, he found it unlocked. He took that as a bad sign.

The place was messier than he remembered from the night before. He saw a couple of empty wine bottles on the floor, one of them broken. He also spotted his Oakleys and bent to collect them. Then he made a quick, cursory check of the entire place, peeking under furniture and in dresser drawers, just to say he had. He found no valuables, no drugs, no notes, no surprises. Also, no sign of his Sig Sauer. Which was also no surprise. His assailant probably considered that a nice bonus.

He had only guesses as to who had knocked him out. Danny was his lead suspect, especially if he thought Hannibal was a threat to Connie. Hannibal would have loved to ask Danny, or Connie, but he had no idea where they might be. In fact, most of the players in this drama were out of reach. But there was one person he figured he could find. That was the man who had delivered him to this little cottage. His name was not that common, so a simple internet search on his phone should turn up a home address.

Hannibal was both pleased and alarmed to learn that Quentin Sands was one of those people who opened their entire life up to scrutiny on social media. As it turned out, Sands lived just a few minutes away in the town of Occoquan. Thirty minutes after he left the house where he had last seen Sands, Hannibal was parked in front of the man's condominium, which was within easy walking distance of the main drag.

Hannibal loved Occoquan, a small town of maybe a thousand residents that celebrated its history, arts and culture. Downtown, if you could call it that, was a peaceful escape from The District with parks, unique shops and home style restaurants. It was a downtown that begged you to leave your car at the edge of town and walk in.

Quentin Sands' flat filled the second floor of a rambling Victorian house with a deep wraparound porch. Entry required you to mount a long wooden outdoor staircase. Hannibal took a deep breath when he got to the top and hesitated before knocking. Sands had set him up and run out on him. He had more than a few choice words for Sands, but he wanted to keep their interaction civil until they were behind closed doors.

Hannibal's knock was polite but insistent. No response. He knocked again. Nothing.

"Quentin, are you in there?" Silence. Reflex drove him to try the knob. A second time in the same day he was surprised to find a door unlocked. And again, he thought it was a bad sign.

Hannibal stepped inside and closed the door behind himself. A quick scan showed Sands to be a good housekeeper for a bachelor. There was a place for everything. The blinds were set to let the maximum amount of sunlight into the front room. Small knickknacks and figurines stood on display on bookcases and the end tables bracketing the leather sofa. A scattering of tiny roses made the wallpaper seem feminine, but the framed paintings of Civil War combat scenes counterbalanced that. The neatness was almost jarring under the circumstances. The only thing out of place in the front room was Quentin himself. He lay spread eagled on the hardwood floor. And with no carpet to absorb liquid, the pool of blood beneath him had spread quite a distance.

Lying face up, Quentin looked more startled than pained. Hannibal stepped as close to the body as he could without touching the blood pool. There was no need to check for a pulse. The pencil-sized hole just above his left eyebrow was pretty definitive. Hannibal knew the picture would not be nearly as neat on the other side, and he had no desire to see it. Powder burns and stippling on the man's forehead told Hannibal that this shooting was done up close. Despite Quentin's final facial expression, he had to have seen it coming.

So, what was your crime, Hannibal silently asked the corpse. Did you get too close to Connie for some other man's comfort? Did you learn too much that someone didn't want you to know? Were you simply in the way? Or was this a punishment for bringing a detective to the house where Danny and Connie thought they couldn't be found?

And why, Hannibal wondered, did his simple runaway trace have to drag him into a murder?

Well, it was his case now, and he sure wanted to get ahead of it before the police became involved because there was a real possibility that the offending bullet would match a handgun registered to him. So, after swallowing hard and snugging his gloves onto his hands he took the next ugly step. He slid his hands into the dead man's pockets to see what clues they might yield.

He didn't bother to count the cash in Quentin's wallet or pay attention to the credit cards. He would not pursue the locks that matched the various keys. He might have taken the time to check the numbers in his cell phone but didn't dare leave with it.

The valuable finds were in the inside pocket of Quentin's jacket. A small address book was overflowing with contact information. Quentin was right to be proud of his connections. Among the entries written in tiny characters with a fine-point pen Hannibal found not only his own name and number but those of Orson Rissik and Sophia Babcock.

So, Quentin was way more deeply involved with this situation than Hannibal had suspected. If Sands knew Sophia, Hannibal's meeting with him was in no way a random event. Was he sharing information with the Fairfax County detective or getting it from him? And how did he know Sophia Babcock? Had he reached out to her with information about her missing daughter?

Those questions would wait while Hannibal followed up on another interesting bit. A handwritten note had fallen out of the address book when Hannibal opened it. The note showed only a date and time written in a decidedly feminine script. Which was no surprise since it was signed Wanda. Again, no surprise since it was ripped from a note pad of a Wanda Young, with her phone number and email address beneath her name. That was all on the bottom. Across the top was the logo of the Virginia Pilot. Quentin had talked about learning from a reporter that she was digging into Danny's connection with MS-13. That made Wanda Young the next person Hannibal needed to talk to, and possibly the next person in danger of gang retaliation.

Chapter 14

The Virginia Pilot was the major newspaper of record for the lower two-thirds of Virginia. Northern Virginia didn't really have its own paper since the Washington Post and Times covered that territory pretty well. The Pilot's main headquarters sat in Norfolk surrounded by military installations. However, Wanda Young worked out of the Virginia Beach offices, at least that was the address on her notepad.

The building was a square block of sandstone with four stories of symmetrical windows, reminding Hannibal of the first drawings of the Daily Planet he saw as a child. He strode through the lobby and chose the stairs to get to the second floor. There he found a huge newsroom, also reminiscent of his first views of Clark Kent's workplace. It was a vast cubicle farm, noisy but at the same time subdued. What struck him most was that everyone he could see was busy. That separated this place from every other office he had ever visited.

There was no approaching the cubicle dwellers without walking past the reception desk. Her name plate said Ashanique and the very dark woman sitting behind it was occupied at a monitor yet alert to newcomers. A mop of tight, thin dreadlocks hung to her elbows, and her full, purple lips matched her eye shadow. Eyes like laser range-finders pinned Hannibal in place.

"Can I help you?" she asked, in a tone that said not to waste her time with small talk.

"Good afternoon," Hannibal said. "I need to speak to Wanda Young. I have some information for her."

"She expecting you?"

"No," Hannibal said, "But she wants to talk to me." He offered his card, thinking that she'd think a private investigator might be working for the paper. Ashanique stood and turned to face the room. In that tight black knit dress her full round bottom demanded his attention until she waved a hand in a specific direction and turned her eyes on him again.

"There," she said aiming a fingernail that he now noticed was the same purple as her lips and eye shadow. "Six desks in. On the phone."

Hannibal thanked her and moved down the narrow aisle wondering how these people could tell which desk was their own. None had any sort of personal items or decoration, not even family photos. He walked up behind Wanda, whose straight, flaxen hair just reached the collar of her conservative-cut, beige suit. Her voice was staccato, almost machine-like. Instead of goodbye she said, "Out" at the end of her call. She hung up and spun her chair to face Hannibal, looking up with an air of expectant disinterest.

"Bad timing. I'm on a deadline. You are?"

Hannibal chose his all-business face and voice, presenting his business card. "Hannibal Jones, private investigator. Working a missing persons case. Connected to you through a Quentin Sands. My case might be connected to a story you're working on. Only need five minutes of your time. Is there someplace we can talk?"

Wanda's eyebrows rose at the mention of Quentin's name. She stared at the card and nodded. Her eyes moved left then right which Hannibal took to be her reflex during decision making. Luckily, she made decisions quickly. She stood, pointed toward a conference room and marched off. Hannibal followed. She moved forward at speed in a pair of brown flats, although he had noticed three-inch pumps under her desk. Her curves stressed the bounds of her knee-length skirt as she swiveled between cubicles and never once looked back to see if he was there.

Wanda swung the door open, revealing a tall fellow seated at the head of a ten-person polished oak table. His tie was pulled down an inch or two and he was half-way through a sub sandwich. The room smelled of oil, onions, and everything Hannibal grouped under the heading "antipasto." Late lunch, he thought.

"Hey, Jimmy," Wanda said, walking in. "I need the room."

The man stood, tossing her a dirty look which Wanda chose not to catch, and gathered up his food and coffee. Hannibal chose to stand outside the threshold until the other man had cleared the area. When he walked in Wanda had settled into the ergonomic chair in the far corner. The walls were a pale green like overcooked cabbage, but the top half of the wall toward the larger room was glass. Wanda had chosen the seat least visible from outside. Hannibal closed the door and sat at the foot of the table, facing her and nearly touching knees, his back to the cube farm.

"So, a missing person," Wanda said. "Should I be recording?"

"I'd rather you didn't."

"All right," she said, glancing at her watch. "How can I help you then?"

"I'm trying to find a young woman. Her family has lost touch with her and fears foul play."

"And you think this is someone I might know?"

"Yes. Her name is Concepción Babcock. You might know her as Connie Babcock. Or maybe Connie Hernandez." In response to Wanda's puzzled expression Hannibal handed over his photo. That raised a smile and a look of recognition.

"Oh, I see. You just crossed up the names. You mean Connie Sands, Quentin's wife. Hernandez is how she's connected to a story I'm working on."

"I see." Hannibal quickly reshuffled his mental deck. Was Quentin close enough to Connie that he could introduce her as his wife? Or was he simply trying to protect her by separating her from Danny Hernandez? Who was lying to whom? He decided to follow the trail of the one connection he could be sure of.

"I take it you are pretty close to Quentin. I guess I should tell you that he's gone missing as well."

"Yes, so you said when you called," Wanda said.

"When I called?"

"This morning," Wanda said with an air of impatience. Then she paused. "You did call, right?"

Hannibal waved her question away. "You said you knew Danny Hernandez, or at least knew of him. What is this story you're working on that ties to him?"

Wanda actually looked left and right before leaning in closer to Hannibal giving him a whiff of a very flowery perfume. "I didn't tell Quentin the specifics, but I'm working on an in-depth expose on the international gang called MS-13 and how it has wormed its way into control of Fairfax County, Virginia."

"Really? I wouldn't think your paper down here would care much about crime up in Fairfax," Hannibal said.

"The hook is their growing influence up there and how their tendrils are slowly snaking their way south toward us. Hernandez promised some serious insider info. This is the kind of investigative journalism that pulls Pulitzers."

"Wait, if you didn't tell Sands then how's he involved with all this?"

Wanda did the eyes-left-eyes-right thing again before she answered. "Okay. Look, Sands thinks he's cool, but really he's just a stringer for the paper. One of those guys, you know? Thinks he's Bugs Bunny but he's really Daffy Duck. He knows I work the crime beat, so he introduced me to his wife because apparently she's got some underworld connections. When I said show me, she connected me to this Hernandez."

"To prove the underworld connection was legit."

"Right," Wanda said. "Maybe I should have warned him about this MS-13 thing. Pretty sure he thought she was hanging with some low level bad boys."

"And you never told him otherwise."

Wanda closed her eyes and shook her head slowly from side to side. "Wanted to keep this to myself. I did warn him about Connie, though. Tried to tell him she's in deeper than he might have thought. Damn, do you think they got to him? What if he found out too much? Might these gang boys have snatched him up? Or done something to him?"

She had slapped her palms down on the table. Hannibal moved one of his gloved hands over to rest on hers. "Anything's possible but even if that was true, it's not on you. But if they were together, don't you think Quentin and Connie might have just run off together?"

"I don't know," Wanda said. "I'm not even all that sure they're actually married. It was awfully soon after…"

Hannibal gave her five seconds to finish her sentence before gently prodding. "After?"

"Well, he was fooling around with Ashanique."

"The receptionist?"

"Yep," Wanda said. "She runs this place and, trust me, she's a lot of woman for the man who can handle her. Quentin took his shot and she dug him. But then he brings this pretty Latina around just a couple weeks after he ran out on her."

Chapter 15

Sunlight stabbed into Hannibal's eyes right through his Oakleys while he drove north from Virginia Beach. The low hanging orb made Beltway traffic move like pebbles dropping through a pool of honey. Hannibal was sandwiched between a tractor trailer and two pickup trucks. But there was no reason to get frustrated. This was life in the seldom-fast lane and he was used to it. He would turn up REO Speedwagon or some other classic rock band he grew up with and fade into the music, right after he made his phone call. He only had six numbers programmed into his phone and he told Black Beauty's dashboard to dial one of them.

During work hours Cindy didn't answer her cell phone, so Hannibal called her office. Gatekeeper Mrs. Abrogast warned him that his girl had had a hard day and he's better not make it any worse before patching him through to Cindy's desk. She must have given Cindy a heads up, judging by the way she answered.

"Hey, sugar! What's the latest from my favorite private dick?"

"That line never gets old, does it?" he thought but didn't say. His actual words were, "Wanted to see how late you'll be at the office."

"Why? You thinking dinner?"

"Well, yes," he said, riding his brake as he ground through late afternoon Beltway traffic. "Dinner, and then I wanted to ask you to come with me to that shelter down in Charles County, Maryland"

"Oh!" He could hear her smile through the phone. "Is this about the missing girl thing? You got a break in the case?"

"Not exactly. But I need to report in to my client. I think the girl has gotten in deep with some pretty bad people. I think this ought to become a police matter, but you know I won't throw a case to them without the client's go-ahead."

"And you think me being there, as a lawyer and maybe just as a woman, will make the lady more likely to make the right choice, right?"

Hannibal chuckled. "Well, that does sound a lot better than 'I just wanted my woman's company for a couple hours' so let's just go with that. Now, what are you in the mood for, foodwise?"

When Hannibal pulled up in front of Cindy's building she was already waiting outside. She hopped into his 850 GLT and he swung around to 19th Street. He had called The Palm for reservations from the car so when they walked in a table was ready and waiting for them. Hannibal liked the fun atmosphere of the place, although the walls, covered with artists renderings of past politicians made him feel as if he was being watched by the worst possible watchers. Cindy called for her usual filet mignon. Hannibal liked the prime bites, which really amounted to a small plate but hey, where else could he get Kobe beef sliders?

In between bites he shared the entire history of his twisted journey in search of one Concepción Babcock, whose mother may or may not have good cause for worry. In any case, pointing a gun at him moved her out of Hannibal's "innocent" category, but she could still be way too deep in something dangerous. Whether or not she thought she had the situation under control she would be better off separated from the MS-13 crowd before Hannibal did something to turn up the heat.

In the restaurant Cindy stayed focused on her steak, allowing the conversation to be more a one-sided briefing. They were back in the car headed south on Crain Highway before she asked Hannibal about his plans.

"Do you really think it will make her safer if Mrs. Babcock reports her as a missing person?"

"Look at how much dust got raised just because I went looking for her?" Hannibal said. "The cops are a bit less subtle than I am, and the bad players she's got herself connected with prefer a lower profile. If the police go stomping around, tossing her name and picture around, the gangster types will likely see her as a liability and cut her loose. When she has no place to go she's most likely to run home to mama, which is all I really want to happen."

"Then what?"

"Then," Hannibal said, "I track down Ozzie Hernandez. I'm betting he can point me to his brother Danny, who sounds like the real gangster here. I figure he's the guy MS-13 really wants to catch up to."

"You think he's the one who knocked you out anyway, right?"

"Well, Danny's a big guy," Hannibal said, "and it was a big guy who wrapped his arms around my neck and put me out. So yeah, I'm betting on him. With any luck, he's got my pistol and I can get it back. Either way, I'll hand him over to big boy Pablo on the condition that nothing blows back on Connie or her mother. I don't know what their business is, but I'm sure it's something dirty so Danny probably gets what he deserves, the girl gets clear, and I get off Pablo's radar."

A fat, pock-marked moon glowed through the crisp night air as Hannibal walked toward the front door of the Angel's Watch Shelter. On the porch he pulled off his Oakleys and stuffed them into an inside jacket pocket.

"Are you alright, lover?" Cindy asked.

"Sure. Why?"

"You're about to break my hand squeezing it like that."

"Oh. Sorry," Hannibal said, trying to pull his hand away.

"No, no," Cindy said, clinging to his fingers. "I didn't say let go. Just don't break any bones, okay?"

Hannibal knocked on the door, knowing he was expected, but not knowing what he should expect in greeting. He felt he had let his client down. He had technically found Connie but didn't know where she was, or even if she was safe. Her mother may be crushed by the news he was bringing. She could be angry, hurt or just disappointed. And if she was upset enough to lapse into Spanish, only Cindy would know what she was saying.

What he didn't expect was for the door to fly open and for Sophia Babcock to leap forward, wrapping her beefy arms around him.

"Oh, Mister Jones, I am so grateful! You are everything they said you were, a miracle worker. Thank you thank you thank you SO much for sending my Concepción back to me!"

Sophia dragged Hannibal into the house with Cindy trailing behind, beaming.

"Well, he is pretty special," Cindy said, "But right now I think he's a little confused."

"When Connie came home yesterday she said she met Mister Jones at a friend's house," Sophia said. Then she turned back to Hannibal, beaming. "She said you seemed like a very nice man."

"Connie is here?" Hannibal asked as Sophia hustled them into seats on the sofa.

"Not now," Sophia called over her shoulder on her way to the kitchen. Three other women sat on the other side of the room in bathrobes and hair curlers, watching a reality show in which a group of beautiful women fought over one handsome man. The women ignored the two new visitors. Hannibal and Cindy exchanged puzzled glances until Sophia returned with a tray of coffee. Hannibal managed to maintain his calm appearance by picking up and sipping his drink.

"So, Connie was here last night?"

"Oh yes," Sophia said, sipping her own coffee. "She apologized for not staying in touch. Her new job as a sales manager involves long hours. But when you told her that I was worried she knew she had to take a break and come see her madre."

Cindy smiled hard at Hannibal, as if she hoped the expression would be contagious. "How about that, honey," she said. "Connie must have come straight here after she met you."

"I think you're right," Hannibal said. "I guess I must have said the right things." He sipped again, enjoying the warmth the coffee spread through his body as he tried to warm to his own story. "So tell me, Sophia. Did you happen to notice what kind of car she was driving?"

"Oh, I didn't see how she got here. Maggie over there opened the door. In fact, I don't think she was driving because that nice young man came and picked her up this afternoon."

"Is that a fact?" Hannibal said. He saw Cindy's smile falter for a moment. She understood, as he did, that Connie could still be in danger. They might have brought her to her mother just to prevent her from involving the police.

"This young man," Cindy said. "Was it someone you know? An old boyfriend maybe?"

"Oh no, I've never seen him before," Sophia said, "but I was happy to see she's with," he hesitated, "well, one of us, you know?"

"I do," Hannibal said. He worked to control his heartbeat, not wanting to panic Sophia. "You know, I might know him. What did he look like?"

Sophia tapped her front teeth with an index finger. "Well he's probably a little shorter than you are, I think, but very muscular. Nice eyes. Too bad about his nose. It's crooked, like maybe it was broken. I thought maybe he was a fighter. Her last boyfriend I think was a wrestler. Maybe it's just the type of boy she likes."

Hannibal nodded and turned to Cindy again. "That sounds like my old pal Juan," he said. If it was Juan it told him a lot. Pablo Rodriguez would never have agreed to Connie visiting her mother, so he didn't find her last night. He probably had someone watching the shelter. When she was spotted, Pablo's boys Juan and Kenny ran down to scoop her up. That only reinforced Hannibal's feeling that Danny was the lead suspect for choking him out last night.

Hannibal could not sit still. He sprang to his feet, despite Cindy tugging on his jacket. The room was feeling small and he walked around Sophia. She spun to follow him around her and back the other way. Things were connecting in his mind in new ways and he wondered how far the connections went.

"Mrs. Babcock, do you know a reporter named Wanda Young?" he asked. "Has she contacted you?"

"Hannibal, sit down," Cindy said.

"No," Sophia said. "No news people come here. What is this about?" Her face had slipped from joy to worry. Her features seemed more familiar with this expression. Hannibal returned to his spot in front of her on the other side of the coffee table but he didn't sit.

"Well, Ma'am, I think this reporter is stirring up trouble that Connie may have gotten caught up in. That fellow that picked her up, I don't think he's a very nice man and the guy he works for is a really bad man." He hated seeing the horror on Sophia's face but he thought it necessary. "I fear that Connie is in some danger right now. And we may have to involve the police."

In a voice Hannibal could barely hear, Sophia said, "Whatever you think is best." Cindy reached out and took her hand.

"Thank you," Hannibal said. "I'll make the arrangements, so you should expect to be interviewed by the police."

"Again?"

The question stopped Hannibal but Cindy squeezed Sophia's hand and leaned in. "Are you saying you've spoken to the police before about Connie?"

"Yes. I thought the officer that came here was Mr. Hannibal's friend. Isn't he?"

Now Hannibal sat, to be on Sophia's eye level. "This policeman. He mentioned my name?"

"Well, yes." Now Sophia's forehead wrinkled, confusion causing her to squint. "I can't remember his name but he was very nice. He listened to my concerns about Connie. He said he didn't think the police could do anything right away. That's why he urged me to hire you to look for her. I wasn't sure but when I saw you that night I knew it was the right thing to do."

Hannibal's mind was spinning now. No one he knew in law enforcement would recommend him to a potential client without telling him about it. "This policeman... was he in uniform or plain clothes?"

Connie's smile returned. "Oh, very plain clothes. I didn't think a policeman would dress that way, but he showed me his badge."

"What did he look like?" Hannibal asked.

"Well, he was an Anglo, a white man, kind of tall and thin. He had this wild brown hair and a little mustache. And he had on a suit like you, but no tie, just one of those Hawaiian shirts with the crazy prints on them. Not a man you would forget, you know?"

Chapter 16

Hannibal was pushing Black Beauty up over eighty miles an hour when Cindy asked, "So the cop who visited Sophia Babcock was really this Quentin Sands?" Out the corner of his eye he saw her backlit by passing headlights. She was even beautiful in bas relief and moonbeams through the windshield only made her glow more than usual.

"From her description it had to be," he said.

"But why would he have set her up to drag you into all this?"

"Good question," Hannibal said, gliding around a Mercedes in the right lane. He wondered if everyone got their windows tinted outside the DC area. "And somebody made sure I won't be able to ask him. For now I'll go with him wanting somebody to hunt Connie down without police involvement. He did manage to steer her away from involving the cops by putting me in the mix."

Cindy leaned back and placed her hand on his leg. "But you're still going to look for her, aren't you?"

"Actually, I'm pretty sure I know where she is," Hannibal said, "And yeah, I will go check on her. I've got other business to clear up there anyway."

Chapter 17

After a long, deep kiss Cindy rested her head on his shoulder and asked, "Are you sure you won't come up. Lover?"

Hannibal smiled, his hand still tangled in her hair. He glanced over his shoulder at her front door then turned his eyes back to her smile, glowing in the dashboard lights. "You know how tempting that is, right? But you've got an early start in the morning and if I come in there is not going to be a lot of sleeping. And, you know…"

"Yeah," Cindy nodded and sighed. "You've got some crazy shit going on tomorrow and you need to be in your own space to prepare, right?" At Hannibal's look of surprise she added, "I know my man. Just promise to dream about me tonight."

Cindy's parting words, and the taste of her goodnight kiss, kept Hannibal smiling on the short drive from Alexandria to his neighborhood in Northeast Washington DC. He pulled into the parking space directly across the street from his own front door, right under a street lamp. For reasons he didn't really understand his neighbors seemed to agree that this was his designated space. No one else ever parked there.

As he climbed out of his car his smile dimmed a bit. Two Hispanic men lounged on his stoop. He evaluated them as he walked toward his front door. One man sat on the left sandstone handrail, with the other opposite him. Both were young, he'd guess under thirty. Both wore clunky brown boots and oversized flannel shirts. Both were showing two or three inches of boxer shorts at their waists above low slung jeans. Was this the approved gang uniform?

The strangers waited until Hannibal set one foot on the first of six steps up to the landing before they stood. Side by side, hands hanging loosely with one shoulder dipped lower than the other, they looked like a pair of avant guard bookends. Gangsta chic, Hannibal would have called it.

"Can I help you gentlemen? Are you lost?"

"You Jones?" the left bookend asked.

"Pretty common name, right?" Hannibal asked, smiling up into their grim stares. "In this case, Hannibal Jones. That who you're looking for?"

Right bookend said, "You been asking a lot of questions. Asking about the wrong shit, making too much noise. You need to quit."

Hannibal stifled a chuckle. "Really? They send you two to threaten me? I'm kind of insulted."

"You don't want to fuck with us," Left bookend said. He lifted his shirt, slowly and dramatically, to let Hannibal see the automatic shoved into his waistband.

"Well hell, son," Hannibal said, thumbing back his jacket far enough to reveal his shoulder holster, knowing it was too dark to see that it was empty. "Everybody's got one of those. Now, you feel like gambling? You want to bet your life you can draw faster than me?"

The right-side gangbanger cracked a smile and elbowed his partner. "Chill, Rafe. We only here to deliver a message. But maybe we should cement it with a good ass kicking. He might hear better without all them teeth in his mouth."

Hannibal tightened his gloves on his hands and slowly moved up the next five steps. "You boys should have done more research before you came to my house. I generally step over boys your size to get into fights." When he was one step down from the man on the left he showed his clenched teeth and said, "You got three seconds."

It took the gang banger two seconds to decide. He snapped his right fist back, aiming down at Hannibal's face. Hannibal's left hand snapped up faster, to slap and grip the man's crotch. Before his eyes could even cross Hannibal's right hand clamped on his throat. Hannibal yanked to his right, pulling the left bookend into his partner, knocking him backward before twisting to toss his first assailant down the sandstone stairs. Hannibal recognized the sound when the falling man's right shoulder hit the steps. That was a dislocation at least.

Spinning back, Hannibal drove his right fist deep into the second man's stomach. He ducked a clumsy right cross, captured the arm, and hauled this man over his shoulder. The second man flew for a second and landed hard on his partner. Hannibal trotted down the steps and snatched number two's gun out of his waist and aimed it down at his two attackers.

"I heard you boys were tough. Can't believe you're the best Rodriguez had to offer."

"Who?" the second man asked, scrambling to get to his feet.

"You're here for Pablo Rodriguez, right?" Faced with blank faces, Hannibal reconsidered. "You are MS-13 right?" The two men looked at each other, then back at the gun in Hannibal's hand. "Wait. You didn't come in here from Virginia… did you?"

One of the men shook his head. Hannibal walked slowly down to them, gun moving smoothly from one to the other. "Of course not. You're DC gangstas. They heard I was poking around in MS-13 business. But you assholes are like any other terrorists, ain't you. Separate cells. Your bosses don't talk to each other. Well, let's put an end to this crap."

Hannibal pushed the pistol close into his first attacker's face. He yanked the man's gun out of his pants, tossed it behind him to the bottom of the stairs, and got a firm grip on the man's injured shoulder. "You delivered your message. Now you can take one back to your boss for me. The business that I'm involved in, it's Virginia business not District business. You boys stay out of my way, I'll stay out of yours. If he's got issues with that, he needs to talk to his

V-A contacts. If any of you boys steps to me again, they'll go home in a body bag. Got it? Now you two hit the road before you really piss me off."

Hannibal released the gangster and took a couple of steps back. He kept the gun on them as they slowly withdrew, looking over their shoulders the whole way. Behind him, Hannibal heard his front door open. He turned to see Sarge, one of his upstairs neighbors, easing the door open, shotgun first. Sarge was a big, beefy, bald black man. He was barefoot but in jeans and a white wifebeater that put the Marine Corps fouled anchor tattoo on his shoulder on display. He took in the tableau and called to Hannibal.

"Heard a ruckus. Trouble?"

"Not so you'd notice," Hannibal said. "Couple of local troublemakers but I took care of it."

"People after you?" Sarge asked.

"Not really," Hannibal said, holstering the pistol he confiscated from the gangsta. "Just turns out I've got more enemies than I thought."

"Yeah, well, that's cause you don't know how to talk to people nice."

Chapter 18

Friday

Bright sunlight flashed up from the driveway flagstones as Hannibal cruised into Pablo Rodriguez' circular driveway. He parked just past the front door and sat for a moment to allow the invisible guards time to evaluate his car and realize they were not under attack. He adjusted his Oakley's on his face, straightened his tie and tightened his gloves on his hands. Then he stood, used the fob to lock his car behind him and stepped up to the front door. He didn't see any point in ringing the bell. He stood for less than a minute before the door opened and he was staring up at Kenny's crooked smile.

"Seriously?" Hannibal said. "You're the doorman too?"

Kenny's brow furrowed in a threatening way. "You got an appointment? Or you just looking for trouble?"

"Come on, man. You know I got business with Pablo. He busy?"

From deeper in the house, Juan's voice said, "Hey, the man says bring him in."

Kenny nodded and took two long steps back. Hannibal matched his movement and held his arms out. Kenny patted him down, raising an eyebrow when he felt the empty shoulder holster. Then he pointed Hannibal toward the office and stepped around him to close the door. So he was sufficiently accepted now that he didn't need to be escorted to the room. Guess they trusted he wouldn't try to steal any of the decorations on his way in. His footsteps clicked on the marble floor and the familiar floral scent met him at the office door. Pablo was in his power chair with Juan standing to his left, arms folded, leaning against the wall. Hannibal stopped in front of the desk and nodded acknowledgement toward Juan before focusing on Pablo.

"So you're the man, eh?" Hannibal said.

"Nah, I employ the man," Pablo said. They locked eyes. After six seconds of silence Pablo said, "To what do I owe this unexpected visit? You got something for me?"

"You've already got it," Hannibal said. "Your man picked up the package already."

"So?"

"So I'm here to get paid," Hannibal said.

Pablo opened his humidor and selected a fresh cigar. His face betrayed nothing while he clipped the tip and lit his cigar with a heavy lighter sitting on his desk. When he looked up at Hannibal he managed an expression of mild surprise. "So, you want to get paid? My man here brought me the Babcock girl, so unless you got Hernandez in your trunk outside, what am I paying you for?"

"Come on, Pablo," Hannibal said. "We both know I'm the reason you've got Connie. I found her, I flushed her out."

"Nice try, Chico." Pablo pointed his cigar at Hannibal. "Truth is, some broad at this shelter called to tell me the girl was home. That broad got a nice reward for that."

"Good for her," Hannibal said. "but I'm the reason she was there. I found her. I talked to her. I told her to go home to her mama. She did. If not for me she'd still be in the wind."

"Really? Funny, that's not her story."

Hannibal leaned forward, planting his palms on the desk. "Oh yeah? What IS her story?"

Juan moved away from the wall but a subtle hand movement from Pablo froze him. The gang boss grinned and nodded. "You trying to play me, player? If you knew she was there, how come you didn't call me?"

"Because some asshole clocked me from behind and knocked me out. Pretty sure it had to be Danny Hernandez. So now I got my own reasons for running that boy down."

Pablo laughed out loud, a harsh barking sound. "So you got your own reasons for finding him now. Just don't let that get in the way of my reasons."

"Hold up," Hannibal said. "I thought you were after Ozzie."

Pablo shook his head. "Keep up, Chico. Connie Babcock was the path to Ozzie Hernandez. Ozzie was the path to his brother Danny."

"Who's on your shit list, because…?"

Pablo slapped a palm on his desk. "That bitch stole from me, and that can't be allowed. You find him, you do what you need to but when you're done you bring him here in condition that he can talk to me. Or, really, so he can talk to Kenny. Kenny, he's real good at getting people to tell him what he needs to know."

"Yeah, I want him but don't get it twisted," Hannibal said. "I ain't bringing you nobody for free. So first we settle this business about Connie Babcock…"

Pablo held up a palm. Hannibal stopped talking and backed off from the desk. Juan returned to his leaning, arms crossed stance. "That business is settled," Pablo said, puffing his cigar. "You ain't getting dick for the girl. But I see you're highly motivated so tell you what. A new deal. Forget Ozzie. Fifty grand for Danny Hernandez. But you deliver him here, in person, not a clue or a lead. Get it?"

"Sure," Hannibal said, holding both palms out, then pointing at Pablo with both index fingers. "And I'm supposed to trust you, right?"

Pablo was not a tall man but he was a big man. He rose from his chair in a manner that was almost majestic, and his black eyes nailed Hannibal to the spot. The fierceness of his gaze was accented by the scar by his eye which reddened. His voice was low, deep, almost a growl.

"You saying you don't trust me? Me, Pablo Rodriguez?"

Hannibal slowly slid his Oakley's off and moved one step closer to the monster on the other side of the desk. "Let's be clear. You are a drug dealer. A pimp. A murderer. You work in extortion. All cash businesses, and it would be a hell of a lot cheaper for you to have me taken out than to hand me fifty K. But with your army of street thugs, you can't find this one punk. I, on the other hand, am a private investigator. My clients generally give me a retainer when I accept work, not threats and bluster. Because they know they need my skills more than I need their business."

Pablo raised his right hand as if he was going to grab Hannibal by the shirt. Hannibal raised his left hand as if he was going to block Pablo's arm.

"That," Hannibal said, "would be a mistake. We wouldn't be doing business anymore. It would become something else."

Pablo took a deep breath. A second. Then reached down to open a desk drawer. He pulled out a short stack of bills and dropped it on his desk.

"Five thousand dollars. A ten percent retainer. That says you're hired to do a job. That says we agree to trust each other. That says you don't stop until the job is done."

Hannibal replaced his glasses and stuffed the money in an inside jacket pocket. "Glad we can do business."

"Well I figure ain't shit gonna intimidate a nigger that grew up with blue eyes," Pablo said, lowering back into his chair. So go get to work."

Only then did Hannibal notice that Juan was leaning forward and had drawn his pistol. Now he smiled, holstered his weapon and leaned back.

"I'm ready to get to it," Hannibal said. "And I'm betting you've got the best clues right here in the building. I need to question Connie Babcock."

Chapter 19

The room made the king bed look small. The open door to his left led to a big walk-in closet. Latin music videos bounced across the 27-inch television facing the love seat to his right. A vase of red roses stood on the dresser against the wall, visually doubled thanks to the mirror that spanned the length of the dresser. A vanity beside it offered three more panels of mirrors, making the room look even bigger. Hannibal's shoes were almost lost in the deep, plush off-white carpet as he stepped into the room. He moved toward the four-poster bed which was dressed in a thick purple satin comforter. Connie Babcock sat in the center of that comforter wrapped in a terrycloth robe that matched the comforter exactly. She neither leaned away nor forward as he approached. Her face seemed totally relaxed. She waited until Hannibal stood at the edge of the bed before she spoke.

"So you are one of them," she said. "Well, be prepared to get rough. I won't tell you any more than I told the others. Which is nothing."

Hannibal nodded. "Message received. You're not scared of me."

"That's totally wrong," Connie said. "I'm fucking terrified. But that don't mean I can't take whatever you got. And I won't turn on my man."

Hannibal grabbed the chair from the vanity and spun it around so the back faced the bed. He dropped onto the chair, straddling its back. "You do know I was telling the truth before, right? Your mother must have told you that she sent me looking for you."

"She said something about a private eye looking for me. Didn't say he was black." Connie picked at a dark shadow under her left eye. In the dim light Hannibal could now see it was a purple bruise resting on her right cheekbone.

"Well, it's me, and I want to get you home safely. I'd also like to know who did that to you. I didn't think Pablo would hurt a guest. Kill you. Sure. Hit you? Not what I'd expect."

A lopsided grin appeared on Connie's face and she faced him squarely, crossing her ankles and offering Hannibal more of a view than he wanted. "What you got in mind, amigo? Are you mi Salvador? You want to save me? You going to throw me on your back and shoot your way out of here?"

"Maybe you don't get this, but they don't really want you," Hannibal said, keeping his eyes on hers, avoiding her creamy thighs and the dark space above. "They don't even want Ozzie. All Pablo wants is your boy Danny. He gets him, he loses interest in you. And since Danny has apparently run off and left you to the wolves, I'm not sure why you haven't given him up. How'd you get hooked up with that loser anyway?"

Connie seemed to notice Hannibal's discomfort. Her brow wrinkled in confusion, then she spun her legs to her left and pulled the robe to cover most of her upper legs. "You know who Greg Howard is? I was with Greg for a while, before Evelyn. He was nice. But then he introduced me to Danny. Greg was good, but Danny runs those fights they set up. I knew that was a step up so I got with Danny. He was good to me but that's not the reason I won't tell these gangsters anything. You really want to know why? Well I'll tell you, after you tell me why you want him so bad. I know it's not just to help me. You on the MS-13 payroll?"

"No, this is personal now," Hannibal said. "Are you really surprised? I was standing there, talking to you. Then, all of a sudden I'm in the dark, then I'm in a wrestling hold from behind. It had to be Danny that knocked me out. That's bad enough. Then he had the nerve to take my gun. Can't have that kind of shit happening. Bad for the rep."

Connie looked at Hannibal as if he might be the next step up. She swung her legs back toward him and slid forward so she was sitting on the edge of the bed, face to face with him. His brow wrinkled as he got a good look at the bruise.

"Between us, Danny's no idiot," she said. "He's probably out of the country by now. But what were you doing at the house that night? How'd you find me? I thought I covered my tracks pretty good."

"No mystery," Hannibal said, thinking about how quickly this girl ran through men. "I met your other man, Quentin in a bar. He led me to the house. I figure you and Danny were both home. Before you opened the door Danny slipped out the back, right? You just distracted me while he went around the house and came in the front door and knocked me out. I'm looking forward to a rematch."

"Not likely," Connie said. "You say Quentin brought you to his rental? That's too rich. He was nowhere to be seen when we came out of the house. But I drove Danny to Quentin's house that night. Danny ran in looking for Quentin but came out and said he wasn't home. So I drove him down to the airport where he keeps his plane"

"Down to?" Hannibal asked.

"He flies out of this podunk place down by Virginia Beach. Knight's Landing I think. Anyway I dropped him down there before I went back to let my mom know I was okay. That turned out to be a bad idea."

"Well that's a pretty good lead," Hannibal said, "Assuming it's the truth. But why didn't you tell Pablo's boys? It might have spared you that shiner."

Connie leaned forward, setting her elbows on the back of Hannibal's chair. "I'll tell you why. They put their hands on me, squeezing my tits, grabbing my ass, didn't even ask or try to pretend I invited it. I got used to boys treating me with a little more respect. That's how I got this on my face. Rodriguez told them not to hurt me, but one of them grabbed my crotch and I tried to claw his eyes out. He hit me before

90

Rodriguez could stop him. So when they started asking questions I just got stupid."

"Well, I appreciate that you didn't get stupid with me."

Connie pushed her face as close to his as she could, making Hannibal lean back. "I told you because you're different from them. You didn't even try to look where that pig stuck his fat hand. So I figure maybe you will try to take me away from here. And maybe I'll let you."

Chapter 20

Kenny was standing in the hall outside Connie's room when Hannibal stepped out. Hannibal felt those eyes on him but ignored the thug as he trotted down the spiral staircase. He dropped his calm demeanor like tossing off a stained shirt. He was breathing deeply when he reached the main floor. He heard the heavy footsteps behind him, but did not slow down. When he reached the familiar door, he burst into Pablo Rodriguez' office uninvited. Pablo looked up, clearly startled, but this time Hannibal didn't steer to the visitor's chair. Instead he turned to his right and walked straight up to Juan. The gangster pulled back against the wall, looking more surprised than threatened. Hannibal almost snarled at him, fists clenched tight.

"Who hit the girl?"

Juan glanced at Pablo, whose face betrayed only amusement. Hannibal heard Kenny enter the room just as he heard a switchblade snap open.

"Don't even try," Hannibal said, not taking his eyes off Juan's. He grabbed Juan's right wrist and slammed his hand back against the wall. "I will shove that little blade right up your Latin ass. Now, who hit the girl?"

Kenny's hand landed on Hannibal's left shoulder. "You need to chill, Nig…"

Kenny's words were lost when Hannibal's right elbow swung up and around into the side of Kenny's head. Then Hannibal swung forward, his right shoulder smashing into Juan's chest, crushing the man into the wall. Pulling Juan's right arm, Hannibal turned just enough to spin Juan into Kenny. Then Hannibal snapped off a crisp right jab into Juan's jaw. Juan dropped, and Hannibal nailed Kenny with a left uppercut. Kenny fell backward, rolled across Pablo's desk and dropped to the floor.

"Stop that shit," Pablo bellowed, aiming a .44 revolver. Hannibal stayed focused on Juan, stepping hard down on his right wrist.

"Who hit the girl?"

Kenny got to his feet and rose to his full height. "Get off my boy." He charged, but Hannibal stepped aside, grabbed Kenny's arm and shoved him head first into the wall with a loud thump. He yanked Kenny back and used a foot sweep to drop him on the floor, half on top of Juan.

"I said quit it," Pablo shouted.

Hannibal turned toward Pablo, all but ignoring the gun. "Kill me and you'll never find Danny and whatever he took from you. Besides, you don't want to bring the violence here to your home. But you took that girl, she ain't done shit to you, and one of your boys punched her. I want to know who."

"It wasn't either of them," Pablo said. "These two don't hurt nobody unless I say."

"Well somebody blackened that eye. You're supposed to be in charge here. Don't you know who?"

"Of course I know," Pablo said, "and it ain't none of your business but I took care of it and that boy won't be stepping out of line again. Now, you know where Danny Hernandez is?"

"I got a strong lead," Hannibal said. "I'm sure I can track him down. Can we get back to business now?"

Pablo lowered his weapon slowly. "Yeah, we need to get back to business. Right after this is finished."

Kenny's looping right came out of nowhere, spun Hannibal's head around and tossed his glasses across the room. The bigger man's punch staggered Hannibal but he did not fall. He readied a counter punch but held it. The two men locked eyes for a second. Then Hannibal dropped his fist.

"All right, Kenny. I'm going to let that go. Now we're even. Yeah?"

Kenny glanced at his boss' impassive face, looked past Hannibal at Juan, and then dropped his own hands. "Yeah, okay, mano." Then he grinned. "You got a hell of a left for a little guy."

Hannibal nodded his thanks for the compliment. He turned to see that Juan was smiling too. "Sorry I thought you might have … I should have known better. You a pro." Then he walked into the corner and bent to retrieve his glasses.

"So, you think you can find Danny," Pablo said. It was not a question.

"I know he has a plane," Hannibal said, slipping his glasses back into place. "I figure he's in the wind with whatever you're looking for. I also figure that even if you knew what airport it was and what kind of plane he had, you still wouldn't know how to figure out where he went."

"And you going to tell me you can?" Pablo asked, setting his gun down on his desk.

Hannibal shrugged. "I'm a detective. This is what I do. But I can't do it alone."

Juan knocked on Pablo's desk with a knuckle. "You want I should back him up, Jefe?"

"I appreciate the offer," Hannibal said, "but that's not what I meant. The only way I can be sure I'm headed to the right place is, I got to take Connie Babcock with me. You turn her over to me, and I'll bring Danny Hernandez right here to you, guaranteed."

Pablo rested his hand on the big revolver in front of him. "Uh-huh. So I'm supposed to trust you now?"

"If I don't come through, I'm not hard to find."

At that Pablo leaned back and laughed his rough bark, then told Juan, "Bring the little bitch down here."

After an awkward ten minute wait Kenny walked into the office, his right hand locked around Connie's upper arm. When he released her she stood right where he left her, in the center of the room, in blue three-inch heels. In that time she had squeezed into skin tight jeans and a tee shirt that said, "I love caviar, Cadillacs and cash." A gift from someone who really knew her, Hannibal thought. She had brushed her hair to one side, with one long wave hanging to partially obscure her bruises.

While she stared at Pablo, Hannibal studied her face. He saw no surprise there or even curiosity about what was happening. Nor did her features reflect fear or anger. It was difficult to put a name to her expression but Hannibal finally settled on a word that surprised even him: calculating.

Pablo stood and pointed his cigar at Connie, but pointed a finger of his left hand at Hannibal. "So, chica. I'm cutting you loose. You his bitch now. Do what he say and he might let you go home to your mama." Then he turned to Hannibal. "Now take your bitch and get the fuck out of my house. Come back when you got what I want."

Connie looked at Hannibal. He jerked his head toward the door, then walked out of the office. He heard her stilettos clicking behind him. They exchanged no words on the way out to his car. He opened the passenger door for her. Her smirk said she was not accustomed to that. She dropped into her seat and sat in silence while he got in, started the engine and drove off. Hannibal still listened to the classic rock of his youth in Europe more than anything else. As he eased his car out of the driveway, David Bowie's voice broke into the quiet, telling his story about changes.

The narrow local streets of Northern Virginia had given way to the four lane bustle of the Beltway before the girl added her voice. "So what now Mister Detective?"

"Now I return you to your mother, which was the job I agreed to."

"Thank you. Then you go after Danny?"

"That was the price of your freedom." Hannibal smiled at the skyscraper trees lining the highway. Leaves were just starting to brown in the sun, preparing for colder days. Some changes were better than others.

"I hope you don't end up getting him killed," she said. The Bee Gees took over the musical background warning of Jive Talking.

"He apparently stole from MS-13," Hannibal said. "I think I can come back without him if I bring whatever he took instead."

Connie nodded, staring into her hands. "Look, they took my stuff. Can I borrow your phone for a minute?"

"No."

"If we're going to the shelter I'd like to let Mama know I'm coming."

After another brief pause Hannibal pulled his phone out of his jacket and handed it to her. She murmured something that might have been thank you, then tapped buttons on the phone. Her eyes expanded in surprise when she heard the ringing through the dashboard. Hannibal's phone was paired through the car for hands free use.

"Can you…?"

"No," Hannibal said. He didn't want to miss any of this particular conversation.

After five rings Sophia Babcock said, "Hello?"

"Mama? It's me, Connie,"

"Madre de Dios! Concepción! Are you all right? Where are you? I was so worried."

"I'm fine Mama. Headed home right now. Maybe forty-five minutes away. This detective found me."

"Mr. Jones found you? He is so nice. Is he there with you?"

Connie glanced at Hannibal but he chose not to speak. "Yes, Mama. He's right here."

"Oh, good. He has been so good to me and I don't want him to get into any trouble. There are policemen here right now and they were asking about him. They say he might have information about a murder."

"Oh my God," Connie said. "Who's dead?"

"They showed me a picture of the policeman who told me I should ask Mr. Jones for help. But they said he's not really a policeman at all. It was all very confusing."

Hannibal's hands tightened on the wheel and he tuned out of the conversation while Connie and her mother said goodbye. So they had found Quentin. And they thought Hannibal might know something. Well, it was possible that some witness had come forward. Maybe a neighbor saw him outside the house. Or some ambitious CSI type may have found some forensic evidence that placed Hannibal in the house or even something on the body that led to him. Well, they would have to wait. He would drop Connie off a couple blocks from the women's shelter and head back to The District. He'd talk to the police later. It would not do to be detained while he was on Pablo Rodriguez's clock.

Besides, before too much time passed, he wanted his gun back.

Chapter 21

Hannibal spun his eyes to the ceiling to accentuate his frustration.

"You mean I came all the way up here to visit Danny and he's checked out already? This can't be real."

"You did say Danny Hernandez, right?" the nurse asked. She was neither cute nor ugly, but her leathery skin made her lean to the latter in Hannibal's eyes. Besides, he never really liked blonde black women. Under other circumstances he'd walk right past her, but in his business he had learned that it was easier to get people on your side if you treated them nicely.

"Look Miss," he glanced at her name tag, "Lincoln is it? Miss Lincoln I drove five hours up from North Carolina after I heard my boy was hurt. Well I guess he wasn't hurt too bad in that accident. You sure he's checked out?"

"I'm looking right at his records," Nurse Lincoln said. "Signed himself out Tuesday night. It's right here."

"Damn," Hannibal said, under his breath. Then he slid his sunglasses off and looked into her eyes as if seeing them for the first time. "So sorry for my language. I'm just sorry I missed him. Haven't seen him in an age. Do you have his address there?"

"Sorry, I'm not supposed to…"

"Please, Miss Lincoln."

One thing Hannibal liked about hospital nurses was that they were too busy to waste time trying to protect personal information. Most had figured out that the fastest way to get someone who was not a patient out of their hair was to tell them what they wanted to know. The nurse sighed, shook her head, and tapped on her keyboard a few more times.

"Sorry, sir, he didn't leave an address."

"Wow," Hannibal said, shaking his head. "I didn't think they could admit you without your address."

He didn't really think it would be that easy to find out where Danny had gone after he left the hospital but it was worth a try. He was about to give up and move on but something made him hang on for a moment. Maybe it was the way Nurse Lincoln stared into his blue eyes again. Then she tapped more keys and arched an eyebrow.

Are you sure you didn't mean Ozzie Hernandez?"

"Ozzie?" Hannibal asked. "That's Danny's brother! Was he here?"

"Yes, looks like he came in to the emergency room, but wasn't admitted. Geez, this must be a bad luck family."

"Ma'am, you have no idea."

While driving into the NoMa apartment's parking garage Hannibal considered how entangled he had become in Hispanic family connections. He didn't really have a good handle on the relationship between Sophia Babcock and her daughter Connie, but he had overheard enough to know that the Hernandez men were tightly bound together.

Of course, Hannibal had checked Ozzie's apartment first. No one was there and nothing had changed. Had he been home he would have had to straighten up at least a little. Hannibal reasoned that if Danny was half as sharp as Connie implied he wouldn't even consider a return to the rented house down in Colchester. But there was that family connection. Nicky kept track of his sons and still doted on them. If anyone knew where Danny had taken off to, it would be Nicky.

Once again Hannibal rang the bell and stood back so his face would be clear to the eye on the other side of the peephole. This time he heard movement inside. After a long minute, locks were thrown inside and the doorknob turned.

The door opened a crack and a single inquisitive eye peered out of the darkness.

"Hello," Hannibal said, sharing a friendly smile. "My name's Hannibal and I'm looking for Danny Hernandez. I visited him in the hospital the other day, but when I went back I found out he's already discharged. Figured he'd come here to visit his old dad."

"How you found my house?"

"Danny gave me the address of course," Hannibal said. "And I must say these are some mighty fine digs. You got Danny recuperating in there?"

"I don't know you."

Hannibal took a deep breath and tried to look wounded. "Seriously? Do you know Greg? Or Connie? I hang with them."

From deeper in the apartment a voice that was not quite Danny's said, "Pop, for crying out loud let him in. If he was trouble he'd have tried to bust in here by now."

The single eye blinked. The door closed. A chain slid out of its moorings. The door opened and Nicky Hernandez waved Hannibal into the apartment.

Nicky was a shorter, rounder version of his boy Danny, with thinning black hair that still managed to cover his whole head. He wore khakis and a wife beater shirt that showed off a wrestler's shoulders that were only now starting to soften. He smiled but didn't offer a hand and his eyes remained suspicious.

"Come on in the kitchen," Nicky said. "I got paella on the stove." His accent was deeply Cuban and in every way he reminded Hannibal of Cindy's father.

The apartment was bright and filled with an eclectic mix of mismatched furniture. It was also filled with the relaxing aromas of saffron and cilantro. The wood floors went through the entire apartment including the kitchen, which boasted new stainless steel appliances and quartz stone countertops. Nicky walked around the white wooden island to grab a big wooden spoon and stir the pot on the stove. To his left a sliding door opened onto a balcony that looked out over the courtyard. And left of that sat a wooden table that would seat four. The man at the table, dressed just like Nicky, was a shorter, thinner version of Danny. His smile was electric, and nervous energy bled off him.

"You have got to be Ozzie," Hannibal said.

"Yep," he said, hopping to his feet and extending a hand. "You say your name is Hannibal? Like the guy who eats people?"

Hannibal shook hands and nodded. "And you're Ozzie like from the old Ozzie and Harriet TV show, right? Except I don't think there was ever anybody Spanish on that show. That would have been Ricky on the Lucy show."

Ozzie's face went blank.

At the stove, Nicky smiled. "Me and Benita, got rest her soul, wanted the boys to sound American, at least on paper. Maybe make it easier to get a job. Why don't you grab a seat and I'll give you a taste of home. At least my home."

Ozzie dropped back onto his chair and Hannibal took the seat at the other end of the small table. "Thanks, but listen. I have to tell you I'm here on some serious business."

Ozzie spun and stabbed a finger in Hannibal's face. "It's Danny, ain't it? He's in trouble. I'm right, ain't I?"

"I'm afraid you are," Hannibal said, dropping his smile. "There's some serious trouble on Danny's trail, but I'm not it. I just might be able to get him out from under this."

"Danny's a good son and a good man," Nicky said, ladling chicken and rice into three bowls. "He's a smart one, and works hard. I could never pay the rent on this place without his help every month. What kind of trouble could he be in?"

Nicky's face was passive but Ozzie's curiosity was more obvious. In the light of his hard stare Hannibal decided to step carefully. "Well, Danny has some seriously bad people looking for him. I think there was a business deal and they think Danny ended up taking something that didn't belong to him. These people…"

"It's them MS-13 assholes, ain't it?" Ozzie asked, slapping a palm down on the table. "I told Danny not to deal with them guys. We was going good with the wrestlers, but he had to let them damn West Coast Salvadorans get involved." Ozzie added a few words of rapid Spanish that Hannibal didn't catch.

Nicky looked up with a straight face and said, "My boy thinks he's slick, but he's no thief. He can just explain it to them." Ozzie fell back against the wall and sent his eyes to the ceiling. Hannibal sensed there were things he had tried to explain to his father about Danny in the past, with no success.

"Seriously, these aren't the kind of people you explain things to," Hannibal said. "They're the kind that break your arms first, and then ask for an explanation."

Conversation stalled while Nicky sat the three bowls on the small table and handed everyone a fork. Then he pulled three cans of Jupina from the refrigerator. Hannibal recognized it as the pineapple flavored soda Cindy and her father Ray sometimes drank. Hannibal pulled off his gloves and the three men sampled the paella. Not as good as Cindy's, Hannibal thought, but he smiled and made the universal sound for "this is delicious."

Ozzie emptied his mouth before continuing. "So, these gang bangers are looking to do Danny bad. What do you think you can do?"

Hannibal took a long drink from his sharp, sweet beverage. "Well, if I get to Danny before they do, I can make him understand the situation. If I get back whatever he took and return it, I'm pretty sure I can get the bad guys to call off the dogs."

"But I don't know where he might be," Nicky said. "He hasn't been home since he left the hospital, and he isn't answering his phone. Could they have found him already?

"I don't think so. I had a chance to talk to this girl Connie he was hanging with," Hannibal said turning toward Ozzie. "You know her, right?"

Ozzie looked down, focused on his food. "Um, yeah, I know her."

"Well, she tells me Danny has a private plane. She says if he really wanted to disappear he'd hop in that bad boy and take off to parts unknown."

Ozzie jumped to his feet so fast he nearly dumped his food. "What the fuck?"

"Ozzie!" Nicky snapped. "Not in this house."

Ozzie ignored his father, rattling off a few words of Spanish with his fists clenched before turning again to Hannibal. "That plane belongs to me! I let him fly from time to time but it's my property. He can't just… just…"

"Take off?" Hannibal offered. "Well in fact it sounds like he can. But don't you have to file a flight plan and such? Maybe if I knew where to go I could head him off and resolve this mess. Don't want the bad guys confiscating your plane thinking it's his, right?"

"You got a fast car?" Ozzie asked. "Mine's in the shop. But you let me grab a jacket and we need to get to the airport before little bro gets away with my wings."

Hannibal was starting to resent the Virginia Beach connection overrunning this case. With Ozzie's guidance he found himself again southbound on I-95. Traffic got ugly by the time he was taking the 295 spur to get around Richmond. It got worse when he bumped onto I-64. Then there was the fifteen long minutes on toll road 168. After a number of turns farther and farther off the beaten track Hannibal started to wonder if Ozzie was lost. Left on one road for a couple miles, then right down another for two or three miles, a couple more such twists and finally onto a road with no name before they came within sight of what had to be the smallest airport Hannibal had ever seen. One runway. No tower. If not for the hangars he might not have known its purpose.

"Not well named," Hannibal said. "Can't imagine why any knight would land here."

The comment went over Ozzie's head. "Naw, it's Knight's Landing because the guy who owns it is named Knight. Swing over that way. That's where my baby sleeps."

"What am I looking for?" Hannibal asked as they pulled up in front of a blue Quonset hut masquerading as a hangar.

"She's just a little green Cessna 150," Ozzie said with evident pride as they walked toward the hangar. "You don't know planes, do you? She's a side-by-side two-seater. Pretty easy to fly and solid as a rock. I'll tell you, she held up pretty damn well under an endless series of bad landings when I was trying to teach Danny how to fly."

"So you couldn't haul anything big in it I take it," Hannibal said as they wandered into the dark, damp space.

"Oh, hell no. You can stash a couple of good-sized duffle bags behind the seats, and there's just about enough room for two people, if they're good friends, you know what I mean? And if neither of them is fat. But I like to solo and… holy shit!"

They had stopped on the cement in between two planes, either one could have been Ozzie's from the description, except for color. Ozzie held his hands forward, as if he was about to throw a tantrum. His voice started low, and slowly increased in volume.

"She's gone. She should be right there. Right there. That son of a bitch took my baby, without even asking me. He's out somewhere with my baby!"

"Don't panic," Hannibal said in what he hoped was a soothing tone. "We can find out where he went, can't we? Don't you have to file a flight plan or something?"

Ozzie waved the comment away. "Man, that don't mean dick. A little plane like mine can go almost anywhere once it's off the ground. And I don't even know how long he's been gone. If he took off yesterday he could have landed in a backwater strip like this, gassed up and took off again."

From off to their left a voice said, "Nope, it was this morning."

Ozzie and Hannibal spun to focus on a thin fellow in a gray windbreaker lying under a small aircraft. It looked to Hannibal like he was performing some sort of maintenance on one of the wheels. Ozzie ran over to stand at the man's feet.

"You saw him take off?"

The slender man rose on his elbows to look at Ozzie. Bright eyes glowed under a shock of white hair. "Sure, must have been around eleven or so."

"You're quite observant," Hannibal said. "You'd probably notice if a pilot was in a great hurry, or just taking a leisurely flight, eh?"

Hannibal stood relaxed with his hands in his pocket. The man under the plan slid out and sat up to face Hannibal.

"Didn't seem like any big rush to me. Haven't seen this fellow around here for quite a while," the older man said, hooking a thumb at Ozzie. "But he treats his plane right. To tell you the truth, I thought it was him, taking somebody up for a joy ride."

"That was my idiot brother," Ozzie said. "Who was he taking with him?"

The man on the ground recoiled from Ozzie's harsh tone. "Look, son, I got no idea who was in the plane. Passenger was already in there when I came in the hangar. I just saw there was a body in the other seat."

"He was skipping town and taking somebody with him, that son of a..." Ozzie stopped himself, and his face fell as a new thought entered his mind. "Or.. Oh, Jesus, suppose they caught up with him. Suppose one of those gangsters forced him to take off, maybe at gunpoint? They could have took him anyplace."

"Let's not get carried away with conjecture," Hannibal said. "Let's thank this nice man for his help and get back on the trail. I've got some resources I haven't made use of yet."

A light coating of dust from the last road into the airport clung to the lower half of Hannibal's car. He was thinking of getting his Volvo detailed while he hit the button that dialed a preset on his phone. When a voice came thru the dashboard Hannibal asked to be connected with Detective Rissik.

"Did you just say Fairfax County Police?" Ozzie asked. "You got a friend on the force?"

"Sort of."

Less than a minute later, a gruff voice said, "Go for Rissik."

"Orson! It's Hannibal. How's your day going?"

"I thought it was about to end," Rissik said. "What new trouble are you bringing me?"

"Actually, I was hoping I could ask a favor."

Hannibal slid back onto a more serious road during Rissik's heavy sigh. "Jones, I got over a million county residents counting on me for protection. Almost 400 square miles of trouble to keep an eye on. What in hell would make me want to do you a favor?"

"Well..." Hannibal cut his eyes toward Ozzie and decided it didn't matter what he heard after all. "It might just make you feel good. I know you want to stick your thumb in the eye of MS-13. I'm on the trail of a guy who stole something Pablo Rodriguez wants back real bad. If I find him first, I can not only piss off the gang boss, but I just might be able to set him up for you to take down."

"Okay, you got my attention," Rissik said. "You can't run this guy down on your own?"

"He's airborne, chief," Hannibal said. "But it's a private plane, stolen. The owner is here with me. It's the runner's brother but he still he wants his plane back, you know. If we give you the bird's call sign, can you check to see if it's turned up anywhere?"

"I ain't your personal bird dog, you know?" Rissik said. "But I guess if you give me the registration number, the tail number, I can check around for it pretty easy."

Ozzie quickly spoke the number at the windshield, and Rissik rang off. The two men rode northbound in silence for a few minutes, each in his own thoughts, until Ozzie broke the silence.

"You know, I don't know shit about you, but you okay."

"Thanks," Hannibal said, keeping his eyes on the road. He didn't want to be rude, but he also didn't feel a need for a friend named Ozzie. Besides, he wondered if Ozzie would like him so much if he knew Hannibal would willingly turn Danny over to Rodriguez if given the chance. It was the job, and Danny had earned whatever was coming to him. To blunt further conversation, Hannibal tapped a button on his steering wheel, and Hall and Oates launched into Private Eyes.

"I never had a cop do a damn thing to help me out before," Ozzie said.

"Rissik's a bit more of a straight shooter than your average cop."

Ozzie turned to face his window, and seemed to be speaking to the air. "You know, I love my little brother, but sometimes he makes some bad choices. Thinks he can get away with anything. And sometimes shit he does blows back on us."

"Has MS-13 come to you looking for Danny?"

"Not exactly," Ozzie said.

"I saw you were in the emergency room the other day and I wondered…"

"Know how I ended up in the hospital? Them crazy Salvadorans ran me off the road. They was looking for Danny for sure, and I think they thought I was him. This big mother comes over to my car after I'm crashed on the shoulder, looks in at me all banged up, and he says, 'Well, hell, it ain't him' and then just walks off and leaves me there."

Hannibal was stuck for a response but was saved by the phone ringing. He pushed the button on the steering wheel and listened to the disembodied voice in the glow of the dashboard lights.

"Jones? It's Orson."

The subtle switch to first name made Hannibal more alert. "Appreciate you calling me back, chief. You find out anything?"

"Yeah I got some news for you."

"That was fast."

"Yeah," Rissik said. "Planes on the move can be a challenge. News of crashes comes pretty quick."

Chapter 22

Hannibal threw back a shot of Laphroaig and gritted his teeth against the flame burning a trail down into his stomach. "So, when you say crash, do you mean like burst-into-a-fireball-nothing-left-but-ashes crash?"

Rissik shook his head and sighed. "That right there, Jones, is the richest single Malt scotch in the world. This," he held up his glass, "is meant to be sipped, not tossed down your throat like cough syrup."

Of course, Hannibal knew Rissik was right. The shot was a reflection of the mild anger he felt for himself. how did he let himself get caught up in all this? All he wanted to do was a good deed, a favor for a worried mother. But sometimes when you pull a loose thread, you can't know how much ugly you'll unravel.

They had landed in The B Side only because Hannibal had asked Rissik where they could get a drink together and it was his favorite bar. In fact, it was the only bar he ever went to. Orson Rissik was the ultimate creature of habit. But since he chose the venue he let Hannibal pick the drink. They both ended up with Hannibal's chosen scotch, of which Rissik approved, but Ozzie ordered tequila, the rail brand.

The B Side was the kind of informal place Hannibal would call a joint. Tucked inside a simple brick building it catered to a mostly younger crowd but it was mostly professionals on the starter rung of the corporate ladder and a bunch of college types so Hannibal didn't complain. The three men sat huddled around a huge bowl of beef fat fries – supposedly healthier and definitely delicious.

"Don't nobody care about your damned scotch," Ozzie said. "What about my plane?"

"What, like I was there?" Rissik said, stuffing a French Fry into his mouth. "All I've got is a report. No details. But the good news is, there was no mention of bodies."

"I'm betting there won't be," Ozzie said. His two drinking partners were in suits and ties, but he was the clear expert in this case and not reluctant to lecture them. "You guys don't fly, do you? Well let me tell you, even if the engine dies completely, little planes like my Piper Cub, they want to be in the air. They're just gliders with propellers stuck on them. And even if you come down rough, that burst into flames crap only happens in the movies. Only a really shitty pilot would get bad hurt bringing her down. Danny ain't the greatest, but he ain't no shitty pilot either. I taught him."

Hannibal raised a gloved hand, signaling the waitress to bring a third round. "Yeah well I don't think he crashed anyway," Hannibal said. "Or at least I don't think the crash was an accident. What you just said makes me more confident that he just ditched the plane. Danny's on the run and he has to know MS-13 can track him no matter what airport, train station or bus station he might turn up at. So he flies to an out of the way place…"

"Yeah, well not quiet," Rissik said. "If this is him, he went down barely five miles from the airport." He was the most relaxed Hannibal had ever seen him. His top button was open, and he had pulled his tie down a full two inches.

Hannibal nodded at the waitress as their drinks arrived. "Didn't get far, eh? Well that kind of supports my theory. He puts the plane down, and he can walk or hitchhike to anywhere. The western half of Virginia, or even up to West Virginia, that whole empty space sounds to me like a damned good place to get lost."

The three men got quiet for a minute, and Hannibal's mind drifted into the soft rock that he could barely hear over the buzz of room noise. He had never even heard of beef fat fries before but he had to admit they were perfect: crunchy and flavorful on the outside, melt-in-your-mouth soft inside.

They took salt and pepper well, and he liked just a tiny dab of catsup. They were a perfect match with the smoky scotch.

Across the table from him, Ozzie was staring into some misty past. Apparently the fries complemented tequila too. He sighed and said, "I wonder if he had this in mind all along." Both Hannibal and Rissik stared at him until he continued. "Getting a plane was Danny's idea. I kinda always wanted to fly, but I didn't even think about actually owning a plane of my own until Danny suggested it. At the time I thought it was all about my little brother finally caring what I wanted to do. Now I'm thinking maybe he was just playing the long game. And playing me."

"So where is he, Ozzie?" Rissik asked. "Where would your little brother go if he was on the run? And who would he take with him?"

"Hell if I know," Ozzie said. "He took off with my plane, remember?"

"Yeah," Rissik said, leaning forward. "But he could have told you. If his life was on the line I'm pretty sure you'd have let him take it. But instead, he sneaked away."

Hannibal turned to Rissik, suddenly remembering that he wasn't just a friend. He was a cop. A really good cop. And even though he had matched Hannibal drink for drink, he looked and sounded stone cold sober.

"Hey, buddy, where you going with this?" Hannibal asked.

Rissik continued in his familiar flat monotone. "Maybe Danny Hernandez was running from more than MS-13. Who gave you that shiner, Ozzie?" Rissik reached out as if to touch Ozzie's face. Ozzie slapped his hand away.

"What the hell? I was in a car crash, man. Some asshole ran me right off the road. I think they was looking for Danny."

"So it didn't happen in a family squabble, right?" Rissik asked.

"Come on, Orson," Hannibal said, resting a hand on Rissik's shoulder. "Where you getting this stuff?"

Rissik swiveled his head around, turning his dangerous blue eyes on Hannibal. "I had a couple of my guys ask around that fight club Danny helps run. When they asked about Danny's big brother, they were told he threatened Danny just a couple days ago."

Chapter 23

After that the night didn't seem as congenial. Hannibal shook Rissik's hand and they exchanged polite but guarded goodbyes. Hannibal watched Rissik climb into his car and head down the street before he led Ozzie to Black Beauty.

"That guy's a cop, right?" Ozzie said, pulling on his seat belt.

"Yep."

"And you're going to drive now, with him knowing you had all that liquor?"

Hannibal chuckled. "That's the thing. He's a cop, he's not a dick. Not every guy with a badge feels like he has to make everybody's life suck. Rissik, he's only interested in the big fish."

Hannibal started his car and pulled up Ozzie's address in the GPS. He thought he could probably find his way back to the apartment, but why bother when the machinery would do it for him? But as the first sign pointing to I-66 came into view Ozzie prodded his shoulder.

"Hey, man, you ever watched one of those mixed martial arts fights?"

"Not in a long time," Hannibal said. "I studied kickboxing for years but these days I just watch the matches on TV. Those guys can be brutal."

"It's a lot better in person, brother," Ozzie said, warming to his subject. "They guys we got ain't the pros but some of them are damned good. We should go by the dojo and watch a match."

Hannibal steered onto the poorly-lit two lane highway and eased into the far left lane. Exit lanes come and go on I-66 and he didn't want to end up taking one by mistake. "I don't know if I'm really up to watching a fight tonight. Rain check?"

Ozzie plopped back into his seat for a few seconds. When next his voice came out of the darkness it was less jovial. "Danny's a smart guy. The whole flight west could have been a fake. And if he was going to go back to anywhere, it would be the dojo to pick up his stuff."

The RHO Martial Arts Academy was fairly quiet when Hannibal and Ozzie arrived. As always, Hannibal's eyes were drawn to the action as soon as he entered. The men in the ring he could see were very skilled, but they were clearly just sparring, not locked in serious combat. A handful of people in exercise gear wandered in and out, all focused on their own actions to the extent that none was likely even aware of the others. Luis was behind the counter, involved in what looked like business paperwork. Maybe he was logging the take from bets, legal or otherwise, on the fights.

Hannibal was just wondering why the Academy smelled so much like an old-school gym when he noticed the deep, spectator space.

"Hey, Ozzie, what gives?" Hannibal asked. "There's all this space for an audience but it's pretty much empty. I'm thinking there's no match scheduled for tonight at all. Didn't you know?"

Hannibal turned to Ozzie, stunned to see him racing toward the counter with murder in his eyes.

"You bastard," Ozzie screamed, "Danny would never have got involved with this shady shit if not for you."

Ozzie's right hand was stretching toward Luis' throat. The smaller man seemed calm to the point of unawareness. Then his right hand gripped Ozzie's an inch from contact. Luis twisted his arm, then his whole body. Ozzie screamed in pain as his body spun on the axis of his right arm. He landed prone, face down on the floor. The thump made

Hannibal clench his teeth. Luis stepped around the counter and dropped into an easy defensive stance.

A couple of people nearby focused on Luis and his attacker and Hannibal imagined he had seen this scene in a dozen martial arts movies. He walked toward the loser on the mat.

"What the hell, Ozzie? Pretty obvious there's no fight scheduled for tonight. So is this the reason you wanted me to bring you here? So you could pick a fight you are clearly not qualified to win?"

Ozzie lurched to his knees, then planted one foot. His face reflected more rage than embarrassment. It was clear that he wasn't finished. Luis stood ready for an attack. Not his first battle outside the ring, Hannibal judged. This might even be worth watching.

Hannibal heard the click before he saw light flash off the steel. He wasn't sure where Ozzie had pulled the switchblade from, but five inches of steel certainly changed the equation. Now Ozzie stood in a more comfortable stance. This was his kind of action, and the outcome was no longer certain.

Ozzie circled slowly, edging closer to Luis. He was actually grinning in a way Hannibal found chilling. Luis pivoted to track his enemy but he no longer looked quite so confident. Hannibal wasn't sure who would win this clash, but he was pretty sure blood would be shed, barring interference.

A low rumble started deep in Ozzie's throat. He was gearing up for a quick dash into his enemy. "My brother ain't no gangster," he said through clenched teeth. "You and your damned gang muscled your way in here and turned a sweet deal into shit. Well now you gonna pay."

With surprising speed Ozzie stabbed at Luis' midsection. But this time it was Hannibal's gloved hand that captured Ozzie's wrist. Hannibal pulled Ozzie into a circle around himself, knife first. He guided the knife hand down, then suddenly up and back. Ozzie had no choice but to follow until the final move. Then he flipped up and back. For an instant he hung suspended in the air, horizontal, before crashing down hard on his back. Hannibal plucked the knife out of his hand to an unexpected round of applause from bystanders.

"Nice move," someone said. "Is that Jiu jitsu or aikido?"

"More krav maga," Marisol said, stepping up behind Hannibal. "That was pretty impressive."

"You just saved him an ass kicking," Luis said, moving in and preparing to stomp Ozzie's face. He raised his right foot but something about Hannibal's manner stopped him.

"Seriously?" Hannibal asked. "Which martial art teaches kicking a man when he's down? Doesn't matter. I've got his arm locked and he's helpless. But if you land that kick it's going to be you and me. And remember, I've seen your moves, but you ain't seen mine."

The two fighters locked eyes over Ozzie's body, then Luis took two steps back.

"I don't need to get my hands dirty," he said. "Juan will kill him for this." Luis looked around the room as if he had just made an important point, then turned and walked out the door.

"Well I guess there's no doubt what team he's on," Hannibal said, helping Ozzie to his feet. Hannibal was startled by a gentle hand stroking his back. He turned to find himself staring into eyes that were perfect matches for Marisol's light brown curls.

"Hey, killer, do you think I could talk to you for just a minute?" He had seen her as tough but now she looked vulnerable, despite the fact that she was his size and was probably every bit the fighter he was.

"Ozzie, go get in the car," Hannibal said, shoving the key fob into his hand and giving him a gentle push. "Get in and lock the door. You seem to have a knack for making enemies and I don't need to get in the middle of any more fights tonight."

After watching Ozzie's back slip out the front door Hannibal let Marisol take his arm and lead him to a back room set up like a small office. The desk and office chair might have come from WalMart and the steel filing cabinet was probably second hand. He wasn't surprised. It wasn't unusual for businesses to spend all their money on the areas customers could see.

Hannibal closed the door and leaned back against it. Marisol sat on the desk facing him, trying to look cute and seductive in her bright blue workout suit. She was sadly out of practice.

"Okay, Marisol, how can I help you?"

Her eyes went to the floor then climbed to Hannibal's sunglasses. "I need you to tell me where Danny is. I miss him and I'm thinking you the man, maybe the only man, who knows where he took off to and when he'll be back."

Marisol absently scratched her forearm while she stared into his eyes. She seemed anxious, as if his answer meant the world. It wasn't until she rubbed her nose that it hit him.

"Oh," he said aloud before he could stop himself. This wasn't love or lust. This was withdrawal.

"Marisol, I hate to disappoint you, but I don't know where Danny is. But I am looking for him, I only came here tonight because Danny's brother said there was a match to watch and I thought Danny might come back to work the event." Marisol's eyes went to the floor and Hannibal ached for a moment to see this girl, who at his first meeting appeared to be a dedicated athlete, looking weak and insecure because of the need for some drug.

"Yeah, okay, well, thanks," she mumbled, then looked up as if a new thought had forced its way into her mind. "Say, we do have a match on tomorrow. Should be pretty good too. A couple of pretty popular fighters facing off. Maybe Danny will come back for that. There's going to be a lot of cash floating around. I know he's going to want to grab some of that." Then she turned and walked off toward the weight stacks as if Hannibal had floated out of her mind and was already forgotten. Not that this bothered him at all. Marisol was a connection he did not need to make.

Chapter 24

Saturday

"So then I take it you took this Ozzie character home," Cindy said. She was pushing eggs around in a frying pan, absently preparing to flip some while others would remain sunny side up.

"Yeah. His daddy wasn't all too thrilled with the news of the day but that wasn't my lookout. I still left there with no clue to where Danny might have run off to."

The kitchen in his modest railroad flat was small, but he had upgraded it with new, stainless steel appliances and mocha-colored tile flooring. Cindy had declared it a joy to cook in and now made it a habit to either drop by or wake up at Hannibal's place on Saturday to make brunch.

Sitting in the next room at the big table with the men he called his chosen family, Hannibal closed his eyes for a moment to drink in the mix of some of his favorite aromas: fresh toast, strong coffee, and the butter in the big pan under the eggs popping and sizzling at Cindy's hand.

Seated across the table, Ray said, "I see you over there Chico. This here is the smell, and the sound of home." The short, bulky, balding Cuban was starting to thicken around the middle. Ray was Hannibal's friend, the owner of a thriving limousine service and one of Hannibal's four upstairs neighbors. He was also Cindy's father.

Not that long ago Hannibal had hired on to close the crack house this building had become. He hired Ray, along with the others at the table – Sarge, Quaker and Virgil – to help him chase the drug dealers out. That effort turned into a pitched battle with local drug lords. The fight got ugly before the end, but it also forged strong bonds of friendship between these five men. Afterward they all decided to stay in the building. Hannibal lived in the ground floor apartment on one side of the building and used the one on the other side for his office. His friends rented the four apartments upstairs.

"Plates," Cindy called, and the men lined up like hungry school children. Each plate held two thick slices of buttered Cuban toast. Cindy worked the spatula like an artist as the men filed past her. She had cooked for this group before, her extended family, so she knew who wanted their eggs on the toast, and who wanted over-easy as opposed to sunny side up.

As they settled back into their seats, Sarge asked, "So what you want with this Danny character anyway? I thought the job was to find the missing girl?" Sarge was a retired Marine, stocky and dark. His scalp shone after his recent decision to shave his head.

"Well it started that way," Hannibal said, sipping his coffee. "but it got kind of twisted. The girl was mixed up with some bad characters. Somehow I got mixed up with them too, and now Pablo Rodriguez expects me to produce this guy and whatever he stole."

"Rodriguez?" Virgil asked in his rolling, booming voice. He was a big black man with yellowed eyes and the puffy hands of an ex-junkie. He was an electrician by trade, but proved most useful to Hannibal because of his street connections. "Isn't he the lead of MS-13 down in Virginia these days?" When Hannibal nodded, Virgil said, "Damn, bro, you don't want to be messing with them South Americans. Them guys don't dance."

"You got that right," Hannibal said, just before biting into his egg-topped toast. "There are a few ways I could get out of this spot, but the easiest will be to find the boy they want."

Hannibal was an expert in the art of the egg sandwich. The trick, as he would have told anyone who asked, is to continually tilt the toast in different directions in order to keep the liquid yolk on the toast until your mouth is sufficiently empty for the next bite. You will of course have guided the bulk of the yolk to the exact area you intended to bite into next.

"You got any good leads?" Quaker asked, attacking his egg with a knife and fork after coating it with a thin layer of salt. Sometimes Hannibal thought Quaker forgot he was the white guy of the bunch, tall and thin with an angular face and brown flyaway hair. But it seemed the rest of the crew forgot as well. And he was a handy guy to have in a building that needed constant work. He had done a fair amount of carpentry work there, in addition to changing all the locks.

Hannibal was sipping strong, hot café con leche out of a mug Cindy handed him. He nodded at Quaker. "Best I've got is the idea that he might return to the dojo he was helping to run. I'm told they're holding a match there tonight. I actually think he was dealing drugs out of that place for MS-13 before he did something that pissed off their boss. He might be on the run, but if he wants to make good with them…"

"He might go back there to make some sales and gather some cash," Cindy said, easing her curvaceous bottom into the chair beside Hannibal. "That would make sense."

"And that would be crazy dangerous too," Sarge said. "He'd have to be nuts."

"Or real desperate," Hannibal said. "The kind of desperate that might make a guy crash a plane on purpose."

Cindy leaned toward Hannibal and smiled. "So, is that where we're going tonight?"

"We?" Hannibal asked.

"Well, I've never seen one of these mixed martial arts shows," Cindy said. "Sounds fun."

"It's not a show," Hannibal said, finishing his breakfast and licking his fingertips. "These fighters are serious, and so are their followers. I expect they'll draw a pretty good crowd tonight. I was thinking about going, but if I do I'll be searching that crowd for Danny Hernandez. I'm afraid I won't be very good company."

Sarge swept his toast around his plate, cleaning up the last bits of egg yolk. "You got a picture of this jamoke? I haven't been to a good fight in a long time. Let's have a look at the target so we can search with you."

"Yeah, we should all go," Ray said, winking at his daughter. "A good night out, we'll see some action in the ring, and we can watch your back if you spot this fool."

"I don't know," Hannibal said. "If one of the old crew spots Hernandez before I do the action might not all be in the ring."

Ray waved the objection aside. "MS-13 ain't nothing but a street gang that's got too big for its britches. And you got to remember. You got a gang too."

Hannibal thought he was exaggerating that morning, but to his surprise RHO Martial Arts Academy was standing room only on Saturday night. The spectators were a thorough mix of the population of The District of Columbia, Maryland and Virginia, what people called the DMV these days. Black and white, Hispanic and Asian, old and young, big and small, and just a touch more male than female. From the ring to the wall they stood shouting at the fighters in a dense variety of languages.

It didn't look like a good matchup to Hannibal. The fellow who entered the octagon first was muscled like a body builder with rippling abs, arms like polished oak and legs that pulsed with power under his chocolate skin. He walked around the ring shouting that he was the champ and the best fighter around. Hannibal hated to see a black fighter with a big mouth, but this boy looked as if his body could cash any check his mouth decided to write.

His opponent approaching the ring was more focused, less showman. He appeared to be twenty pounds lighter than the other fighter, his foot pads and gloves making his hands and feet look disproportionately big for his arms and legs. The only thing that recommended the slender, wiry Latino was his smooth, round shoulders. That is, until he walked into his corner and threw a couple of practice jabs.

The smaller man's hand all but disappeared halfway out from his body to reappear there an instant later. He was fast in a way that only real martial artists become. Suddenly the balance shifted and Hannibal put his mental wager on the smaller man.

"What do you think?" Sarge asked at Hannibal's elbow.

"The contender," Hannibal said. "Focus and speed over muscle and mouth. But it could get real interesting."

"We put our money on the same horse," Sarge said. "I'm heading over to the other corner. Virgil, Ray and Quaker are spread out okay too. If your boy comes in the room one of us will spot him for sure. Meantime I am going to enjoy this rumble."

Two steps away Sarge disappeared into the screaming crowd. Hannibal wondered if he would see Danny even if he was here. At least Ray was watching Luis. If Danny did come back to do business Hannibal figured he'd touch base with his old contact.

To be less evident, Hannibal wore jeans and a blue golf shirt that evening. Without his usual Oakley sunglasses and suit most people who knew him would walk right past him. Beside him Cindy was also in jeans with a simple sweat shirt, but her outfit didn't make her any less sexy.

The crowd quieted when the announcer stepped into the ring. Cindy gripped his arm and bounced with excitement during the opening announcements. To Hannibal's eye this part of the evening was the same whether it was a boxing match, kick boxing like Hannibal used to do, or an MMA match. Rules are explained, fighters are introduced, and scoring is discussed while the opponents flex and stare each other down.

The bigger man, Tony Makee, walked the edge of the ring with arms raised when his name and weight were given, pumping up the crowd again. In contrast, the smaller man, called Baby Boy Aldo, waved his hands but his eyes never left the other fighter. He was in the zone, just waiting for the bell.

When that first bell sounded the two men circled each other, testing with tentative punches and kicks. Cindy became part of the crowd, screaming random disjointed comments of encouragement at both men in the ring. The world became a roiling mass of squirming humanity. Informal bets changed hands and a whoop arose every time one of the fighters landed a punch or kick.

Hannibal was an island, his own personal eye of the storm, scanning for one face in that mass of humanity. He mentally screened out all women, blacks and men below a certain height. All others got a cursory examination before being pushed into his mental reject pile. He would sift and filter the people there until his on board facial recognition software spotted a match.

Makee managed to land a solid right, backing the smaller Aldo against the net surrounding the octagon. The crowd roared, perhaps smelling blood in the water. But then Aldo came back with four jabs too fast to follow and a crashing overhand right that put Makee on the canvas. Aldo landed hard on him, hooking a leg and slamming a few follow up punches to the bigger man's head.

Across the room, Hannibal spotted Marisol. Tonight she wore a bright yellow work out set with black piping, a zippered sweat shirt and tights that hugged her body in a way that would be distracting to any male opponent. She also was an island, slipping through the crowd like a quicksilver wraith. It was not her seductive body that held his attention, but rather her serious expression and disregard for the fight. Perhaps she was hunting Danny as well, or even better, searching out contacts for him. Tracking her could lead him to his quarry.

Hannibal stole a glance at Cindy, wondering if she would react to him staring at another woman. Nothing to worry about there. She was totally engaged in the fight. Both men were moving more slowly now, circling each other warily. Makee drove forward hoping to take Aldo to the ground but the smaller man anticipated the attack and landed a sweeping roundhouse kick to Makee's head. Makee again went down, and Aldo landed on him, getting an arm around his opponent's neck and both legs around his waist. If he had the strength he could press for a submission from there.

Hannibal zeroed back in on Marisol in time for a surprise. She bumped into a big white guy in a corduroy sport coat and jeans but as she moved away her right hand was not empty. Had he seen it right? Did she just pick that man's pocket?

It was a perfect hunting ground for a good pick pocket. A big crowd with people packed close together, jumping, shouting and jostling each other constantly. Everyone focused on the same central point. And Marisol turned out to be quite skilled. He watched her make another touch, never looking around or revealing a hint of nervousness. Stuffing the wallet inside her zippered workout jacket she moved toward the back room.

"Back in a minute, honey," Hannibal told Cindy, dropping a kiss on her cheek. She gave him a quick hug, but then the crowd roared as the referee ended the second round forcing the fighters apart.

Hannibal hung back when Marisol entered the back room. Less than a minute later she reappeared carrying her gym bag and followed the wall around the room to get to the door. She walked right past Ray, who had never gone far past the entrance. Then Hannibal noticed that the reception counter was unattended. He broke from the crowd to stand beside his friend.

"From the sound of things I'm missing one hell of a match," Ray said as soon as Hannibal was close enough to hear.

"I'm afraid so," Hannibal said. "Where the hell is Luis?"

"Oh, he left before the bell for round two," Ray said. "I didn't think you wanted me to track him."

"No no. I didn't expect him to just take off. But I got a feeling he'll end up the same place as the lead I'm tracking. When Cindy comes looking for me, let her know I'm following a lead and I'll let her know if I get someplace. You'll get her home after this, right?"

"You know it, Chico," Ray said. "Still need me at the door?"

"No, I don't think the guy I need is here. I think he's at the end of the trail I'm following."

"Okay then," Ray said. "Go do the job. I'm going in to catch the big finish."

Hannibal gave Ray a thumbs up and pushed out the door. After the close, muggy standing arena inside, the cool night air hit him like water thrown in his face. He spotted Marisol already nearly a block away, grateful for the bright colors she wore that day.

Marisol crossed the street and moved away at a quick march. Tailing a suspect was a regular part of Hannibal's job but in this case he was grateful that he was in running shoes for a change. He darted in front of a Yellow Cab, which was in fact gray in color, and fell into a gentle jog to keep the distance between him and Marisol constant. He smiled as he ran, dragging the crisp night air into his lungs. He never felt more alive than when he was on a healthy run at a moderate pace.

But Marisol was both fit and in a hurry. After a couple of blocks she started to run, using her long stride to best advantage. Hannibal's lungs were burning but he would not let her get away. For all he knew she was meeting Danny to exchange her stolen treasures and cash for drugs.

Followed only by the sound of his own soft footsteps Hannibal soon lost track of the distance. Marisol wandered from the sidewalk to the street and back, but otherwise ran in a pretty straight line, generally north and east. As they moved, streets got narrow and buildings became less attractive and more run down, except for the occasional place some new owner had decided to grace with a bright and often ugly coat of paint.

When she hit New Jersey Avenue, Marisol cut sharp left and Hannibal sprinted forward, afraid of losing her. When he reached the corner she was still in sight, but slowed to a walk. Hannibal did the same, careful not to stumble on the brick sidewalk, clinging to the deep shadows of the curbside trees.

When she stopped, so did Hannibal, crouching behind a car of indeterminate age and make. She glanced around the deserted street, stared up at where the stars should have been for a moment, then hopped up the steps of one of the buildings. As she closed the door behind her Hannibal was already moving to that flight of stairs. He climbed silently and paused on the brownstone stoop. Two voices reached him, but they were too distant to understand. He thought the sound came from upstairs, and one was stronger than the other.

He gripped the doorknob and turned it very slowly, listening for anything that could indicate he was noticed. She must have been in one hell of a hurry to leave it unlocked behind her. He pressed the door inward until it was open by about a foot. After exhaling he slipped through the space and inside the apartment.

The room was dimly lit but nicely furnished. The whole space of the apartment was one big room set up like a living room in the front with the kitchen at the back of the space. The décor was simple, Contemporary IKEA with African masks on the walls. He appreciated the deep pile carpet. It allowed him to step all the way in and close the door.

A wooden staircase stood against the left wall of the apartment, leading up to a mezzanine-like space which Hannibal assumed would hold a bedroom. The voices came from there, and the male voice was rising. Hannibal recognized that voice, and it was not Danny's.

Hannibal moved up the stairs, keeping to the inside edge to reduce any creaking noises. He was within reach of the door at the top when he heard the crack of a solid slap. A body hit the floor and he could hear the person skittering across the floor. When he burst through the door his eyes focused in on Marisol, sitting in a corner, cowering with one arm raised. Tears stood in her eyes but by the light of a single bedside lamp her expression was more shame and regret than fear or pain, almost as if she felt she deserved the next backhand blow that was set to fall in less than a second.

Hannibal was not.

"You don't want to do that, Luis," he said from the doorway.

Chapter 25

Luis spun and snapped into a fighting ready stance, but his fists lowered a couple of inches as recognition dawned.

"Jones. I didn't recognize you at first. What the fuck are you doing here?"

Hannibal didn't answer right away. Instead he moved slowly across the carpet, sidestepping until he stood between Luis and Marisol. His hands were up too, but open. "I was trailing the girl. Thought she might lead me to Danny. Looks like I was wrong. And I don't need to be in the middle of your argument, whatever it is."

"So bounce," Luis said, moving forward, shoulders hunched in the universal threat signal.

"I would, dude, I really would, but I still need to talk to her. Besides, I can't just walk away when you're slapping a girl around."

"So I guess I have to kick your ass too."

"Really?" Hannibal asked. "Are you high too?"

In response Luis hopped forward and swung a hard wheel kick. Hannibal blocked it with his right arm. He also blocked the follow-up right and left fists before landing his own solid left jab on Luis's nose.

Luis hopped back, eyes wild and wary, his heavy breathing in sharp contrast to Hannibal's calm and steady respiration.

"You can leave now," Hannibal said, "Or you can try again, only next time I'll come back at you and likely break something you might need."

Then Hannibal smiled and threw his right shoulder forward in a feint that made Luis jump back. Then he took one long step toward the door.

"All right, chump, you got ten minutes. You go ahead and talk, but you better be gone when I get back."

Hannibal listened to Luis stomp down the stairs and slam the door behind himself, then turned to Marisol. She was on one knee, just starting to stand. She looked at Hannibal, her face seeking understanding his eyes did not reflect.

"What the hell?" Hannibal asked. "I'd have bet money you could kick that boy's ass without breaking a sweat. Why you let him treat you like that?"

Marisol's eyes went to the floor. "I don't know. When I need a fix I get... different. Besides, if I hurt him, or even piss him off... I need it and he's the connection."

"Luis is your dealer?" Hannibal asked. "Is this his place? If there's drugs here I'm surprised he'd go."

"No," Marisol said. "This is my apartment. He made me give him a key. He waits here for me with my stuff. I bring him the money, then I give him whatever else he wants that night, then he goes so I can get high."

Hannibal's heart ached to see this young athlete in such a state, and to hear her admit her debasement in such a matter-of-fact manner. He never really understood what narcotics did to people's minds.

"I'm surprised these people can push dope in a dojo," Hannibal said. "I'd expect people who go there to be proud of their bodies."

"People who go there want to excel, to be the best. Sometimes the right drugs can push you to the next level. Some of us just choose the wrong drugs. Then they own you. Do you think you can help me?" Marisol stood, tried to effect a sexy smile, and reached to put her arms around Hannibal's neck. He stepped back just out of her reach.

"So Danny was working for Luis?"

"No way. Danny was different. He mostly just ran the club. Luis works for Greg."

"Greg Howard?" Hannibal asked.

"Yeah, he's the one who started bringing in the drugs. The dojo was clean before that. But Greg is connected."

"You know Greg," Hannibal said, beginning to pace the room. "And you're scoring from Luis. So why were you looking for Danny? Was he your supplier before?"

Again, Marisol averted her eyes. "Danny was a hustler but he was, well, kinder. Never mean. It was just business. When he found out I was hooked he started taking care of me, but he never tried to get anything but money for the stuff. If I could score from him I didn't have to do things I didn't want to do."

"I see," Hannibal said. "That's why you were hoping he'd be back."

"Well, after we got down I thought he'd want to come back. And I was still hoping he'd be able to bring me what I needed."

Again Marisol reached for him, perhaps looking for comfort, perhaps something more. Hannibal took her hand and said, "Let's go down to the living room where it's a little brighter."

Marisol seemed to gain strength as they moved down the stairs. It really was a nice little apartment, remodeled to make best use of the space. Light colored hardwood floors reflected light from the two small chandeliers. A faux leather sofa on the wall to the left of the door was separated from the brick fireplace by an amoeba shaped coffee table. Plush chairs sat on either side of the fireplace. Beyond that was a glass table with four chairs, then the low divider wall that held the sink and marked off the kitchen area.

As Marisol settled on the couch Hannibal said, "You and Danny? I'm confused. I thought he didn't make you do things."

"Oh, Danny didn't have to make me do anything. He was sweet, and gentle, and so handsome. I had a thing for him. And to be honest, I thought he might take me away from this place. But then he just flew off."

Hannibal had stepped into the kitchen to get them glasses of water. He had just opened the refrigerator when her words froze him in place.

"He flew off? How did you know?"

She perked up and a smile spread on her face. "Well, me and Danny was tight. This one night we had a little party, you know. Then he took me with him to pick up some drugs. Hey, there's iced tea in there if you want that. Anyway, we had a good time in the car, too. See, I know what to do when I want to. He nearly drove us off the road. We drove around most of the night. He told me he had a plane and I said, sure you do. Men always want you to think they got more than they do, you know. But then he drove me to this airport and showed me. He really did have a plane. Damn."

"Did he take you for a ride?" Hannibal asked, handing her a glass.

"No, dammit," Marisol said. "But he told me he was leaving soon, told me exactly when he planned to go. I begged him to take me with him, but he just said maybe. So I figured, shit, if I show up at the right time and give him what I gave him before, he'll take me with him. So I borrowed a friend's ride and packed a couple things and went to meet him, but I was just a little too late."

They both sipped through a few seconds of silence while Marisol's mind drifted back to her missed opportunity. Hannibal was fighting to keep his voice level despite his interest in this new information. "So did you miss him by much? Did you actually see him take off?"

Marisol's smile dimmed as her memories became darker. "Well, it was a long drive and I didn't want to be, you know, sniffing and scratching when I met him. So I kind of stayed there in the airport parking lot to shoot up. Then I kind of nodded. Then when I heard the engines it was too late. So yeah, I saw his plane take off. I freaked out. I started the car and followed him on the road for a few minutes. It was like he was following 95 for a while. I was really too high to be driving. I think I drove off the road a bit. Then…"

Her right hand rose as if she wanted to draw what she saw. "Then something must have gone wrong. I saw the plane pointed down toward the ground."

Hannibal walked around to stare into her widely dilated pupils. "Are you saying you saw the crash?"

"I saw it crash, kind of up on a hill," Marisol said, staring right through Hannibal as if she was watching the event again on a wide screen. "But then I'm pretty sure I saw a man running through the woods away from the crash."

"You're pretty sure?" Hannibal eased down into the chair to the left of the fireplace.

"Well, yeah. You know. I was pretty high right then. I had just shot up and that was some good shit. Pretty sure I passed out for a while so I don't know if I saw the running man right after the crash or maybe it was later. But I kept hoping it was Danny and if it was he'd come back to me."

Hannibal had more questions and was about to ask them when the door flew open and Luis followed a silver .44 Magnum revolver into the room.

"I told you to be gone when I got back, nigger."

Chapter 26

Luis was showing all his teeth but Hannibal wasn't sure he'd call that a smile. Marisol sucked in enough air for a loud scream but nothing came out. Her hands went slack and her glass fell. The crash on the hardwood floor was louder than expected, and shards flew in all directions. The shattering glass drew Luis' attention. In that moment Hannibal threw his glass as hard and fast as he could. Luis' face jerked forward just in time for the bottom of the glass to crash into his nose. His head snapped back, the gun waved to the side, and half a second after the impact, Hannibal's left shoulder forced the air out of Luis' diaphragm. Luis' feet left the floor and his back slammed the front door shut.

Hannibal backed off a step and straightened up with Luis still on his shoulder. He flipped the body backward and was rewarded by the sound of Luis crashing down onto and through the coffee table. Hannibal didn't have to guess where he was and there was no time to turn and look. He just fell backward, swinging his right elbow down hard. He wasn't sure if he hit ribs or Luis' solar plexus, but he heard the surprised cry of pain and that was good enough for him.

To his right he saw that Marisol had pulled her legs up on the sofa. Her eyes seemed big and round as silver dollars. He was lying on Luis' right arm and to his left he saw the big pistol that had thrown him into action. He snatched it up with his left hand and jammed the barrel up under Luis' chin.

"You arrogant little asshole I ought to blow your brains out your head."

Luis stunk of fear. He was barely able to stutter "Please, please no." Hannibal held that pose for a few seconds just to make sure his enemy understood his position. Then he slowly got to his feet keeping the pistol's front sight fixed on Luis' face.

"Now plant your ass in that chair, asshole, while I decide if I should call the cops or just blow both your kneecaps off and call it a day."

"Hey, you don't want to do that," Luis said, tossing false bravado while taking the seat as instructed. "I'm a player, man. I'm Greg Howard's partner, you know, and Greg's connected. He's somebody with MS-13. So, take me out, you got MS-13 on your ass, just like Danny. And trust me, you don't want MS-13 on your ass."

Hannibal stared at Luis over the gun's sights. "You moron. I already got MS-13 on my ass. So nothing to lose there. But since we're talking, just why are they so hot after Danny anyway?"

Luis squirmed a little, his eyes on Marisol. Hannibal considered the situation. Even with a gun to his head, a small time gangster's ego might force him to act tough in front of a woman he had dominated. And Hannibal wanted the information more than he wanted to humiliate Luis. He turned to the girl and nodded his head toward the stairs.

"Hey, Marisol, why don't you go on back upstairs? This could get ugly, and you don't need to be a witness to anything ugly I might have to do. I'll come get you when this is done."

Hannibal's eyes followed her up the narrow staircase, and he noticed that Luis was watching her too. When she reached the top he waited for her to close the bedroom door. Then he turned back to Luis and stepped closer. He wanted the boy to be able to see into the barrel, to see the forty-four caliber death that was poised to come flying out of that barrel and ruin his day.

"You were saying?"

Luis nodded, either in defeat or as a gesture of thanks. "They after Danny cause he double crossed Greg. Him and Greg was tight, at least everybody thought so, but Greg was the one who was the real player. At first, Danny was helping Greg sell his shit. Then Danny started selling even when he hadn't scored from Greg. That shit pissed MS-13 off."

"So Danny was selling for somebody else," Hannibal said. "I can see how that got Greg pissed off, but that's a small time local beef. Why would Rodriguez get involved in this petty bullshit."

"Cause Danny fucked up," Luis said, showing an unexpected anger. "He started getting with another gang. And he ripped us off."

"Slow down," Hannibal said, lowering himself onto the couch. "There's another gang involved? Do you get drugs from them?

"Oh, hell no," Luis said. "You think I want to get dead. I follow the rules all the way." As he talked he slapped the edge of his left hand into his right palm. Hannibal chuckled, but the gun did not waver.

"Look at you, all company man and shit. Alright, who do you get your supply from?"

Luis shrugged. "MS-13. I told you…"

"No no no," Hannibal said, waving the gun back and forth. "I need a name. With Greg apparently out of the picture, who do you get supply from?"

Luis hesitated just long enough to make Hannibal raise the gun barrel to target Luis' forehead. "All I know is Young. That's what people call him. Greg copped from him and now so do I. He works for a guy he always calls V. Just V. I don't know who after that but I know it goes back to MS-13."

"And you say Danny was getting drugs from somebody else? Well, I know MS-13 is the eight hundred pound gorilla nationwide, so who's got the balls to step into MS-13 territory?"

"I don't know any names, but I know they the Nine Trey Gangsters down out of New York. When Danny hooked up with them, he fingered Greg as their competition. That's what got Greg stabbed. When Greg went to the hospital Danny ripped him off. His whole last shipment of drugs."

Hannibal sat back and took in a sharp breath. He didn't think anybody would try to move into MS-13 territory. They had a couple thousand soldiers in Virginia alone and maybe as many in Maryland. But he didn't know their strength in The District. And the Nine Trey Gangsters were affiliated with the Bloods, so they could reach out for muscle if they had to. Stabbing Greg might have been the first strike in a major gang war.

"They left Greg breathing, so he was a warning, or a message," Hannibal said aloud, but really talking to himself. "He's not back out on the street dealing so where is he?"

"Hiding out," Luis said. Hannibal looked up, surprised that Luis knew more. "Greg was my homey. He could see where things was at, and he had lost a week's worth of blow and pills. So when he left the hospital he went underground. I ain't seen him but I get messages back and forth once in a while through Young."

Hannibal stood and leaned toward Luis until the muzzle of his big pistol was two inches from Luis's nose. He wanted to say, "Take me to Young so I can take out one drug dealer at least."

He wanted to say, "Starting today you get out of the drug dealing business for good, or else."

He wanted to walk up the stairs and say, "Marisol, get yourself into a rehab program first thing tomorrow and never touch narcotics again."

But he knew that was just not the way things worked. Instead he held out his right hand and said, "Give me the key. I know you got one."

Luis knew what he meant. He fished in his pocket and pulled out a key ring. With shaking hands he managed to disconnect one key from the ring and dropped it into Hannibal's hand. He looked up, as if asked if there was anything else he needed to do.

"You won't need the key because you will never come to this place again. Right?" Hannibal glared, and Luis nodded. "And that girl upstairs, you don't touch her again. You don't even think about touching her. In fact, if you even dream about touching her you better wake up apologizing. If I ever hear you put your hand on Marisol again, in any way, shape, form or manner, I will hunt you down and break something that you will surely miss. Clear?"

Luis nodded vigorously. Hannibal took a step back and waved the revolver toward the door.

"Now get the hell out of here before I change my mind. And I'll keep the pistol, thanks. It's a fine piece of machinery and I'm starting a little collection since somebody stole one from me."

Chapter 27

Sunday

Even after Labor Day, the sun can be fierce in The District and summer weather usually hangs on. Hannibal pulled on a pair of gym shorts and brewed a fresh cup in his French press, then carried it to his front room, hoping the sun would burn away some of the fear and frustration he had carried home the night before.

Most Sunday mornings the foot traffic in front of his building offered good people watching. Standing at the big bay window that faced the street he enjoyed the moving fashion show. For a couple of hours everybody he saw would be all dressed up. It was an interesting mix, and it was easy to tell which neighbors were just coming home from the party, and which were on their way to church. In the suburbs things had changed. Saturday night was for jeans and sweatshirts in some places, and people attended services in casual clothes. But there in the inner city people still put on their classiest threads for drinking and dancing, and others still saved their best and most formal clothing for their weekly visits to The Lord's house.

What he didn't expect to see was two men in khakis and blazers across the street, leaning on the front and rear bumpers of his car. Juan, at the front of the car, stroked his Fu Manchu mustache and rubbed the top of one cowboy boot against the back of his pants. Like him, Kenny made a point of looking everywhere except into Hannibal's window. They were trying to look harmless, but this was not what he wanted to bring into his neighborhood.

It took Hannibal less than two minutes to pull on a pair of jeans and a polo shirt, slip into sneakers, and text his four upstairs neighbors, asking anyone who was awake and unoccupied to join him downstairs. Then he stepped down the hall and out onto the stoop. When he appeared, Juan and Kenny looked up as if surprised to see him. He strolled across the street, nodding good morning to people walking past.

"First, get off my car," Hannibal said when he reached the driver's side door. "And what the hell are you two doing here?"

Kenny pushed his hands into his pockets. "El Jefe wanted you to know the chain of command is long. But there is one."

"This is about the two boys who met me on the steps."

Kenny nodded. "Their boss works for a guy who works for a guy who works for Senior Rodriguez. You understand shooters and hitters only get told what they need to know." Kenny paused to let his words sink in. It took the smile five seconds to appear on Hannibal's face.

"They work for him, but they didn't know my involvement with him," Hannibal said. Kenny nodded. "They were following standard protocol for people who get too nosy. This is Pablo Rodriquez's way of apologizing." He had to grin at his visitors' obvious embarrassment, but silently gave a nod to their boss for having a little class.

"So tell him I said thanks," Hannibal said, "and I hope I didn't hurt his boys too badly. And while you guys are here, do you know anything about the Nine Trey Gangsters?"

Kenny kicked at an imaginary turd in the road. "Vicious gang of killers. No respect for nobody but themselves. Think they can just take over everybody else's business."

"Oh," Hannibal said, "You mean respectable businesses like drug dealing and human trafficking"

"They don't bring nobody in," Juan said. "They just figure they can steal girls and turn them out. Or hijack drugs

and sell them. There's going to be a lot of blood when..."
Juan fell silent at a sharp look from Kenny.

"Yeah, well, nobody wants a gang war," Hannibal said. Standing in the street he weighed possible risks against potential rewards. He pondered the lesser of two evils. And he considered the devil you know versus the unknown threat. Just as the two gang members moved to leave he said, "Why don't you boys come into my office for a minute."

Inside Hannibal pulled a second chair from the next room and sat it in front of his desk beside his usual visitor chair. He circled around to sit at his desk and waved Juan and Kenny into the chairs. Neither sat.

"Look I'm going to be straight with you," Hannibal said. "You boys have a rep for being way too violent. You recruit them young and initiate with beatdowns and rapes. And the only way out of the gang seems to be in a body bag. There's nothing good about MS-13. But having another bloodthirsty gang of thugs in town can only make things worse. So tell me what you know about these jokers and maybe I can help the cops block them from getting a foothold in here."

Kenny looked at Juan. Not hard to tell who the decision maker was between them. Juan nodded and turned to Hannibal. Just as he was about to talk the door opened and Sarge walked in carrying a baseball bat.

"These guys trouble, Hannibal?"

"Not right now," Hannibal said. "Fellows this here is Sarge, one of my neighbors upstairs. He's just here as an observer. Now, you were saying Juan?"

Kenny took a long close look at Sarge, standing beside the door with arms crossed, then turned back to Hannibal. "The Nine Trey Gangsters is a kind of a franchise of the Bloods out west. They work down in VA mostly. They was getting real strong down in the Hampton Roads zone. For a while they owned that area. Then a couple years ago their boss got busted and sent up for forty years. That knocked them back a bit. Now they coming back hard, and think they need to push north, up into our turf. Tell you the truth, I'm surprised you not working with them."

"Me?" Hannibal's eyebrows went up. "Why the hell would I side with any gang?"

"Cause they black," Virgil said, slipping through the door and moving to the opposite side of the door from Sarge. Juan eyed Virgil so hard Hannibal was afraid there might be a confrontation but both men stayed in place.

"Okay, they a black gang," Kenny said, "and they do all the old school Bloods stuff with gang signs and the tats and shit."

"Tats?" Hannibal asked.

"You know, those three dots they call the dog paws," Kenny said. "They don't do the girls much, mostly drugs and guns. And, you know, murder for hire and shit."

"So they don't have a leader cell up here in The District?" Hannibal asked.

"No they haven't pushed hard yet," Kenny said. "But I know it's coming. They crazy."

"Yeah, they crazy as you boys." It was Quaker walking in, and the visitors looked shocked to see a white man with wild hair and crazy eyes join the group. Ray strolled in right behind him and moved over to the window. Juan kept his hands near his waist, where Hannibal assumed his weapons were. Kenny leaned forward, put both hands on Hannibal's desk and stared at his host as if asking a silent question. Hannibal smiled back.

"This is my posse," he said, pulling a desk drawer open. "So now you boys know how I felt sitting in front of Rodriguez's desk."

"What? Am I supposed to be scared?"

"No," Hannibal said, "but I know you are. For now you can tell your boss thanks for the apology. You can tell your other gang bangers that I've been threatened by three of you so far." He pulled a semi-automatic pistol out of the drawer and slapped it on the desk. "I took this from one of them." He pulled out the second pistol. "I took this off another." Finally he produced the silver revolver. "And I took this off the third. I kind of like this one. Pretty. Any of your South American friends want to contribute to my collection you tell them to come on after me. But let them know that these gentlemen right here might want to talk more than just their guns."

Chapter 28

Monday

The Fairfax County Government Center was that rare government building that actually had a big enough parking lot. Hannibal was parked in it ten minutes before 9am. He wanted to be the first person Orson Rissik saw that day aside from other police. He had a lot of information Rissik needed and he hoped to be part of the planning to deal with it. The thought of a serious gang war in the DMV chilled him, and these two monster gangs really could overwhelm the law enforcement resources of The District, Maryland and Virginia.

Hannibal was dressed for business in his usual black suit and white shirt, Oakley sunglasses in place and driving gloves snug on his hands. Unlike most business trips, he was travelling this time without a firearm. Neither the Glock 17 nor the Colt M1911 he took from the pair that met him at his door had been maintained well enough for him to trust them. Luis' .44 Magnum revolver fit poorly in Hannibal's holster and he was happy to leave it in his glove compartment that morning.

Once inside he slipped through the metal detectors as part of a long line of men and women on their way to court to plead their cases, victims coming to plead for aid, and citizens reporting for jury duty. Unlike the vast majority of them, he knew exactly where he was headed.

The high-ceilinged halls echoed with the crowd's footsteps. Uniformed security personnel looked bored but were in fact very alert. That early in the morning the air carried an antiseptic smell. Despite the bland tile floors and cream colored walls, the entire building made you feel as if you were already in prison.

Hannibal stepped into the large shared anteroom that you had to pass through to reach Rissik. It was a stark but comfortable waiting room, brightly lit and almost uncomfortably clean and neat. To reach Rissik you really had to pass his administrative assistant, a brunette of indeterminate age whose desk nameplate labelled her as Ms. Petersen.

"Good morning, Gert," Hannibal said with a smile. "Is the boss in yet?"

Her eyes flashed to Rissik's inner door and back to Hannibal's lenses. Her severely cut tan suit made her look even more serious than she was. "We've been here for an hour Mr. Jones, but Detective Rissik has a visitor right now. Is your matter of importance?"

"It is, but I can wait for a few minutes. Can you just let him know I'm here?"

Gert seemed to consider the question very seriously for a moment before pressing a button on her desk phone which apparently doubled as an intercom. "Sir, Mr. Hannibal Jones is here to speak with you on a matter of some urgency. Shall I have him wait?"

"No," Rissik responded. "Send him on in."

Hannibal nodded to Gert and pushed through to the inner office. Rissik sat behind his obsessively orderly desk in a conservative gray suit and crisply starched white shirt, his Structure tie pulled up tight to his throat. The three familiar framed citations hung behind him, as well as the poster Hannibal liked so much. It was a picture of a pelican trying to eat a frog. His head already in the bird's mouth, the frog had reached out and wrapped a hand around the pelican's throat, preventing it from swallowing him. A caption under the picture said, "Never Give Up".

All of that was familiar and comfortable to Hannibal. The surprise was the woman in the visitor's chair wearing the unseasonable white and yellow sundress and white pumps.

"Good morning, Hannibal," Rissik said. "I believe you know Miss Blanco."

Hannibal smiled a good morning at the girl, wondering if their meeting here could be a coincidence. Then he looked again at the three framed citations hanging on the wall to the left and right of Rissik's desk that he thought must have been put there using a T-square and a laser sight. Although he had not called ahead, Hannibal rejected the notion that anything that happened in Orson Rissik's world was a coincidence.

Rissik leaned back, his head supported by interlaced fingers. "I'm glad you're here, Hannibal. I was just getting a statement from Miss Blanco here. I sent a car to bring her down this morning. She is being very cooperative and I think some of what she knows might relate to that missing person's matter you and I discussed. Is your news related to that same case too?"

"As a matter of fact, it is," Hannibal said. He was looking around for a place to lite when Gert appeared, pushing an upright wooden chair. Hannibal thanked her and dropped onto the seat. "As it turns out, Danny Hernandez appears to have been at the center of a lot of crazy stuff. My sources tell me that he ripped off a guy running drugs for MS-13. That was his friend, and Connie's, Greg Howard. Greg got stabbed because Danny fingered him as MS-13."

At this, Connie gasped. "You saying Greg was in that gang?"

Hannibal ignored her. "Thing is, rather than do the deed himself, Danny got some new friends to handle it. Members of the Nine Trey Gangsters."

Rissik sat forward, palms on his desk. "What? That mob that got started up in Riker's, and is now practically running the underworld down in the Tidewater? Crap, this is bad. I wonder if Hernandez knows what he might have started. I can't have a full-on gang war ripping across my county."

"Word is the stabbing was a way for Hernandez to grab some drugs that came from a dealer named Young. Do you know about this guy?"

Rissik shook his head. "I know most of the significant names in Virginia and The District, but I don't know a drug dealer named Young. So doesn't sound like that's going anywhere. And for all we know this Hernandez clown is lying dead in the woods somewhere."

"Actually, that seems unlikely," Hannibal said. He watched Connie in his peripheral vision as he spoke. "I found a witness to the crash. She was drugged up pretty bad, so might not be the most reliable witness, but she swears she saw a man get up and run away from that crash. So I think the odds are good that Danny is out there somewhere, waiting for the heat to die down so he can sell the stolen drugs and get out with a fortune."

Connie's smile expanded a bit but her eyebrows didn't rise, her eyes didn't widen and if he could have taken her pulse Hannibal was sure he'd detect no change. No indication that the idea of her boyfriend surviving the crash was a surprise. She looked happy, or at least was trying to look happy, but her response seemed very understated. Hannibal wasn't sure what that meant. The room was quiet for a moment while Rissik went to his coffee machine for a refill and poured for Hannibal while he was there. A cup sat by Connie on Rissik's desk, but it looked like she hadn't even sipped it. Handing Hannibal a cup he said, "I'm kind of glad to hear that. I hope your witness wasn't just hallucinating."

Back in his chair, Rissik continued. "Our interests may have aligned. Tell me, do you know a fellow named Quentin Sands?"

At that moment Hannibal was glad he rarely removed his sunglasses when on a case. One can control many of their natural micro-expressions but widening irises are outside the reach of any amount of training. Rissik had just dropped a name Hannibal never expected to hear from him.

"We met," Hannibal said. "He was one of the people I interviewed on the trail of Miss Blanco here. In fact, he's the guy that led me to her. Haven't seen him since that night, though."

"Well, you won't see him again," Rissik said, sipping his coffee. "He's the reason I asked Miss Blanco to come in and give a statement. He's dead. Murdered."

"Sorry to hear that," Hannibal said. Then to Connie, "and sorry for the loss of your friend." Her grateful smile was warm, but her eyes were guarded. "But Orson, I'm not sure I understand what that has to do with me, or how this case ties in with mine."

Rissik stared over the edge of his coffee cup at Hannibal. It was his disappointed look. He expected more, but certainly would not ask for it. His dangerous blue eyes said he would play out the game as it lay.

After a brief pause and a deep sigh, Rissik said, "Our cases overlap because you and I are looking for the same man. You see, Sands was found dead in in his own home. No signs of forced entry. When the techs went over the house they found Hernandez' fingerprints. That was enough to make him the lead suspect in Sands' murder, or at the very least a person of interest. So, I'm going to need you to bring your witness in for questioning. Not that I doubt your abilities but even a drugged up witness can sometimes remember details better in one of my interrogation rooms."

"Of course," Hannibal said, glancing at Connie. "But you know I'm looking for Hernandez for other reasons."

"And, if Hernandez is alive and on the run, you now know he's wanted," Rissik said. "If you find him first, you'll give me a call and I'll come take him off your hands. Right?"

"Orson, don't I always cooperate with the police?" Hannibal spread his hands wide as if he was stating the obvious. "Besides, I'm off the hook if he ends up in police custody. Nobody would expect me to bring him in if he's under arrest."

"Thanks," Rissik said. "I knew I could count on your help. And you know that, with or without you, I will bring the killer to justice."

Rissick stared at Hannibal over his desk trays, the ones with the full out box. Hannibal had never seen anything in the inbox. Things that got passed to Orson Rissik got handled right away. The message was subtle but clear.

"Then Rissik played his next card.

"The more I think about it, the more I think we could get closer to the truth if the two of you were to compare notes. What do you think, Hannibal?"

Hannibal got to his feet, nodding. "That might not be a bad idea. Miss Blanco, do you need a ride home?"

Chapter 29

Hannibal held the door for Connie to step into his passenger seat and closed it after her. As he started the car she reached up to open his sun roof. He let it pass. Whatever made her comfortable was good.

Pulling into traffic he noticed her scent. Subtle and floral, different from what she was wearing when he'd seen her before. Her hair was freshly done. Her nails had been done in the last day or so too and a quick glance down told him both fingers and toes had been attended to.

"Came into some money," he said as he pushed into the left lane on I-66. Traffic was still heavy. In Northern Virginia, Monday morning rush hour could last until noon.

Connie stared out the window. "Was that a question? And is that really any of your business?"

"Fair, but unexpected question, that. You seem a bit more self-possessed now than when I met you," Hannibal countered. "Is this an act? Or was that?"

"Look, I'm just a girl trying to get along," She said. "I'm not helpless by any means, but I hope you don't imagine me some great femme fatale." She stabbed at the console, and Led Zeppelin filled the car. The singer had been dazed and confused for so long it wasn't true.

Traffic brought them to a stop and Hannibal was able to look at her for a moment. "Look, I understand the reason young women sometimes pretend to be dumber than they are. It's a useful defense mechanism, a way to get over when dealing with us arrogant males. I don't hold any of that against you. Just don't play stupid with me anymore, all right?"

Connie slowly brushed her hair back with her right hand. Her head tilted forward and she twisted her face toward him, looking out through a veil of hair. "Tell you what, dude. I know I'm in some real shit here. And you saved my ass when you didn't have to. So here's the deal. I'll be real with you if you don't try to hang all this shit on me."

"I can work with that," Hannibal said, again focusing on the road. As soon as he cleared the ramp onto the Beltway he set his cruise control to sixty, five miles per hour over the limit, and settled back. "So how involved were you with Danny's hustle?"

"You mean the whole drug thing you were talking about in the cop's office? First I heard."

"You said you were going to be real with me," Hannibal said. "Connie you are too smart not to know what Danny was up to. If you were really his girl." When she didn't respond he asked outright. "So... you and Danny?"

"Yes," she said with a thin smile.

"You and Ozzie?"

An open mouthed sigh, then, "Yes."

"You and Sands?"

"No! Not once, even though he sure wanted it."

A purple Mazda ripped past Hannibal doing at least 80. Hannibal pressed the accelerator to follow him. "So why did Rissik have you pulled in?"

"Somebody told him I was staying at Quentin's rental."

"So he figured you might know if Danny was at Quentin's own place."

"Yeah," she said. "For a cop he's pretty bright."

Hannibal spotted a police car on the shoulder and took his foot off the accelerator. "And did you?"

"I did," she said. "I drove him there that night."

The music rolled to Pink Floyd. Now the singer was comfortably numb, but Hannibal was on high alert. He watched the police car pull away from the side of the road running lights and siren. He pulled the Mazda to the shoulder. Hannibal passed them at the speed limit.

"I'm thinking Danny was pretty pissed that Quentin Sands took me to the rental you guys were staying in. He had to know Sands had the hots for you. Damn, maybe he did kill Sands."

Connie shook her head slowly but did not comment on Hannibal's suppositions. She shifted her body so she was turned toward Hannibal. "I know Quentin took you to the cottage to find me. What I don't get is how you ended up looking for me in the first place."

"Funny," Hannibal said. "I thought it was just random. Your mom knew me from working at the shelter. But as it turns out Sands brought me into the case. He told your mom to hire me. Since he went to so much trouble to put me on the train, I have to think it was no coincidence I met him in Virginia Beach. That was all a setup. Now I'm thinking he went to all that trouble hoping I'd separate you from Danny and give him a clear field to you. Guess Danny disagreed with that plan."

Connie leaned toward Hannibal, resting her hand on his leg the way a woman does when she's already been intimate with someone. "I don't believe it," she said. "Danny was a smart guy, and a hustler, but he wasn't no killer."

Hannibal reached down and with a gentle tug lifted her hand and placed it on the seat. "If not Danny, then who?"

The song ended and AC/DC rolled in screaming about a highway to hell.

"What is this shit you listen to?" Connie asked.

"I think the proper term is classic rock," Hannibal said. "Before your time, when actual musicians played instruments to make music instead of letting computer programmers do it. Now answer the question. Who do you think took Quentin out?"

"If I had to guess I'd say it was Rodriguez' man, Juan," Connie said. "I think Quentin was getting too close to the facts on MS-13, prepping to break his big Pulitzer winning story, so Rodriguez sent Juan to take him out."

Chapter 30

By the time Hannibal got home he was ready for lunch, perhaps a nice ham and cheese sandwich and fresh brewed coffee. His visit to the police station had not been all he wanted it to be, and delivering Connie Babcock to her mother was starting to get old. He entered his building and paused for a moment in the front hall. To the left, a relaxed lunch in his apartment. To the right, consolidating his notes and checking for messages in his office. As usual, business won out over pleasure. In the time it took to walk to his office door he had the key out of his pocket. But for the third time in recent days he found a door unlocked that should not have been. And for the third time he took it as a bad sign.

The knob made no noise as he released it and backed away. He managed to get out the door without making a sound and returned to his car to retrieve the silver .44 he had tucked into the glove compartment. Now two major gangs had his name. If there were people in his office looking for trouble, he had every intention of giving them some.

The big revolver filled his left hand and he held it pointed toward the ceiling as he again turned the knob and pushed his way into his office. One man sat inside and Hannibal levelled the gun at his uninvited visitor before he realized that he was not a threat.

"Getting jumpy in your old age?" Orson Rissik asked from the chair in the corner to the left of the door.

"Yeah, well, most people who come to see me don't let themselves in." Hannibal rested the revolver on his desk.

"Well if you're going to stay in this business you have got to get yourself a better lock." Rissik was the kind of calm men are when they know you need them more than they need you. Hannibal went to the coffee maker and saw that his visitor had at least brewed a fresh pot. He nodded his thanks to Rissik and poured himself a mug full of energy. Then he turned and leaned back against his desk.

"Okay, Orson, what can I do for you? And why am I doing it here?"

Rissik sipped his own coffee and tugged his tie down a couple of inches from his throat. "I'm here because I wanted to talk. Informally. Unofficially. Before you do something that makes me have to deal with you in an official capacity."

"That almost sounds like a threat, Orson," Hannibal said. "But you and me, we ain't like that. So just say it. What do you need?"

"Well first, I want to know why you're still looking for Danny Hernandez."

Hannibal inhaled the rich aroma from his mug before answering. "You know I was after him originally as the best link to Connie Babcock."

"And you found her," Rissik said. "So, why are you looking for Danny Hernandez?"

Hannibal drank slowly. He knew Rissik would be patient while he thought it through. He was in the position to be doing a bad thing for a bad man but so what? Ultimately, would it hurt him for Rissik to know the truth?

"I'll be straight with you, Orson," Hannibal said. "After I found Connie, MS-13 snatched her up. I went to get her back. When I found her, Rodriguez had her."

"Wait. Pablo Rodriguez himself? You talked to him?"

"Yeah. Danny ripped him off and he wants that boy bad. Rodriguez figured Connie knew where he was or maybe she could reach him to get him back. Anyway, I cut a deal. Said I'd find out where Danny went in exchange for Connie's freedom."

Rissik stood up and let out a long low whistle. "So you're working for him now. You actually took on MS-13 as a client."

"Well when you put it like that…"

"That's how it is," Rissik said, pointing at Hannibal. Then he put his cup on Hannibal's desk, slid his hands into his pockets and walked over to the window to stare out at the street.

"That's why I'm hoping to help you with your investigation. If I find Danny I point you to him. I figure getting him into police custody puts me off the hook with Rodriguez. Didn't you say he's your prime suspect for the Sands murder?"

Rissik leaned back and sat on the narrow window sill, his arms folded. "Well here's the thing, Hannibal. We did find Danny Hernandez's prints in Sands' condo. But we also have an eye witness who puts you at the scene. She says she saw you leaving the place."

Hannibal took a deep breath. No way around it, that added him to the suspect list. "Yeah, I was there, Orson, but I know your techs will verify the gap between the time of death and my visit. Sands had been dead for hours when I got there."

Rissik stood again and turned to face the glass. The sunlight painted a corona around his body that made him hard to look at. "You found him," Rissik said, almost biting off the words. "You found him and didn't report the body."

"Come on, Orson. There's no law says I have to tell you when I come up on a dead man."

"No but it does make me wonder." Rissik faced, turning his dangerous blue eyes like lasers on his host. "Are you investigating a murder, Hannibal? Or are you covering one up?"

Hannibal walked closer and lowered his voice. "I think you know me better than that, Orson. I saw he was dead and got the hell out of there."

"No, I figure you didn't stay long," Rissik asked. "Didn't search the house did you?"

Hannibal could feel a freight train heading his way and realized that he could not get off the tracks this time. It was

Rissik's game and he had to play along. "I know your boys did. They're thorough. And I got a bad feeling I know what they found."

"Yep. Right there in the kitchen trash can. I don't know what kind of an idiot guns a man down at close range and then tosses his gun in the trash at the scene of the crime, just a few feet from the victim. But there it was. That pretty Sig Sauer 40 caliber registered to you." Rissik turned his head to eye Hannibal over his shoulder. "Now, do I have to tell you what the ballistic report showed?"

Hannibal paced from his desk to the door and back again. "I can guess, and if I'm right you got enough to take me in, Orson. But you'd never be able to get a conviction. First off, I just met Sands, so I had no motive to kill him. And nobody who's read my record would think I'd leave my gun in such an obvious place. Besides all that, what did they give you for the time of death?"

Rissik turned, tracking Hannibal back and forth. "They're saying between midnight and two a.m. Why, you got an alibi?"

"Orson I was unconscious on the lawn at Sands' rental at midnight. Danny, or whoever knocked me out, took my gun and let the air out of two of my tires. I was stuck out there for a good couple of hours waiting for Triple A to come out and get me moving again."

Rissik nodded his head, then stepped forward to put a hand out, stopping Hannibal's pacing. "That's a good story at least. You got any witnesses? Did anybody see you out there?"

Hannibal froze, and a slow smile spread across his face. "As a matter of fact, there was this couple that drove by. I didn't know how to tell the tow truck where I was so I flagged them down and they told me where we were. We talked for a few minutes. I'm sure they'd recognize me."

Surprise put a grin on Rissik's face. "Well now you've got something. I'd much rather bring these folks in to make a statement than bring you in. Did you get their names?"

"Tina," Hannibal said. "Tina and Vic. White couple. He was driving a navy blue Lexis."

Rissik nodded again. "The prosecutor would want to meet them. Thing is, I can't devote resources to…"

"Just give me a couple of days, Orson," Hannibal said. "I got enough, I know I can find them pretty quick."

Rissik seemed to make up his mind about something, slapped Hannibal's shoulder and moved toward the door. "Bring them in in the next forty-eight hours and we're good." He rested his hand on the doorknob and turned to Hannibal as if to say goodbye but instead said, "Any idea how Miss Babcock might have known Sands? I didn't get a read on her reaction to his death, but I definitely felt something there."

"Interesting," Hannibal said. "Did she tell you she drove Danny to Sands' place the night he was killed?"

"What? No, she didn't mention that. I knew it was a good idea to put you two together."

It was Hannibal's turn to grin. "I had a feeling you were working an angle there. Yeah, that's what she told me, but I'm not so sure she was happy with the outcome. Connie had a lot of men in her life, but I got the feeling maybe she had a thing for Quentin Sands."

Chapter 31

Tuesday

Early morning was Hannibal's time. Even when Cindy stayed over he always rose before dawn, got in a good run and had a full breakfast before starting his work day. His neighbors were not all so eager to greet the sunrise so he asked for the meeting to begin at nine o'clock, after he had been up for three hours.

His team, as he thought of them, were arrayed in no particular pattern around his office, facing him. He stood in front of his desk, jacket off and sleeves rolled up. Ray, over to his left, had opened the window and sat right in front of it. His daughter Cindy, dressed for business in a navy blue suit, perched on the window sill right beside him. Sarge had claimed the padded visitor's chair, while Quaker and Virgil dropped into folding chairs. Everyone had coffee and a donut from the box on Hannibal's desk. None of them looked particularly awake but Hannibal knew those brains were buzzing with the thought of getting involved in another investigation.

"So here's the deal, my friends," Hannibal said. "You all know what I'm involved in, and you know that the key to the whole case is the location of this Danny Hernandez, hustler and drug dealer. He is a very wanted man. Wanted by the police for a murder. And worse for him, wanted by the local MS-13 boss for double crossing them. What you might not know is that Hernandez wasn't working along. It looks like he was working with another gang called the Nine Trey Gangsters. So in the process of ripping off MS-13,

Hernandez might have kicked off a war between these two street mobs."

"Them dudes is vicious, bro," Sarge said. "Both are known for cutting the throats of anybody gets in their way. You sure you want to get in the middle of this?"

"Oh, hell no!" Hannibal said. "But I need to find out where Hernandez went, and one of them might have a clue. Hernandez scored from a Nine Trey dealer named Young. That's all I got, except that he operates in The District. He might be the one person Hernandez would trust with his plans."

"So, you looking to find this Young?" Ray asked. "You know, if he's dealing in DC and he's not getting supply from MS-13, he's keeping a real low profile, Chico. It's not like he'll be hanging a shingle out or handing out business cards with his address on them."

"Truth," Virgil said. "Them kind of independent dudes work on a personal referral basis. This might not be easy."

"That's why I'm asking for your help," Hannibal said. "You've all got your ears to the ground and good connections in the city. I'm asking you to poke around, listen and find this guy for me. Usual pay for you, even though I'm not getting paid for this one. If we divide up the city we should be able to run this guy down and get some answers."

Virgil spoke up, his voice rumbling forth like Eeyore on a bad day. "We can find him. Worse case, we can get one more drug dealer off the street." Virgil had the puffy arms and red eyes that marked him as a former addict. Hannibal had no doubt he was eager to take this one on.

"I'm confident one of you will find this Young. Just be careful and stay in contact, okay?"

The four male visitors rose to their feet as one. Cindy dropped into the chair her father vacated. The men thanked Hannibal and shook his hand or bumped his fist. Once they were gone he turned his attention to Cindy.

"So, what's the plan for today? Need a ride downtown?

"Actually, things are pretty smooth at the office," Cindy said, smoothing her skirt. "I was thinking of taking a mental health day. So tell me, if I were to take a day off do you have any ideas of something we could do with it?"

Hannibal watched her hemline slide back up to where it was more comfortable. "Well my investigation is kind of stalled for the moment, so if you are free I think I might like to…"

A familiar jangle cut him off and got Cindy to giggling.

"… answer the phone?" she asked, finishing his sentence with a chuckle.

Stifling a sign of frustration Hannibal picked up the receiver and answers in his usual professional manner. His eyes widened when he heard the voice from the other end and the stifled sigh turned to one of relief.

"Mr. Jones, it is so good to hear you. This is Tina Unser. You might not remember, but we meet a few days ago, really nights ago. You were having car trouble."

"Yes of course I remember you," Hannibal said. "And I'm very glad to hear from you."

"Really?" Tina said. "That's flattering. And it's nice because I'm calling because, well, you gave me your card and I could use your help."

"You mean professionally?" Hannibal asked. "I'm in my office right now if you want to…"

"Actually, travelling is a bit inconvenient for me right now," Tina said. "I know it's asking a lot but could you possibly come to me? I'll gladly pay for your time and inconvenience."

He covered the receiver with his hand and turned to Cindy. "Feel like taking a ride down into the Virginia countryside?"

"I'm down for whatever, lover,"

To Tina he said, "I could be there by noon or so, if you don't mind my bringing a business associate with me."

While Hannibal drove Cindy fiddled with the GPS until she found a route to Tina's house that got them off the highway as early as possible. At her insistence they rode with the sun roof open and windows half down. Her smile was biggest when they reached roads pressed on both sides by tall, majestic evergreens. Steering with his left hand, his right resting on Cindy's thigh, Hannibal had time to consider how good his life was. For a murder suspect being threatened by murderous gangs, He was certainly blessed.

He pointed when they rolled past Sands' little rental house where so much had happened in the last few days. Ten minutes later the street widened and smoothed, and the houses grew but their styles drifted into the past, as if they had found a corner of the universe where time stood still. A woman jogged by in Spandex and two hundred dollar running shoes, and a mature gentleman walked a suitably stately golden retriever. When they pulled into Tina's driveway Cindy almost gasped.

"Oh, Hannibal. This is how people should live."

The house was a vast, rambling affair, white with baby blue trim. gabled roof, corner rooms like storybook towers, and a deep porch that stretched across the front of the house and along the right side. Beside the door, Tina rocked in what was surely an antique chair, reading. When she saw her guests she rose and stood to welcome them.

They stepped out of the car and Cindy did a slow pan of the house to take it all in. The outdoors here smelled exactly like the stuff Hannibal sprayed in his apartment when he was going to have company. Instead of chirping, birds sang in a way Hannibal found oddly Disneyesque.

"Mr. Jones, thank you so much for coming out to me," Tina said. The middle-aged brunette was fashionably dressed but not in an aggressive way. She was a bit taller than Hannibal expected, thanks to the red, three-inch heels. She wore a matching dress that hung well past her knees, a light jacket, and a shy smile.

Mounting the steps, Hannibal said, "Tina Unser, this is Cindy Santiago. Cindy is an attorney and she often helps me with cases. You can count on her confidentiality."

The women exchanged smiles and Tina said, "You are both most welcome. I don't get many visitors. Come inside. There's iced tea and I made brownies if you like those."

"Are there people who don't like brownies?" Cindy asked.

Stepping across the porch, Hannibal commented, "I see you and your neighbors have those same yellow flowers in front of your houses too, just like the house where we met that night. Buttercups, and what are those other things?"

"Clematis," Cindy said, in that tone that asked how anyone could possibly not know.

"We all grow them," Tina said, holding the door open. "I for one love to see the deer wandering through my yard in the morning and just before twilight. Sadly, they eat most pretty flowers, but they won't eat these so they are the choice."

They moved through the house to a sun room furnished with Queen Anne tables and chairs and overlooking a lush green setting that provided the illusion of being the only humans for miles. While Tina poured iced tea Cindy leaned close to Hannibal and whispered, "Deer wandering in the yard," in the tone of voice some people reserve for their favorite dessert.

Tina settled into a chair but sat stiffly, her knees pressed together as if she were holding some dark secret there. Hannibal waved to get her attention.

"You know, I was about to start a search for you, but clearly you called me for your own reasons. So tell me, what prompted you to give me a call?" He sipped his tea and shivered a bit.

Cindy grinned. "Tina, dear, do you have any sugar?"

"Oh, did you want sweet tea?" she asked. She pulled a round sliver server from a side table, tilted the top open and used silver tongs to drop two sugar cubes into Hannibal's glass. "So sorry, I should have asked. And yes, when we met you were in a little trouble and I think I helped you out some. Now, just like that, I'm the one in trouble."

"The fact that you saw me last time could turn out to be very good fortune for me," Hannibal said, sipping from his glass again and returning a broad smile. "But right now, let's focus on your troubles."

Tina settled back into her seat and sighed as if screwing up her courage for a tough climb. "Well, you see, it's Vic. He's gone."

"You're saying your husband left you?" Hannibal asked. "Not to make light, but I saw you together barely a week ago. Sometimes guys just need to take off for a couple of days. Are you sure he's really…"

"He took the Lexus," she said. "That's why I asked you to come down here. And he cleaned out our joint account. Just shy of two hundred thousand dollars. I have assets of course, but not much that's liquid so this is a bit of a challenge."

Cindy whistled and looked at Hannibal. He nodded, having formed an immediate picture. Tina the ingénue with money. Vic the gold digger. He wondered, but didn't ask, how much married bliss there had been. Instead he asked, "Did something happen to make him want to leave? An argument?"

"It was right after the police came. I guess they're looking for the people who were renting that house where we met you. I don't know why. But they came around and questioned everybody living nearby. I suppose I shouldn't have said anything but it was the police. I couldn't lie to the police, could I?"

When Hannibal hesitated Cindy blurted, "Of course not." Again the women traded smiles and Hannibal was glad Cindy was there to put Tina at ease. He put his hands together, elbows on the table, and leaned forward.

"What did you know that you were so reluctant to share?" Hannibal asked.

"No, the truth is I wanted to tell someone." Tina said. "They asked me if I had ever been to that house, and I had to say yes, even though I didn't go inside."

Hannibal couldn't imagine Tina having any business with Danny or Connie, but people did sometimes surprise you. "What was it that drew you to the house, Tina."

"I went there," she began, then squared her shoulders in a defiant stance. "I followed Vic there. I think he went there to see that girl."

"I see. Well that must have been disturbing."

"You mean Connie Babcock?" Cindy asked.

"Is that her name?"

Hannibal sat back. He wished he was surprised, but there was no shock in the idea that Vic might be one more charm Connie added to her boyfriend bracelet. He was getting to know her pretty well. Vic, on the other hand, was still much of a mystery. While the house displayed a tasteful amount of idyllic artwork, he saw no pictures of people. No family members, friends, or shots of favorite vacations.

"You don't seem like the type of woman who is easily fooled by a man," Hannibal said. "How did you meet Vic? Is he from down your way?"

"Oh, no, he's a DC boy," Tina said. "Actually, he was Air Force, so in a way he's not from anywhere anymore. We met last year, and I was just bowled over." She turned to Cindy and added, "Those shoulders." Then her eyes wandered into the past, and Hannibal let her go. When she came back her dreamy eyes narrowed.

"So, Mr. Jones, can I hire you to find Vic and at least get my car back? And the money of course, if there's any left."

"Tina, if I can count on you to talk to the police one more time, I'll be happy to take the case."

"What else can I tell them? I don't expect much help finding a runaway husband."

"I'll handle that," Hannibal said. "Done it more often than you'd think in the last couple of years. All I need you to do is give an honest statement about where and more importantly, when we met."

"Well, sure," Tina said. "The truth is the easiest story to tell. But do you really think you can find Vic?"

"I think the odds are in my favor," Hannibal said with an easy smile. "He's probably still driving the Lexus. You give me the plate number and I can have people watching for him. I didn't get a very good look at him so I'll want a description, or…"

"I have selfies of us on my phone," Tina said. "I can text a couple to you."

"Even better," Hannibal said. "And if you can tell me some of the places he likes to hang out, I can start there."

Tina smiled, warming to the process. "Yes, that would help, wouldn't it? When we met it was on a golf course. He's quite the athlete you know. Even though he was Air Force he liked the course on Fort Belvoir, so we went there a few times. And he liked to watch fights. Once he took me to this place where they have these martial arts fights. Wrestling, I guess, but real, not like the guys on TV. That was pretty exciting. I think he used to go there a lot."

"Interesting coincidence," Hannibal said, although he didn't believe in such things. Now he wondered if Vic went to the rental house to see Danny, rather than Connie. "I've been spending time in just such a place lately. Maybe they know Vic there."

"Oh, I'm sure," Tina said.

"Well then, I guess I'd better get on the job," Hannibal said, rising.

To his surprise, Cindy did not stand. "Mrs. Unser…"

"Tina. Please."

" Well, Tina, it sounds as if you're going through some stuff. I'm sure Hannibal wants to get right to work on his new case, but would you like to just sit and have another glass of tea and just relax for a bit? And while I'm here I can show you how to use Uber and Lyft so you won't feel trapped in the house."

"I would love that," Tina said.

Hannibal took the hint from his woman. "Well if that's all you can think of, Tina I'll leave you two to get better acquainted." Tina started to rise but Hannibal waved her back down. He could find his way out and didn't want to interrupt whatever bonding might be happening between the women.

So Vic had connections to the RHO Academy. Just like that, Hannibal saw there were fewer than six degrees of separation between Tina and Connie. As he opened the door he mentally flipped through the faces and names connected to that case and realized they did not seem to be in the same camp. Who Vic knew there might matter, or rather, who knew him. If Danny was one of his contacts he might even have some useful information. Yes, who he might be connected to at the Academy might matter a lot.

Standing on the threshold, Hannibal decided that one or two more questions couldn't hurt. He turned to head back in, but hesitated. Something had changed. They were not chatting like they were before, with a jovial air. Cindy was listening attentively, while Tina spoke in low tones. She looked upset, almost distraught. Hannibal stood for a moment, teetering between the warmth of the outdoor sunshine and the cooler, more somber atmosphere inside. Before he could commit to a next action, Tina's eyes flickered up toward him, and Cindy turned to glare over her shoulder.

"Hannibal. I thought you were already gone. What is it?"

"I was going to ask Tina for some names," he muttered. "If she," he shifted his focus, "If you remember any of the people he spoke to."

"Names?" Tina repeated, staring up at her old memories. "No I don't think he ever called anyone by name. But wait."

She stood and stepped toward the door, her face lit up as a new thought came to her. "None of the people he talked to, but this might be useful. The night we went to the fights a couple of the people there called Vic by a different name. Apparently, he also goes by his middle name. Greg."

Chapter 32

Wednesday

Twenty-four hours later, Hannibal was still shaking his head. All that he had learned in his years as an investigator made him distrustful of luck. Good luck at least. Bad luck was reliable, even predictable. Good luck? Well it just didn't happen, and when it did, it often turned out to be bad luck in disguise.

But it now seemed very likely that Vic Unser, Tina's husband, was also Greg Howard, the good friend Danny Hernandez had double-crossed and gotten stabbed in order to rip off half a million dollars' worth of drugs. Here was another drug dealer Hannibal would love to see behind bars, and since he was being paid to find him, it could happen.

On a different track he considered how Cindy and Tina had hit it off. Cindy had called him soon after he woke up that morning just to chat.

"We had a fine lunch at Tina's place yesterday," she had told him. "She was born to money but she sure doesn't act like it. I mean, that woman can cook. She pulled out some ham, and made these buttermilk hushpuppies. I mean like, damn. And I learned about fried green tomatoes. Then it was mint julips and we just talked. And what a lovely place she's got down there. And such a quiet area. We actually saw deer wander through the back yard while we sipped our drinks."

"Yes, dear," Hannibal had said, "I was there, remember?"

"Yes, honey, I'm sorry. Anyway, I really called to let you know that I convinced her to take me with her on her important errand this morning."

"That's nice," Hannibal said. "I'm glad you've made a new friend."

At which, she had lowered her voice and said, "Honestly, she had me at 'my man left me'."

Of course, Hannibal wondered if there was more to it than that. Perhaps, like Hannibal, she had been struck by Tina's evident lack of anger. Then he remembered that parting scene.

"Cindy, when I turned around at the door Tina looked kind of upset. Would it be okay to tell me why?"

Seconds passed and Hannibal wondered if he had just asked his woman to violate some code. The words "never mind" were forming on his lips just as she spoke.

"There are things a girl will say to another girl that she'd never tell a man," Cindy said. "The truth is she hates that she was taken in. Nonetheless, Vic was her man and she's hurting that he's gone. It doesn't matter what he's done, she misses him."

Hannibal nodded as if Cindy could see him on the other end of the phone. Vic had done Tina wrong in the classic sense but there was little doubt she still loved him. So, what if Hannibal found him? He would want this man to pay for what he had done to her. But, would Tina be okay with him going to jail?

He was thinking through all the possible ways the next events might unfold when his office phone rang.

"Jones? Rissik."

"Good morning, Orson," Hannibal said. "Got some good news for me?"

"As a matter of fact I do," Rissik said. "I just had a visit from a Mrs. Tina Unser and her attorney, who happens to be your girlfriend. Mrs. Unser gave us a statement that appears to establish a solid alibi for you. This takes you out of our suspect pool for the Sands murder. She was very kind and cooperative, considering she was taking an Uber for the first time in her life and she hauled all the way up to my office from Colchester."

"Yes, I'm on the job hunting her stolen car," Hannibal said, smiling. Juggling the phone from hand to hand he pulled off his suit coat and slipped into his empty shoulder holster. "I think this means you have something of mine. Mind if I swing by to retrieve it?"

The Fairfax County evidence room was as big a surprise to Hannibal as everything else associated with their operation. It was bright and clean with a cement floor and rows of steel racks holding well-organized boxes of material. Of course, Hannibal observed all this through a wire screen. Rissik filled out forms and received in return a plastic bag full of Sig Sauer. He thanked the clerk and led Hannibal back to his office. Once behind his own office door he handed the bag to Hannibal.

"You know this is still the murder weapon of record, right?"

"Of course," Hannibal said, pulling his pistol from the bag. He looked it over, dropped the magazine and pulled the slide back to be sure it was cleared. After a good look at the chamber he let the slide go forward and pushed it down into its holster. He felt stronger already. "You have all the ballistic records so you don't really need the material evidence. But I also know you're going out on a limb returning this to me. And yeah, I know some defense lawyer may call for it at some point and you know I will return it if needed."

"You haven't given me any reason to distrust you," Rissik said. "And I'm counting on you to keep it that way. So, what's your next step? You any closer to turning up Danny Hernandez? My people are getting nowhere so far."

"Not really making progress there, Orson," Hannibal said "But I might have a lead on the guy he double-crossed, Greg Howard. He could lead me to the owner of some stolen drugs, the guy Danny really ripped off. I figure his people are still looking for Danny so, who knows. They might have something useful. And even if they don't..." Hannibal lowered his voice and leaned closer. "I'm working on the germ of an idea that could get me out from under MS-13. If it works it'll mean good news for you too, but you got to trust me and not ask any questions if I call."

Rissik literally stroked his chin with thumb and forefinger. Hannibal had never seen anyone do that in real life. Then he looked into Hannibal's dark glasses. "In for a penny, in for a buck I guess. Just remember you only get one chance to screw me over."

Luis was still the man behind the counter at the RHO Martial Arts Academy. It was quiet in the early afternoon, with only a couple of people in the main room working out. When Hannibal walked in Luis hopped to his feet and put on his best hard look. Hannibal stayed relaxed, as if he had never met the other man. He smiled but maintained eye contact, leaning one elbow on the counter.

"What's up, Luis? Can we talk a minute?"

"You stole my gun," Luis said, but in a low tone. Hannibal judged he wanted to sound tough, but all the fight was taken out of him in their last encounter. He'd defend his ego in another fight, but really didn't want the beating that they both knew he'd get. That was all fine with Hannibal.

"You know where my office is?" Hannibal dropped a card on the counter. "You're welcome to come by sometime and try to take it from me. In the meantime, I need to know if your old pal Greg has been around here in the last couple of days. I heard he was trying to get back in the old racket."

Luis' face contorted in conflict, the way a man's does when he's trying to decide which squirrel to run over on the highway. Hannibal waited patiently through the silence. When Luis shook his head and tapped the counter with his finger, Hannibal figured he turned out to be the less offending squirrel.

"Yeah, that bastard stepped through here last night," Luis said, keeping his eyes down the whole time. "He was looking to hook up with all his old contacts. Said he wanted to move some product fast. Not a word about cutting me into the action. Acted like I didn't count at all."

Hannibal thought exactly that but saw no reason to say so. "Well, as it happens, I'm running a special on pest removal this week. I'd be happy to get him out of your hair. Where can I find him?"

"I got no idea," Luis said. "But if he sets foot back in here you'll be my first call. I don't need that asshole in here poking into my business. I bet he's scoring from his old crew again, and I don't want to be in the middle of that shit between them Hampton Roads boys and MS-13, you feel me?"

Hannibal nodded and would have said more but his phone started vibrating in his inside jacket pocket. So he turned, tossed a "check back with you later" over his shoulder and headed back outside. He answered the call as soon as he was out the door.

"Hey man, it's Virgil."

"What's up, brother?" Hannibal asked, getting into his car. Virgil's voice always made Hannibal think of Eyore, the animated stuffed donkey in Winnie the Pooh cartoons.

"I'm down here on New Jersey Avenue," Virgil said. "Been poking around like I needed a fix and I think I found your man. Kind of a surprise, though."

"What? You found Young? The drug dealer?"

"Yep, but it ain't like you think. Dude's Indian or Pakistani or something. I think his name is probably J-u-n-g, get it?"

Hannibal fired up his Volvo while he processed that latest intel. "Don't sound like Nine-Trey but hey, he can still probably take me to Greg Howard and that's all I care about right now. Do you think you can keep him in our sights?"

"Don't worry, man," Virgil said. "As soon as I spotted him I called the rest of the team. We got a plan."

"Cool," Hannibal said, pulling out into midtown traffic. "I'm on my way to you."

"You'd be better off heading a couple of blocks north of me," Virgil said. "That way you can hook up with Sarge. You know, if there's an operation going on he's going to take charge of it. I'm walking, but let me get to the corner. Once I know where I am I can steer you right to Sarge."

To Hannibal's mind, if he didn't make it into heaven his eternal punishment would be driving through The District at the tail end of rush hour. Nothing so clearly defined hell to him better than creeping forward in jumps and starts, seeing a stop light ahead that you could not reach before it turned red, and sitting at an intersection ten seconds after the light went green because drivers from the left and right felt just because the car in front of them went through they should too. So the sun was dipping low before he spotted Sarge leaning against the wrought iron fence in front of an ill-kept yard. As he pulled even, Sarge jumped into the passenger seat.

"Head on up this way. I'll tell you when to turn."

"Where's Jung?" Hannibal asked, easing down the narrow lane, "And does he know he's being followed? Drug dealers I've been after are pretty good at spotting a tail."

Sarge chuckled. "Yeah, well this asshole ain't as slick as he thinks he is. Yeah, he's aware, but he got three big-ass brothers flanking him for protection. They keep their distance so customers can approach him, but they think nobody knows they're watching out for him. So we don't have to follow him. We just need to keep them in our sights. Virgil is tailing Jung's tail gunner."

"Okay, I get that. But what happens if he turns off? Or gets in a car?"

"Will you relax?" Sarge asked, leaning back. "Quaker's out in front of them. Nobody ever spots the tail that's in front of them. If they turn left I'll see them cross the intersection up ahead and I'll follow directly. If they turn right Ray's got them on the other side. We all shift, see?"

"Pretty slick," Hannibal said. "And if they get in a car…"

"That's what you're here for, son," Sarge said. "But I figure we're pretty close to home ground for these birds. They walking like they on their way home."

Hannibal had relied on Sarge's Marine Corps training often enough to just relax and let it be. They all moved slowly through the narrow streets until Virgil's text came through that their quarry had gone into a building leaving two of his muscle men outside. Hannibal found a place to park and walked with Sarge to the nearby corner. Virgil came down the block from the opposite end to meet them.

"I got the street number."

"Good, but I'm pretty sure I know which door to go in," Hannibal said. "I've been here before, recently."

"Good for you," Virgil said. "You see the boy sitting on the stoop? The other one's across the street, two doors down. Quaker and Ray are ready to deal with him."

"Virgil and I can get the boy at the door out of the way," Sarge said. "Then you can breach. You good with that?"

"I figure you got all the details worked out so you don't need me working it out. Let's just do it."

"Okay then," Sarge said. "Let's you and me go back to the car."

Hannibal saw Ray and Quaker walk down the street and step into the doorway across the street from the target building, on either side of the bodyguard who clearly didn't know he had been identified as such. Virgil was staggering down the street, not badly but just enough. Hannibal started driving down the street, stopping and starting as if he was looking for an address. He was almost even with the target door when Virgil engaged bodyguard number two.

"Hey, man," Virgil said, "I was looking to score. I heard this was the place to…"

"Get lost," the guard said, standing to make sure Virgil could see how big he was.

"Come on," Virgil whined. "Look, I got the cash."

Virgil's hand went into his pocket. The guard watched that hand closely and stepped closer to Virgil. With Virgil's frame blocking his view he didn't see Sarge burst out of Hannibal's vehicle. It took only four quick steps for Sarge to get within striking distance. Virgil twisted to the side, allowing Sarge's baseball bat to swing past his head and smack into the bodyguard's. Virgil caught him and eased him to the street. Sarge pulled out a couple of zip ties and yanked the guard's hands behind his back.

Bodyguard number one across the street was focused and alert. He snapped to his feet and started across the street but before he was off the sidewalk Quaker had one arm and Ray had the other. In unison they kicked his feet forward out from under him and slammed him down hard on his back.

Seeing that the situation was under control Hannibal hopped out of his car. Sarge and Virgil pulled their captive into Hannibal's back seat. Sarge took the wheel while Ray and Quaker manhandled their stunned captive into the car beside his partner.

Hannibal hardly registered what his teammates were doing. He had to get inside quickly before the drug dealer could prepare for company. While running to the door he fished his key ring out of his pocket. He needed to defeat the lock on the first try and he knew he had the right key for this one.

It's called a bump key, and every tumbler lock can be opened with the right one. Hannibal carried a half dozen with him. He knew of ten all told and one of them would open 90 percent of all tumbler locks. Because he was familiar with this apartment, Hannibal was confident he had the right key in his hand. He just had to slide the key into place and give it a solid smack. He chose to do that with the side of his automatic. The tumblers fell into place with a solid click and Hannibal shoved the door open, braced for action. Bump keys are easy to use and reliable, but they are not popular with burglars because they are not quiet.

Hannibal stepped forward, gun first, into a frozen tableau. The man on the sofa with his right hand under his windbreaker had to be Jung. His expression was a mix of fear, shock and anger but he didn't move and his eyes locked on the muzzle of Hannibal's automatic. The girl, sitting beside him, had been sorting small plastic bags. When she looked up, her face showed more shame and sorrow than fear.

"I'm a little disappointed, Marisol," Hannibal said, pushing the door closed behind himself. "Disappointed, but I guess I shouldn't be surprised. At the end of the day, you had to find a supplier."

Jung turned to Marisol with questions in his eyes. When he saw that she was not prepared to answer them he turned back to Hannibal. No words, just waiting for the next step. A professional, which made Hannibal a lot more comfortable. There would be no Luis-style nonsense.

"You are Jung?" Hannibal asked. That netted a nod. "First, I'm not here to kill you. I'm not here to rob you. I'm here for information. Sit your piece on the floor in front of you, we'll have a chat, and I'll get out of your business."

Jung almost smiled, and very slowly drew his weapon out using just his thumb and forefinger. Watching Hannibal closely, he sat the gun on the floor, being oddly careful not to scratch the hardwood. Hannibal sat in the chair facing him and leaned forward to retrieve the gun.

"Nine millimeter Smith and Wesson. I might need to keep this one. You'll just have to consider it part of the cost of doing business."

This time Jung really did smile. He pushed his fingers back through his straight black hair and waited. When Hannibal sat back, Jung sat back. Hannibal rested his own pistol on his leg, muzzle toward Jung. Jung kept his hands in plain sight. Marisol shrank into the far corner of the couch.

"So, what can I do for you, Mr...." Jung had an accent that you'd only notice if you were looking for it. He was probably under 40 years old and Hannibal thought he was from a Japanese background. He reminded Hannibal a lot of the actor who played Mr. Sulu on the old Star Trek television show.

"Jones. Hannibal Jones. Not a cop, just a private detective."

Jung nodded. "You are the one they call The Troubleshooter. I do not intend to give you any trouble to shoot. And my men?"

"Alive," Hannibal said. "Bumps and bruises."

"Thank you," Jung said to Hannibal's surprise. "What is it you need to know?"

"I'm looking for someone," Hannibal said. "This fellow used to sell for you, and I think he might be back at it."

"I see," Jung said. "And this fellow's name?"

"Greg Howard. He also goes by Vic Unser."

"Ahh... V," Jung said. "Yes he has indeed returned to the streets, and has been asking about getting back into business." Jung shook his head, as if the idea was too foolish to consider.

Hannibal nodded, staring hard at Jung. Jung relaxed and let him. After a few seconds Hannibal said, "You know, I was asked to find Howard because he was dishonest with his woman. Now I'm wondering if he's been lying to everyone. For example, he told people that you worked for him, dealing for MS-13. True?"

Jung stifled a laugh. "Really? V was a minor player, not long ago. He was one of my flock of birds. The one time I trusted him with some real weight he let himself get robbed."

"Yes. By his best friend as I understand it. So what brings him back?"

"Now he claims to have some product that he would like to dispose of before he leaves the area," Jung said. "Not sure where he came by this supply. Perhaps he robbed someone else. I don't know. But if I can increase my inventory for thirty cents on the dollar I won't pass it up."

"So you haven't done the deal yet."

"No," Jung said, glancing down at the transparent bags he and Marisol had been tallying. "This is previous inventory. V was going to meet with me tonight, to exchange cash for product. Unless of course you would rather I didn't."

Hannibal stood, his pistol hanging at arms' length, pointing at the floor. "Look, I'm not going to get involved in your drug business, but I'm also not going to help you put more poison on the street. So here's how this goes. You take me to Vic. As soon as I make eye contact with this bastard, you can go about your business. I don't pursue you. But what happens to Vic and the drugs he is trying to sell is no concern of yours. We good?"

Jung got to his feet. "No cops? No bruises? No violence I have to watch? Yeah, we good."

Chapter 33

Hannibal felt Marisol's eyes on his back as he escorted Jung out the door. His car was parked right in front of Marisol's place. The second Hannibal closed the door behind himself Sarge hopped out of the driver's seat and Ray slid out of the passenger's side, holding the seat back forward. Jung took the hint and dropped into the back seat beside Virgil. Jung smiled up into that dark face and the eyes whose whites looked brown. Virgil did not smile back. Ray pushed in beside Jung and pulled the door closed. Five seconds later Hannibal was driving down the narrow street with Sarge riding shotgun.

Jung leaned forward between the bucket seat. "Take a left up here and then just keep going straight. It'll be maybe ten blocks. Your friends don't seem to like me Mr. Jones."

"I don't like drug dealers much," Ray said.

Jung sat back and turned to his left, appraising Virgil's puffy forearms. "He sounds like a total outsider but you, my friend, have the look of a long-time customer. Maybe you can explain the service we provide in a capitalist country."

"That was a lot of years ago," Virgil snarled through clenched teeth, staring down at Jung. "I went through hell to get clean, and if I could get my hands on the bastard who sold me that first fix I'd rip his head off and shit down his neck."

Jung sat back and faced straight ahead for the remainder of the ride. Within 15 minutes he directed Hannibal to park in front of a run down brownstone just over the invisible line into Maryland. Hannibal couldn't tell you when The District had become Silver Spring, but Ray had been a limo driver in the city long enough to have a sense of where he was.

All five passengers left the car, although Ray just walked around to lean against the driver's door. Jung pointed to a basement apartment. Virgil parked himself at the top of the steps. Jung led the way to the door with Sarge and Hannibal at his back. A glance at Hannibal got Jung the nod he expected and he rapped three times on the door.

"Yo, Vic. It's Jung. I brought the cash. Let's do this."

Hannibal stepped in front of the door as soon as he heard movement inside. Virgil reached down and gripped the back of Jung's collar. "Let's get you home," he said in a low voice.

Locks flipped. Hannibal heard a chain, a dead bolt and a doorknob lock. The door opened about three inches and the man inside stared out to confirm the identity of his visitor. Hannibal snapped a hard left through the narrow opening, snapping the man's head back. Sarge's shoulder shoved the door fully open. Hannibal stepped inside, driving a hard right into the man's stomach. A left cross put him on the floor. Hannibal stood over him, tightening his gloves.

"I'm going to take it that you're Vic Unser, AKA Greg Howard: failed fight promoter, failed drug dealer, failed suitor of Connie Babcock, and runaway husband to Tina Unser. How's life, loser?"

"Who the hell are you? What are you busting down my door for? What did I ever do to you?"

Looking around, Hannibal saw that this apartment was set up very much like Marisol's but furnished and decorated in a more haphazard manner. Nothing hanging on the walls, no curios or knickknacks. No one considered this their home, just a place to crash.

Staring down, Hannibal was struck by two surprises. First, Vic was bigger than expected, easily Danny Hernandez's size, but compact as you might expect a wrestler to be, in jeans and a golf shirt stretched to its limits by his massive shoulders and neck. Despite the muscles, Hannibal was amazed at the fear bursting out of the wide brown eyes cowering beneath tousled brown hair. This guy was no gangster, or even a player. What had happened to him in the past to break his spirit? And how had he found himself in this game with serious bad men?

"My name is Hannibal Jones. Tina sent me. Now get up off the floor."

Greg rolled onto his knees, keeping an eye on Hannibal all the while, then lumbered up onto his brown corduroy sofa. Both hands went to his face.

"I think you broke my nose."

"I ought to crack your skull," Hannibal snapped. "So you go by Vic now? Or are you still Greg?"

"Greg is my middle name. I started using it when I opened the dojo. I thought it sounded tougher than Victor."

"Right." Hannibal kicked the cheap coffee table out of the way and began pacing in front of his captive. "Greg the tough guy. Vic the hustler. But you were neither. And frankly, I don't give a shit. I'm just here for my client. You took a chunk of change from your girl, Tina. A couple of hundred grand. And her Lexus. I'm here to get them back."

Greg stared into Hannibal's lenses for a second, then looked away. "I can't. I mean, the car's okay, in a garage downtown. But I ain't got the money no more."

"Bullshit," Hannibal said. He raised his right fist. Greg raised open hands and shrank back into the couch. Behind Hannibal, Sarge chuckled.

"I swear to God I ain't got the money no more," Greg said. "But if you give me a chance I can get it. Tell Tina I love her, and I can pay her back in a couple of days."

"A couple of days?" Hannibal stepped back and dropped on the Naugahyde chair against the wall. "Just where did you stash her money, Greg?"

"Not stashed," Greg said, palms forward. "Invested."

"In what?" Sarge asked. "Diamonds? You got the hook up with some smugglers or some shit?"

"No no no." Now Greg was leaning forward, rolling into a sales pitch. "Look, you brought Jung to my door so I guess you know who he is and what he does. I did big business with him not too long ago."

"Don't have patience for a long story," Hannibal said. "Get to the punch line."

"Okay, okay." Greg took a deep breath. "I used to run with this guy called Danny Hernandez. When I hooked up with Jung to help him move his product, me and Danny kind of drifted apart. But then one day I got ripped off by a rival gang."

"Really?" Hannibal shook his head, more amused than amazed.

"These things happen. But when it did, Danny and his girl Connie had my back. Jung, he wasn't so nice. I guess he works for MS-13 and them guys got no sense of humor. So I had to lay low for a while, switched it up, got papers for a false identity."

"Nice try, smartass, but you put the double identity out there months ago, before all this started. Tina wouldn't have married you overnight."

Greg waved his hands in surrender. "Okay, okay, you're right, it was already in place. The gig with Tina was sweet and she didn't know nothing about the drug stuff. But after I got ripped off I just stuck to the Vic side. Things was going okay and Tina, she took pretty good care of me if you know what I mean. But then Danny caught up with me. Turns out he managed to get his hands on the drugs I got stabbed for."

Hannibal sat up straighter. "Wait. You heard from Danny? When?"

"This is, I don't know, maybe a week ago?" Greg said. "I figured if I returned the drugs to Jung I could square things with him and get back in the game. The night I left Tina I headed straight to Danny. I handed him cash, he handed me a duffle bag full of white powder, and I ain't seen or heard from him since. But on the street the dope is probably worth half again what I paid him."

"You expect Jung to give you what it's worth?"

"Of course not. But I bet he'll give me what I paid for it. And if you fellows will just cut me a little slack, I can take the cash back to Tina and square things with her. Make sense?"

Of course it didn't but Hannibal didn't want to get into it with this clown. He drew his Sig Sauer and held it on Greg.

"Whoa. Whoa. It ain't got to be like that."

"You just sit still on that couch and it won't be," Hannibal said. With his right hand he waved to Sarge to follow him into the kitchen. They sat at the small wooden table, out of Greg's hearing range but Hannibal still had a clear view of the door. He kept his pistol pointed in that direction.

"What do you think?"

"What do you want?" Sarge asked.

"Want? Really? I want to throw this asshole in jail. I want to find Danny Hernandez and find out if he killed Quentin Sands. But more important, I want to get my client her money and her car back."

"Yeah," Sarge said. "But you also want to get clear of MS-13, brother. That bag of dope would probably buy you out of their pockets. You ought to think about that."

Hannibal closed his eyes and gritted his teeth. Sometimes he hated it when his good friend was right. He also hated the idea of disappointing a client, but the money was gone and there was no reasonable way to get it back. He had to make a move and besides, his left arm was getting tired. He stared down his pistol's front sight at Greg Howard, then started walking, following the invisible string that led to Greg's eyes. When he stopped in front of his target, gun still raised, he could smell the sweat of fear.

"Me and my friend here been talking, and we decided this can go one of two ways," Hannibal said.

Greg wiped his hands down his thighs. He was listening very closely, but all he could get his parched throat to release was, "Okay."

"One, I can put one of these 40 caliber hollow points through your dome, go home and tell Tina that you pissed away the money and your death is the consolation prize."

"Or?"

"Or you can take me to where you stashed the drugs. I relieve you of that burden, and you get to disappear back into the woodwork with the rest of the cockroaches. Oh, and Tina never sees you again."

"Don't worry," Greg said. "I got other plans. Although I don't know if that plan will still run with me if I don't have the money…"

Union Station was as much busy shopping mall as train station. Just blocks from the Capitol Building, it appealed to Hannibal mostly because it retained its historical feel despite being nicely restored for contemporary use. The Station was also Amtrak's headquarters. Hannibal had driven them there at Greg's direction. They followed him down to the Amtrak concourse and over to the Gate A counter. The clerk didn't look like he could be out of his teens, and wore the bored, defiant expression of a kid out of the Grease musical. He accepted Greg's ticket and cash with a heavy sigh and moved off to some hidden back room. He soon returned dragging a gray duffle bag as if it was more than his delicate constitution could handle.

"One of y'all want to give me a hand with this?" Greg asked. Sarge blew out a derisive burst of air, gripped the handle, and slung the bag up onto his shoulder.

"We done?" Greg asked Hannibal.

"Not quite. Where's the car? It wasn't parked near your house."

"I didn't want to make it too easy for that... my wife to find me," Greg said. "Actually it's in the station parking garage. Why?"

Hannibal held out his hand, palm us. Greg said, "Shit" under his breath, but pulled the key out of his pocket and dropped it onto Hannibal's palm.

"Why don't you take the Lexus and take this clown home?" Sarge asked. "I'll toss the luggage in your trunk and meet you there."

"Yeah, not anxious to have that bag in my car overnight, but it's the only thing that makes sense. Got a big day tomorrow."

Chapter 34

Thursday

Bright sunshine and low hanging clouds. Morning brought one of those days that made Hannibal feel strong and confident. Sometimes he wondered if he was solar powered. Gray days sapped his energy, but days like this energized him. In this case, that was good because he was about to step into the lion's den again.

The earlier part of the morning had been more pleasant. He heard a happy squeal outside his office scant minutes after 9am. A moment later, Tina Unser bounced through the door, walked around his desk and bent to give him a tight bear hug where he sat.

"You are a doll," she said. "Thank you for bringing my baby home."

"You're welcome, but it's not totally earned. I mean, you understand I didn't actually succeed."

Tina sat on the end of his desk, still grinning. "I get it. You can't recover money he already spent. But you found that little shit and recovered my car without a scratch. I'm grateful for that. Now where is he?"

Hannibal stood to get a little distance from his grateful client. "I don't really know, Tina. It wasn't a very pleasant encounter. But if he's still in the area, I'm pretty confident he'll be in jail before too very long. Looks like he was involved in a drug deal."

"Really? I guess I didn't really know my man at all. Time to file for divorce I guess."

"You don't seem too concerned about the money," Hannibal said.

"It's a big loss," Tina said, her smile dimming for a moment. "But you know the old saying. If you fall for a man and he takes your money and runs off and you never see him again, it was probably worth it."

"Well, even though I didn't recover your money I'm pretty sure I can guarantee you'll never see that boy again."

"Just as well," Tina said, waving her hands as if to dismiss her husband for good. "I'm just happy to be rolling again. I need to get into Washington this morning. Cindy and I are trying a new lunch place called The Royal. That girl of yours, she's just a sweetheart. You should join us."

"No, you girls go on and have a good time," Hannibal said. "I've got a very important errand to run."

It was a perfect day for a drive and Hannibal's first stop led him back down into Virginia. The Potomac glistened thru the line of trees that was just beginning to lose its leafy covering. Hannibal took a deep breath as he coasted slowly into Pablo Rodriguez' circular driveway. He took a moment to stare at the house that Cindy would love to have, then nodded at the two familiar door men as they appeared. Juan and Kenny stationed themselves on either side of the front door like a pair of mismatched lawn jockeys.

Hannibal closed his eyes for a second and took one more deep breath. "Fix your face," he told himself. "It's showtime."

Holding his most relaxed smile, Hannibal stepped out onto the flagstones. Without a word he popped his trunk and hefted the duffle bag onto his shoulder. He sauntered to the door, both hands gripping the shoulder strap so the two muscle men could see them at all times. When he was within two steps, Kenny reached over to open the door. Hannibal marched through the carpet to the familiar office. This time Pablo was standing behind his desk. He held a fat cigar clenched between his teeth, and Hannibal had not seen him wearing a shoulder holster before. He hoped that wasn't a bad sign. Pablo stood quiet until Hannibal stopped in front of the big desk and Juan and Kenny were on station on either side of the entrance. Juan pushed the door closed. The latch clicked like the period at the end of a long sentence.

"All right, boy," Pablo said. "Last night I got a call that Connie Babcock was home. So I was thinking I had reason to trust you. Then, when you called this morning and said you had something for me, I thought maybe you meant you had Danny Hernandez in your trunk. That would have made me very happy. But I'm looking at this bag and it ain't big enough to hold a body. So why am I burning my morning looking at you."

"Because I think you want what's in this bag," Hannibal said. "Maybe even as much as you want Danny."

Hannibal flipped the bag down onto the desk with a hard thump. Then he took two steps back and folded his arms. Rodriguez seemed to consider for a moment, puffed his cigar, and finally reached down to pull the long zipper. His eyes got bigger the farther the bag opened. His face made it clear that he was familiar with the big cellophane packs, each secured shut with a strip of duct tape. He pushed a hand into the bag to be certain there was nothing else beneath the evident contents.

"So what the hell is this?"

"Figured that would be obvious to a pro like you," Hannibal said, maintaining his smile. "I'm no expert but I figure that's got to be a quarter mill, or maybe three hundred K worth of heroin."

Pablo broke into a grin that matched Hannibal's. "I'm guessing you're right. Now the question is, where did it come from?"

"I was on Danny's trail. Got a tip that he had sold the drugs he stole. As it turned out the dope was easier to track down that Danny was. I figured you didn't really want Danny, you wanted what he took from your dealer."

"So you bring them to me? You want to sell me my own product?"

"Don't say it like that," Hannibal said. "The dope is all yours. I thought it might be the mechanism through which I could end our one-sided relationship in a friendly manner. And, honestly, I was thinking maybe a modest finder's fee was in order. Say... ten percent?"

Pablo took the cigar out of his mouth, threw his head back and roared with laughter. "You got some balls Jones. You know, word on the street is that Jung had the connect to my drugs. But he wasn't reaching out to me to give them back. This I found very insulting."

"So?"

"So bad luck befalls those who insult me," Pablo said. "As it happens, Jung got hit by a car early this morning."

"You don't say," Hannibal said. A chill rolled up his spine, but this was not the time to show it. Pablo was pulling packs of drugs out of the duffle bag and stacking them on his desk. Then he pulled out a paper bag and gave a puzzled expression.

"What the hell is this?"

Hannibal chuckled. "Like you guessed, I had to deal with this Jung guy. He drew on me and I had to slap him down. I took his gun, but I sure don't want it, and I damned sure don't want it connected to me. So I threw it in with the drugs, sort of like a prize in the Crackerjack box. I'm guessing you can always use another gun, especially one that will trace back to somebody else."

Pablo looked inside the bag at the gun, then dropped it back in the duffle. "You one crazy nigger, Jones. But yeah, okay, you been straight with me so maybe we'll do this your way."

"Got one other request," Hannibal said. Now his smiled dimmed a bit as Pablo stared at him. "We're done, you and me. I figure a quarter million in drugs is enough to get me out of your pocket for good. I want us to be square. Deal?"

"Yeah, I think we can go with that," Pablo said, opening a desk drawer. He dumped the gun out of the paper bag and replaced it with three stacks of bills. Then he tossed the bag to Hannibal.

"Our business is done. Now you go home and forget who I am, forget where I live, forget every conversation we ever had."

"With pleasure," Hannibal said. "I just want to be out of all of this for good. Love the house, Pablo, but don't invite me over for a cookout any time soon, okay?"

Hannibal turned and walked quickly for the door, his two shadows on his heels. Once he felt the sun on his face he gathered a deep breath and his smile returned. It was a beautiful day and getting better. After a few steps toward his car he turned left and wandered to the edge of the driveway. From there, thru the thin stand of trees he could see lights glinting off the surface of the Potomac. He stood still for a moment, absorbing the tranquility that being near water so often brings, until he felt the two gangsters move in close behind.

"Okay, what do you think you're doing?" Juan asked over Hannibal's right shoulder.

Hannibal released a long sigh and dropped his chin to his chest. "Well, honestly Juan I was just relaxing for a minute and enjoying the peace and quiet this environment offers. And admiring this beautiful view your boss has paid for. And waiting for my friends to get into position."

Hannibal spun fast and hard, putting everything he had into a left hook that smashed into Juan's solar plexus and doubled him over. Kenny's right hand flashed to his pistol but before he could get his barrel pointed at Hannibal he felt a similar cold steel tube pressed against the back of his head.

"Give me an excuse," Rissik said through clenched teeth. As he stepped out of the trees an armored SWAT team appeared, each man scanning the area with an assault rifle. They swarmed toward the front door like ants on a dropped candy bar. Two of them slung their rifles on their shoulders to pull Juan's and Kenny's hands behind them while Rissik kept his service revolver on them. The officers secured the gangsters' wrists with zip ties. Only when the pair was led away toward an armored truck did Rissik holster his weapon.

"That was ballsy as hell," Rissik said, "But it looks like it all worked. Guess Rodriguez really did think he could trust his control over you. Well, we've got him now for sure, but just having his body won't mean a thing without solid evidence. What are we going to find in there?"

"Well, unless he's a lot faster than I think, you'll find a crapload of heroin in a big gray duffle bag."

"And we're looking for a drug dealer's gun?" Rissik asked, turning his eyes to the same view Hannibal was reviewing. Behind them the screaming indicated that there were a lot more people in the house than Hannibal had been aware of. They were pouring out the door in single file, again like ants, with police driving the long line forward.

"No, actually I've got that gun," Hannibal said. "What you'll actually find in there is my gun. The pistol used to kill Quinten Sands. I figure finding the murder weapon in Pablo Rodriguez' possession should take me off the suspect list and make his legal defense a bit more complicated."

Rissik turned to his friend and raised an eyebrow. "You know damned well he didn't pop Sands. In fact, he might be the only person I know didn't. But I'm not too proud to admit that he's an important catch and I'll take anything that helps land his ass in jail."

"I guess that will include the word of a private detective about what he saw in the house," Hannibal said.

"Yeah, well as long as you'll testify that you were being held here against your will," Rissik said. "That was the only way I was able to get a warrant for this place."

"Orson," Hannibal turned to the cop. "I understand the narrative here. I wrote it, man. I won't let you down. With luck this will deal a serious blow to MS-13 in your county."

"Yeah," Rissik said. "A good day's work, and it ain't even noon."

"I suppose so," Hannibal said, heading for his car. "But I've got another stop to make, remember?"

Chapter 35

Hannibal waited almost a full minute after he knocked on the door. He heard reluctance in the slow turning of locks, then the door swung inward very slowly. Marisol's face hung low, her eyes looking out from under her light brown curls.

"Come on, don't be playing shy. Let me in, unless you're busy. Where's your boy Jung?"

Marisol stepped back from the door, her head almost hanging. "He left. He came back last night after you took him away. He walked in, grabbed his clothes and shit and just… just left."

"Uh-huh," Hannibal said, pushing into the room. "And what about Luis?"

"He ain't been back since you put him down."

Hannibal nodded. "I figured as much. I don't know why you were messing with those little guys anyway. You are too big a woman to be letting these little guys push you around."

"Don't be mean," Marisol said. "You know why I do it. Why I do everything." She waved a hand at the new coffee table, at the tiny Polyethylene bags scattered across it. Hannibal wondered for a second if Jung had replaced the table he put Luis through.

"Yeah, I know. You need to get yourself clean girl. Go back to being the athlete you used to be. I know a couple of good programs."

Marisol stared at his shoes for a moment. When she looked up it was as if all of the life had been drained out of her. Or may, Hannibal thought, life had drained her of everything.

"I can't. I just can't. I know I need to, but I'm just not that strong."

"Yeah, I was afraid you'd say that," Hannibal said, stepping past her. "So I figured I'd help you out."

Hannibal reached back to the door and let Orson Rissik in. Marisol's eyes grew to the size of saucers but she was paralyzed, not quite knowing which way to jump. She and Rissik both stared at the coffee table, before Rissik raised his gaze to Hannibal.

"Seriously, Jones? Just possession? That is one hell of a stretch with this much stuff in plain sight."

"Come on, Orson," Hannibal said, waving toward Marisol. "This look like a criminal kingpin to you? She don't need a long stretch inside. She needs rehab. She can shake loose from this drug thing if you give her a chance."

Rissik set off Marisol's startle response when he turned to her. "Is he right, girl? Can you get away from drugs for good? Or are you just a career criminal with a pretty face that fooled this big sucker?"

Marisol appeared to teeter on the edge of indecision until she caught Hannibal's eyes. His facial expression was asking her the same question. "It's on you, Marisol," he said. "This is it, the rest of your life is right here, right now."

She licked her lips, stared at the table heavy with the little packets of white powder, and clenched her eyes tight. Hannibal raised a hand to Rissik determined to give Marisol time to come to the right decision on her own. Finally she opened her eyes but looked only at Rissik.

"Yes," she said, raising her fists facing each other as if she was inviting handcuffs . "I can't keep doing this. If you can get me help, I'll do whatever I need to. Can you really get me into rehab?"

Rissik gave her a sad smile and waved her hands down. "We don't need cuffs on you. And yes, I'm pretty sure I can get you on that path. I can see you're no big deal in the drug world, so come on and I'll take you in and we'll see what we can do."

As the three moved toward the door together, Rissik asked, "You knew Danny Hernandez, right?"

"Oh, sure," she said. "Danny and I were… well, yeah, I knew him."

"Then I'm sure you knew some of his friends," Rissik said, pulling out his cell phone. "I'd just like to try some photos." He held the phone up to her face and began flipping pictures. "This guy?"

"That's Greg, Danny's partner."

"Him?"

"Danny's brother Ozzie."

"And her?"

Marisol rolled her eyes. "Connie Babcock. He was butt over boots for that bitch."

"Is that like head over heels?"

"Yeah. But that bitch was screwing every player in town."

Rissik didn't intend for the next photo to be part of his array, but Marisol reacted to the photo as much as the others.

"Yeah, that's Quentin."

"Wait, you know him?" Hannibal asked.

"Well, yeah," Marisol said, as if it was obvious. "He used to hang with Danny too. He wasn't a gangster but it always felt like he had his own agenda. Pretty sure he was banging Connie too. Him and Danny, them two had serious beef. Wouldn't surprise me if he capped Danny."

"Or vice versa," Rissik muttered under his breath. He had brought only one officer with him on this trip, at Hannibal's request. As that man eased Marisol into the back seat of the patrol car, Hannibal turned to the only policeman he called friend.

"Listen, Orson, thanks for doing this. I know you could have been a hard ass about it but that girl's not…"

"Hey, I get it," Rissik said. "You handed me the head of Fairfax County MS-13. I was glad I could do something in return."

Hannibal nodded. "Like you said earlier, a good day's work. So where you off to now?"

Rissik reached for the cruiser's passenger door. "Not the most fun part of the job. On the way here I got the call that they found Danny Hernandez. Headed down to the county morgue. Want to be there when he's identified by the family."

"What?" Hannibal snapped. "You got Danny's body? I wasn't even sure he was dead. And it sounds like you were not even going to tell me."

Rissik had just opened the car door. Now he paused, took a deep breath, waved to his driver, and closed it. Then he took Hannibal by the arm and pulled him a few steps away.

"Hey, you get that this is police business, right?" he said in a low tone. "You found the girl you were hired to find and escorted her home. You found the man you were hired to find and, maybe you didn't get everything the client wanted but you closed the case. You got on the wrong side of a killer mob but squirmed your way out from under all that. So tell me, what's Danny Hernandez' death to you?"

"Well, I could say that backtracking Danny's movements might possibly lead me to the cash Greg gave him for the drugs, cash that technically belongs to a client. But we both know that would be bull. The truth is, Danny Hernandez is unfinished business. And so is Quentin Sands for that matter. Danny's cause of death could yield clues to what the hell happened here."

"Yes and it's my job to make good use of those clues," Rissik said.

"Yep, your job," Hannibal said with palms raised toward Rissik. "No question. But there's a puzzle here begging to be solved. I'd really like to follow through on this."

Rissik considered for a minute, then glanced at the patrol car. "Think you can stay out of my way?"

"Guaranteed. So, can I come with?"

"Okay, I guess, if you feel like wasting the rest of this beautiful day on the road."

Chapter 36

Hannibal followed Rissik's car in his Volvo to drop Marisol at the detention center in Fairfax. Then he followed Rissik to the nearby Subway to pick up lunch to eat in the car on their unexpected drive south.

"So, Fairfax County doesn't have a medical examiner?" Hannibal was talking to his dashboard, listening to Rissik chewing his ham and cheese sandwich in the car in front of the Volvo. "I figured you'd have your own guy there in the government complex."

"Some detective," Rissik replied. "All corpses in Virginia are handled by a state medical examiner system. When an autopsy is required it's done in one of four offices scattered around Virginia. Each of the four offices is staffed by its own forensic pathologists, death investigators and other morgue personnel."

"But you got some control over the nearest one, right?"

Hannibal heard Rissik chuckle through the speaker. "Fact is, nobody controls the medical examiners. They're real independent. And we're not going to the nearest one anyhow. That would be Manassas. I know those folks pretty well and when I have a murder in my county they do right by me. But whose case it is doesn't matter. It's where the body is found. Since Danny Hernandez was found by some hikers just inside the Tidewater District, his body is being handled by the folks in the Norfolk office."

After yet another three-hour drive, Hannibal followed Rissik's vehicle though the Midtown Tunnel to a modest building clinging to the edge of the Sentara Norfolk General Hospital grounds. He parked beside Rissik's vehicle and headed for the door. Rissik caught his arm.

"Ground rules, Jones. In there I'm a cop investigating a murder and you're a private citizen consulting on the case. Listen, observe, and keep your mouth shut."

"Relax Chief," Hannibal said. "I won't embarrass you."

Hannibal was surprised at how relaxed security was inside. But then he realized that no one would have much cause to break into a morgue, and the inmates were unlikely to try to leave. He did note two burly armed men in uniform standing on either side of the divided swinging doors he assumed led to the examination room. While Rissik signed them in at the reception counter, Hannibal eased over toward the guards, one black and one white. When Hannibal saw them raise their awareness levels he slowed his walk and produced his credentials. They looked, nodded and relaxed. Hannibal stepped close enough for some confidential conversation.

"This has got to be the easiest security gig on the planet," Hannibal said with a smirk.

The white guard, whose nametag said "Lutz" blew out a skeptical puff of air. His partner, labeled Parker, said, "You think? Brother you don't know the kind of drama that goes on in here when people come to identify the remains."

"Yeah, man," Lutz said. "People get to yelling about how it ain't fair, she was too young, that other driver ought to hang, or the drug dealer ought to be shot. There's a lot of anger, a lot of pain, and sometimes they want to take it out on the furniture or the windows. That's when we earn our pay."

"Yeah," Parker said in hushed tones. "We see it every day, but a lot of people don't get it, what we know. Every death is unfair. Everybody dies too soon."

Rissik slapped Hannibal on the shoulder and the two men pushed through the doors. The next room had high ceilings and soft lighting. Comfortable chairs sat back against cream colored walls. A tall woman in a lab coat stood facing Nicky and Ozzie. Their faces were hard to read beyond the obvious grief. The woman wore an expression of well-practiced sympathy. Her face was ghostly pale behind lipstick that was barely a shade darker than her skin. Even her auburn hair, limp and straight, appeared to be in mourning. When she turned to the newcomers she showed no curiosity or interest.

"You are the police," she said in a dry, pinched voice. "Doctor Audrey Staub. I'll be with you in a moment. These gentlemen are here for an identification."

Nicky Hernandez turned to Hannibal with an outstretched hand. Hannibal didn't imagine why. Perhaps he just felt he needed to do something but didn't know what. Hannibal gave him a firm handshake.

"Sorry for your loss." It was what he knew to say.

"Nice to see a familiar face," Nicky said. "I guess you been looking for Danny for a while. Hell of a thing but it looks like they found him."

Staub, in front of a large window, said, "When we received and found his ID in a pocket we reached out to his father and brother. We recommended an internet ID using video but they both insisted on coming in."

"I got to know for sure if this is my Danny," Nicky said. "Ain't natural, a father burying his son, but I got to be sure,"

Rissik faced the bereaved father. "Sir, we are here to speak with the medical personnel in as part of investigating the death of your son. If you like we can wait outside until after you…"

"No," Nicky said. "Stay. If it's true, my Danny won't care who's here. If it's not, it won't matter at all."

Staub walked to the end of the window and put her hand on a control knob. "I have to warn you, this will be difficult."

Nicky and Ozzie moved close to the window. Hannibal and Rissik stepped back in concert as if they had rehearsed it. Staub turned the knob and a curtain drew to the side. Hannibal limited his gasp but couldn't contain it entirely. On the other side of the glass a mangled body lay on a table. He still wore tattered trousers and part of a tee shirt. Face and arms were covered with second and third degree burned flesh. Ozzie clenched his eyes and turned away, then slowly turned back to look closely. The corpse's face was almost gone but, unlike in comic books, most of us don't need to see someone's face to recognize them.

Ozzie broke the silence first. "Those are his chinos, papa."

"His hands," Nicky said. "I know my Danny's hands. My boy. My boy."

Rissik put an arm around Nicky's shoulders. "Sir let me help you with the paperwork. I know you have some tough decisions to make, and you'll want to going and start making the final arrangements."

Ozzie held his father's arm and the three men walked off toward another waiting room. Hannibal hung back. Staub looked up and this time showed some curiosity.

"Doctor, are you the forensic pathologist who will be performing the autopsy?"

"My actual title is death investigator."

"Well I was hoping to share some background information with you," Hannibal said. "With all due respect to your profession, I know that sometimes the cause of a death can seem pretty obvious."

"Well, when you find a pilot in a ditch covered with fallen foliage not far from the plane he was flying…"

"Yes ma'am," Hannibal said. "I just wanted to share some reasons I suspect it might be more complicated than that."

Staub stared at her clipboard for a moment. "Rissik brought you in on this?"

"Yes. This death overlaps with a case I was working."

She nodded. "Let's step into my office."

"Will you let me take a look at the body?"

"No," Staub said, shaking her head.

"Well then there's no point," Hannibal said. "I can tell you what you need to know right here." When Staub huffed her impatience he continued. "Look, I'm pretty sure this fellow was being pursued by not one but two different domestic drug cartels. He stole money or drugs from some very bad people. I think it's possible that someone figured a way to kill him after he took off. You're obviously a skilled professional and you wouldn't want them putting anything over on you, right? I'm just saying, take a closer look."

Staub turned her head so that her hair fell to one side and she stared at Hannibal out the corner of her pale blue eyes. "And just what do you think I should be looking for?"

"I don't know," Hannibal said, reaching to touch her elbow. "A cut that might not be caused by the crash, like a knife wound."

"Or a bullet wound?" she asked with raised eyebrows. "Yes, we often overlook those."

Hannibal pulled off his sunglasses to make firmer eye contact. "What about a small needle mark on his neck? Or a perimortem bruise at the back of his head, like if someone knocked him out…"

"Perimortem?" Staub almost chuckled. "That means at the time of death. All of his injuries will be, or should be, perimortem. I think the word you're looking for is Antemortem."

Hannibal looked down, shaking his head at himself. "Sorry, I don't have your level of expertise of course. And I'm not trying to tell you how to do your job, Doctor."

"Audrey," she said. She laid her empty hand on his, the one holding her elbow.

He knew she could see his discomfort and maybe that softened her attitude. "Thank you. Audrey. I'm Hannibal. And I guess I thought if you saw defensive wounds or evidence of death caused by anything other than the impact…"

"I understand," she said. "And I appreciate your sincerity. Tell you what. I'll keep an open mind on this one when I do my examination. And if anything looks out of the ordinary to me, I'll give you a call."

"Oh, I'd very much appreciate a call from you," Hannibal said, handing her his business card. "And if you find anything worth talking about... well, I won't turn down an invitation into your office a second time."

Chapter 37

When Hannibal caught up with Rissik in the outer waiting room, Nicky and Ozzie were still there. Nicky's eyes glowed with anger, although Hannibal could see he was on the downside of that phase of his grief.

"I know he was mixed up with those gangsters," Nicky said. "If I can find the boss I'll make him pay myself. I got some tough friends too, you know."

Hannibal noticed Ozzie starting to slide away toward the parking lot. Hannibal gripped his sleeve and gently but firmly steered him back toward Rissik.

"What's up Ozzie?" Hannibal asked. "Your dad's ready to kill whoever got Danny popped but you look more scared than angry."

Nicky turned to his son, whispering something in Spanish Hannibal didn't catch. Then Rissik turned his sharp blue eyes on Ozzie, who wilted under that stern gaze like a lily in the sun."

"I didn't want Pop to know but I did some work for the gang too. They were part owners of the dojo. They moved some drugs through there for sure, but the big money came from fixing the fights. Pretty hard to do that with boxing these days, but the MMA is still pretty open to it. That was Danny's main hustle, setting up the fighters to take a dive. If they took him out, I might have a target on my chest too."

"I wouldn't worry about it too much" Rissik said. "We were able to find the man at the top of the local MS-13 machine. You'll be happy to know he's in custody and I expect he'll be behind bars for some decades to come."

"It was a fruitful morning," Hannibal said. "but I've got some other things to take care of. I'll catch up with you later, Orson."

Hannibal headed off to his car having had enough of death and even the thought of it for one day. Opening his car door, he gazed up for a moment at the perfect clear sky. A bank of dark clouds was rolling in from the west. It reminded him that in his life, the clear sunny days never lasted very long.

Comfortable behind the wheel, Hannibal started the engine, kicked on the air conditioning and pulled out his phone to check for messages. He saw that his friends had all heard the news about the raid on MS-13 and Rodriguez's arrest. Four notes reworded the same message: they were all glad that threat was over and hoped that Hannibal didn't get dragged back into the trial. He smiled thinking how happy he would be to testify against Rodriguez. He had just put the car into gear, about to move off, when his passenger side door opened and he found himself with unexpected company. For some reason, he found her smile disconcerting.

"Well good afternoon Ms. Babcock. To what do I owe the joy of your company?"

Her smile was as bland and joyless as always, as if she was exactly where he should have expected her to be and there was nothing unusual about it. "Well, that nice Officer Rissik asked me to come down, you know, to help with the identification of poor Danny. Then he said I should come over and talk to you."

"Orson called you in on this?"

"Well, not really," she said. "But I was there when Ozzie got the call. I spent the weekend with him. So we were sort of a package deal."

"Of course. You were there to mourn poor Danny," Hannibal said, with more of an edge to his voice than intended.

Connie Babcock didn't seem to notice. "Yes, poor Danny. He just never had a chance. The last time I saw him we were sharing a quiet dinner and he was talking about going straight. He was just waiting for some money."

"Money? Let me guess. He was going to get some from his old friend Greg Howard."

A wave of emotion passed over Connie's face. Hannibal thought it might actually be surprise. "Why, yes. How did you know? He said he had scored some drugs and Greg was going to buy them off him."

"Let me get this straight," Hannibal said. "Danny bought drugs for resale?"

Connie looked down at her hands. "I guess it doesn't matter now, but I think Danny might have stolen the drugs from that gang he was working for. He wanted them out of the dojo so maybe this was his way of trying to hurt them."

"So he steals drugs from MS-13 and turns around and sells them to Greg?" Hannibal said, mostly to himself. "Gutsy move."

"Yeah, Danny was a good guy, kind of heroic," Connie said. "I'm pretty sure that was why he went to see Sands at his place. I think he was giving him the dirt that would sink the gangsters."

Hannibal started his car and slipped it into gear. The black Volvo was rolling slowly toward the parking lot exit. Connie didn't react. Apparently she was ready to go wherever Hannibal decided to take her. "You know, Sands took me to the rental that night when I found you." He said. "After Danny or somebody knocked me out and dumped me on the lawn, I'm pretty sure Sands took my gun. Now he's dead. But if you got the story right, maybe some MS-13 goon gunned him down. If Danny and Sands were hanging together, Rodriguez would have figured they were partners. What I don't get is why I get pulled into this whole thing to begin with. Why was your mom maneuvered into calling me for help?"

Connie gave a high, breathy laugh. "Well that part's pretty obvious, silly. Quentin liked me but he was terrified of Danny. I think he brought you over there that night so you would fight Danny. He sure wouldn't have had a chance against him, but you look like you might have kicked Danny's ass if you'd had a fair shot at him."

Hannibal was driving in a slow aimless circle around the facility. His mind worked better when he wasn't sitting still. "I guess that makes a kind of sense, but if you're right about all that, it would make Quentin Sands a bit of a dick."

"I'll admit it was kind of a dirty trick," Connie said, "But not much harm done. I mean, both you and Danny survived the night okay. If Danny had been quicker he might be alive today. I mean, he knew the gangsters were closing in on him. He was smart to run, but maybe shouldn't have tried to rat on them. I'm thinking Quentin met him at the airport and maybe they got into it." She stared into Hannibal's eyes as if a new thought had just struck her. "Gee, do you think Quentin might have killed him?"

Hannibal spotted Nicky and Ozzie Hernandez just pulling out of their parking space. He swung around in front of them and stopped. "I think this is your stop," he said, looking straight ahead, not at Connie. She nodded, smiled, and got out of the Volvo. As soon she shut the door Hannibal hit the gas.

Connie appeared to be right at the edge of a lot of criminal activity. She was involved one way or another with almost every man associated with this case. She had given him quite a bit of data to process. He was pulling the timeline apart and putting it back together in a variety of ways. Some of those possibilities made more sense than others, but in all of the likely patterns one element didn't fit well to him.

How did Connie Babcock know that Danny was going to the airport?

Chapter 38

Friday

Hannibal sat in the car until the last note of Wanted Dead or Alive faded out, then cut the engine and got out. It was a gray day, the clouds looking not so much angry as complacent. Or maybe disillusioned. A sharp breeze foreshadowed a strong rain but he figured it was hours off. Incoming storms had their own scent and he could smell it coming. He crunched across the parking lot hoping he wouldn't be driving home in a storm for nothing.

Not much more than twenty-four hours had passed since Hannibal had passed through the doors of the Tidewater District's Medical Examiner's Office. The receptionist recognized him, pushed a button on her phone and waved him on to the waiting area.

The air conditioner was working a little too hard that day, so Hannibal paced for awhile instead of sitting. He couldn't keep from glancing at the drawn curtain every few seconds, remembering yesterday's ugly view, like a horror film on a high definition television. After three minutes that felt like half an hour Dr. Staub stepped into the room carrying her ever-present clipboard.

"Good morning, Doctor. Thank you so much for agreeing to speak with me."

"No need for such formality," Staub said, sounding very formal to Hannibal. "Detective Rissik asked my office to cooperate with you as much as possible. We did fast track the autopsy in question and honestly, you didn't need to drive all the way down her to discuss the results."

"Yeah, I feel kind of stupid now for driving all the way home yesterday," Hannibal said, "But I know I do better with facts in person. Things get lost on the phone. Up close and personal is just my style I guess."

"Well in that case," Staub turned quickly, and Hannibal noted that the lab coat disguised a pleasing figure when it hung static. She waved to him to follow and seconds later he stood in an even colder room appointed with the kind of medical props he was used to seeing in television operating rooms. Was the formaldehyde smell that strong, or were his senses just filling in what was expected?

Staub hitched up her skirt just enough to sit comfortably on a tall stool. "I want you to know I'm very glad you were here yesterday. Your insistence that the obvious cause of death may not be the final answer got me thinking. I'll tell you now that there were no defensive wounds as you put it, and no bullet wounds or knife wounds." She paused to shake the grin that was pushing onto her face. Hannibal appreciated that she was having a little fun with him and said, "Yeah, that was pretty silly, eh?"

"Still I decided to do a few things I might not have done otherwise. I don't usually do a blood panel in the case of an accident. I also decided to check stomach contents. A few surprises surfaced."

He hated this game but so many people loved to play it. "So tell me, Doctor, what kind of surprises did you find?"

She smiled big and rubbed her hands together. "Well for one thing, the initial screening came back negative, but I'll do some more focused blood work."

"What would prompt you to do such a thing?" Hannibal asked. He dropped onto another stool and lean forward like a student who didn't want to miss anything.

"Well, the first clue was his tongue," she said. "He had bitten it."

"Could that have happened at the moment of the crash?" Hannibal asked.

"No, this was more like he chewed it." She shook a finger at him to make her point. And her smile said she was proud of her observational skills.

"And that means…"

"Not much by itself," she said, showing her palms the way a magician might at the moment a coin disappears. "But his stomach didn't look quite right either. And then I saw the blistering in his intestines."

Hannibal's head snapped back. "What the hell?"

"Yes, that might indicate the presence of toxins, perhaps highly toxic alkaloids."

"So, he was poisoned?" Hannibal said. "That would certainly make flying a plane difficult."

Staub shook her head. "That would depend on any number of things. The dosage for example, and the timing."

"But it sounds like you're saying Danny couldn't have gotten into the plane to fly it."

Staub shrugged. "Well, I guess he could have committed suicide. Taken off and drunk some sort of poison cocktail after he was in the air. Or someone could have made him drink it after takeoff." Now she pushed her face very close to his, and there was a twinkle in her eye. "But that's not what happened."

Staub jumped when Hannibal's phone buzzed. He yanked it out of his jacket pocket, annoyed when he saw the caller's name. Then his irritation faded when he realized that he had news to share. He held a palm to pause her while he talked.

"Orson! This is a surprise. I told you where I was going this morning, but I thought you had no further interest in Danny Hernandez' death. That, of course, is a big mistake because, if you haven't seen the autopsy report…"

"Jones, I hate to interrupt you but this woman's been bugging me all morning," Rissik said.

"Woman?"

"Sophia Babcock," Rissik said through clenched teeth. "Apparently she doesn't have, or want, your number, but she sure knows how to get hold of me."

Hannibal's smile dropped. "Is she okay?"

"She's fine," Rissik said. "But her cockamamie daughter is missing again. She's afraid the mob found the girl again and honestly, I couldn't tell her with any certainty it isn't true. I thought maybe you'd go down there and lay some of that P.I. charm on her, and…"

"Yeah, yeah, yeah," Hannibal said. "I'm pretty much done here anyway. I'll go see her and see if I can get a clue to the missing daughter's whereabouts. I got a feeling I'm going to want to talk to her anyway to get this crazy case figured out. Now that I know Danny was murdered, somebody's going to have to pay that bill."

Chapter 39

From Norfolk, Virginia to Charles County, Maryland, was a long drive leaving Hannibal with lots of time to think. This time he decided to dodge the expressway as long as he could, heading north through small town Virginia on Route 17, also called the Tidewater Trail by almost nobody anymore, but a solid drive without that "interstate" feel. He hooked right at the four corners onto A.P. Hill Boulevard which was really Rte 301 to everybody he knew. The four-lane blacktop ran straight through Virginia farm country until it stretched over the bridge across the Rappahannock and continued its run through Maryland farm country. Fall foliage appeared to be coming out early in this area, which helped him relax while his mind tried in vain to Tetris the timeline of Danny Hernandez's last few days into a pattern that would point to his killer.

The Angel's Watch Shelter was where this whole mess had started, at least for Hannibal. He pulled up to a curb two blocks away out of habit and strolled to the building. From outside, this looked like a warm, loving home for some well-to-do family. But as is so often the case, the truth was a pale shadow of the appearance. He paused for a moment to consider what he was walking into, but just as his foot landed on the first porch step, Sophia Babcock burst through the door, arms outstretched, ample bosom bouncing left and right.

"Mr. Jones! I knew you would come if I called. You found my beautiful little girl once, but now I need you to save her." She slammed into Hannibal, nearly knocking him over, her thick arms squeezing him, grinding the twin pillows on her chest into him.

"Take it easy, Mrs. Babcock," Hannibal said, gasping for breath. "I'm sure it will all be fine. Let's have a seat and you tell me what's going on."

Hannibal managed to settle into one of the white wicker chairs on the porch and motion her into another before the verbal dam burst.

"They took her, Mr. Jones. They came and took my baby."

"And just who are they?" he asked.

"You know," Sophia almost sobbed out the words. "Those gangsters. Those killers. She told me how you rescued her from them before."

"Gang members?" Hannibal asked, leaning closer. "They came here? You saw them?"

"No no. I don't... at least I didn't see them. But I know it. She's gone."

Hannibal mustered a comforting smile. "Mrs. Babcock, gone appears to be Connie's default setting. And the gang boss who pursued her before is in jail now. I saw him hauled away. Besides he no longer has any reason to be after her."

"But that's not true. One of them came here looking for her just last night."

Hannibal paused for moment. It wasn't so far-fetched that someone in MS-13 imagined Connie was involved in their recent troubles and was bent on revenge. Every member he could identify was being held but there were a lot more of them running loose, hidden but always on the move like roaches in a tenement.

"You said someone came looking for her?" Hannibal asked. "I don't see how they could have found her here, but I know they did before. A man I assume. He came alone?"

"Si."

"Hispanic?" he felt silly, but he had to ask.

"Oh yes," Sophia said. "One of those street boys in khaki pants and a big shirt. It didn't hide the big shoulders or the bulge in his belt. Short and thin but a lot of muscles. And jumpy like maybe he was on drugs or something. They called me to the door and he asked me where Connie was, like he knew her. I was so scared, but I didn't tell him nothing."

Hannibal nodded. "You spoke to him? Salvadorans you think? The gang that caused all this trouble, their leaders are all South American."

"No, not this one," Sophia said. "His Spanish was Cuban. Is different."

Hannibal knew she could not be mistaken. He might not be able to spot the difference, but Sophia Babcock would no more confuse a Cuban with a Salvadoran than a Korean would confuse a Thai with one of his own countrymen. So, this was no high-level gangster. Which meant that Connie was not a major priority. And the fact that he was armed didn't mean much. He figured they all were most of the time.

"Ma'am I don't want any harm to come to your daughter, but I have to tell you she's pretty good at hiding herself."

Sophia used a fingertip to wipe an errant drop of water from the corner of her eye. "Yes, Connie is very good at taking care of herself. She tells me that all the time. But I can't stop thinking that they found her once. These people are everywhere and they never stop."

Hannibal sat back to consider that. The girl had shown a lot of heart in the face of some pretty scary characters, but she had been found because of what appeared to be her primary weakness. She had too many connections to too many men, and most of them walked on the dark side of the street one way or the other. On the other hand, he didn't want to make a career out of rescuing this one girl with a weakness for bad boys.

"Ma'am, have you spoken to the police about any of this?"

"What good would that do?" she asked. "They don't care about my little girl. You are the only one who has helped us. Won't you help us again now? I have some money…"

"No, no, don't worry about my fee," Hannibal said. "I don't know if I can help at all this time, but I'll give it a try. You've spoken to her in the last few days. Do you have any idea where she might go if she's scared?"

Sophia shook her head and Hannibal could almost see the worry flying off her. "No. That is one reason I am so worried. She has no one she can trust. She has no home, no safe place. She told me the one boy she was dating has been killed. And another man she was friends with was murdered. All in just the last few days. She has no place to go."

Hannibal sighed, considering how Connie's ties to humanity were being cut. But he did know one possible connection not yet severed.

"Okay Mrs. Babcock," he said, standing. "I might have an idea of one person she might turn to if she's in trouble. I'll go ask a few questions and let you know what I find out. There just might be one man willing to help her after all."

On the drive back to The, District Hannibal considered how much mileage he had put on his car during this case. He might have to trade Black Beauty in soon, and a lot of his recent road time had been in pursuit of Connie Babcock. Pulling into a space in the M Street garage he recalled that he was not the only man who had logged serious mileage chasing Connie for a variety of reasons. She seemed to be the catalyst that kicked off a lot of reactions.

Nicky Hernandez looked haggard and drawn when he opened the door. Because he was shorter, Hannibal was always surveying the top of his head which today had gone without attention. His thinning hair wandered without direction, revealing much of a balding skull. His once proud shoulders sagged and even his eyes were at half mast, mourning the death of his son.

"Mr. Hernandez. I didn't get a chance before to tell you how sorry I am for your loss," Hannibal said. "May I come in?"

Nicky slouched back into the house with Hannibal following. He pulled two beers from the refrigerator without asking, and Hannibal dropped into the same seat he had taken there before. Everything looked the same to him, but he knew the world must look different to a man who has lost his son. Nicky settled onto the chair on the other side of the table, took a long drink, and finally focused on Hannibal.

"You have more questions for me." It was more statement than question. "You want to know why my Daniel is gone. How this could happen. Who to blame. I do not know the details, but I know who is to blame. It is his Papa, who could not steer him in the right direction."

"With all due respect, Nicky, there is evidence that Danny may have died because someone was trying to rob him," Hannibal said. "There is no way that guilt attaches to you. And I did not come her to try to get more answers from you or to get to the bottom of anything. I really just wanted to know if his girl had come by to pay her respects."

"His girl?' Nicky asked

"Yes. Connie Babcock?" His girl as much as anyone's Hannibal thought. "She was at the medical examiner's office."

"Oh yes," Nicky said. "That girl. She did seem close to Danny. But no, I haven't seen her since we went to identify the... identify him."

Hannibal smiled as he watched his best lead evaporate, and washed the loss down with another swallow of beer. He looked around before asking his next question.

"Do you know if Ozzie has seen her?"

"Ozzie?" Nicky glanced around as if he had lost his second son unexpectedly, as if his next move would be to look behind the couch. "I don't really know. Was he home today? Oh yes. He was angry about something. He was so upset about Danny's death. He was." Again his eyes swung up to focus on Hannibal. "Yes. He was looking for the girl."

"Looking for Connie?"

"The same girl you asked about," Nicky said. "He was looking for her. She told him she was staying with her mother but he says she wasn't there. He thought she might know who really caused Danny's death. I told him it didn't matter. Danny was gone and nothing he did would bring him back. Instead we should be praying for his immortal soul."

Things got quiet while images rushed in on Hannibal unbidden. Sophia's description of the gangster who had come looking for Connie could match up with Ozzie. But no, why would Connie be avoiding Ozzie? He was the last man she could trust. Or, might she be afraid of him? What could have happened since yesterday morning? Could Ozzie be right? Could Connie have information about Danny's killing somehow? Or, was Ozzie just stepping up as the last remaining boyfriend, only to be rejected by the girl he had tried to keep safe when his brother was in the hospital?

Hannibal had thought Ozzie would in fact be her go-to man for protection. Hannibal had come to Nicky Hernandez because he thought this apartment might be Connie's emergency safe haven. Now, with no car of her own and knowing how easy it was to monitor airports, bus stations and train stations, she would want to go to ground someplace. She'd need a safe hiding place. But where?

When the one idea wandered into Hannibal's head it brought a surge of adrenalin with it. He was energized because he realized that if it occurred to him it would occur to others. And if he was right, Connie's best chance for survival was for Hannibal to be the first to guess and arrive before anyone else.

Hannibal stood quickly and drained his beer. "Nicky, thank you for your hospitality, but I need to get back to work. Again, I'm sorry about Danny, and I hope you and Ozzie come through this okay."

"I can only hope Ozzie will learn from this experience and not do anything stupid," Nicky said. "I don't think I could survive losing both my boys."

Hannibal whispered amen as he headed for the door.

Hannibal gritted his teeth and blasted his stereo all the way down to Colchester, Virginia. He drove two blocks past the little white one-story house and pulled over to the edge of the sidewalk-free road. It was a long drive if he was wrong but well worth the gamble.

Walking slowly toward the house, he considered how everything fell into place when he looked at the whole case and put Connie Babcock at its center. If each of the men he had encountered was a circle on his Venn diagram, this house was the single point of overlap. The house Quentin Sands owned and had rented to Danny Hernandez to conceal her, that Ozzie hid in with her, that even Greg Howard visited looking for Connie. If she considered anyplace a home base, this would have to be it. And it might be the one location that unforgiving MS-13 killers did not know about.

He crunched up the long, gravel driveway and up the steps to the front door. It was locked of course, but that didn't mean it was vacant. He could open it but decided to do the polite thing. He rang the bell. He heard no answer. After ten seconds he pressed the button again. This time a twenty second wait. Might he be wrong? Feeling a little foolish he called out.

"Are you all right? You mother is worried."

"Go away!" It was Connie Babcock's voice, but it carried something he had not heard before. Fear. Even captured and beaten by murderous gang members she had not sounded afraid.

"Connie, I can't just leave," Hannibal said. "Let's talk, okay?"

"All right," she said.

Hannibal allowed a few more seconds of silence before he said, "Let me in, Connie."

Footsteps. Then the sound of locks being flipped. After another half minute he gave up and tried the knob. The door opened. He took two steps into the house and froze.

Connie stood with her back to the kitchen island. Her hair was a tangled mass and the bruises healing on her face reminded him of a peach that had been left out too long. He wasn't sure but there may have been a new one. Two of the nails on her right hand were broken, but she was holding the nine-millimeter pistol just fine.

Hannibal hated the taste of déjà vu, especially when it was garnished with irony.

"Close it," she said. Hannibal pushed the door behind him and moved to his right so he could see both Connie and the front door. He had memories of this place and he was not inclined to repeat mistakes.

"Is there some reason you are holding a gun on me?" he asked. "I understood it the first time, but…"

"I can't trust anybody," she said. "One day you saved me, next day I heard you were working for MS-13."

Hannibal pointed at his own face but he meant hers. "Are you all right?"

"Hitchhiked here," she said. "Driver got rude. I think he looks worse than I do."

Hannibal chuckled. "Somehow I believe that. Why don't we go get you some attention for that?"

Connie raised the gun a few inches higher. "How did you find me?"

"Seriously? Where else would you go? This was your safe haven before, the one place that maybe even vengeful gangsters might not find you. Your mother has no idea where this place is. Danny, who tried to hide you here, is dead. Sands, the owner, is dead. Greg, who came here to visit you, is in the wind. There's pretty much nobody to point in this direction."

"You're so fucking clever," Connie said, emphasizing the profanity the way people do when they don't generally use such words. "You think you know it all, don't you?"

"Not at all," Hannibal said, leaning back and crossing his arms. "There's a lot I don't know. The distance from the earth to the moon. The airspeed of an unladen African swallow. Or, how you knew that Danny went to the airport before anyone told you."

Connie showed no startle response, as if she had expected Hannibal's question. The pistol lowered in her hand.

"Yes, that was a slip, wasn't it? Well I don't mind telling you the truth. I knew when Danny went to the airport because I drove him there. He needed to get out, so I gave him a ride out there thinking I'd end up with his car. So I drive him out there. And guess who's car I spot in their little parking area? Yep, Quentin Sands. That kind of surprised me, but I dropped Danny and got out of there. I didn't want any part of any shady dealings between them. I thought at the time Sands was looking for insider info for his newspaper article. But it turns out he was really after me."

"Yeah," Hannibal said. "Every boy wants Connie."

"Don't make fun," she said. "I'm trying to tell you what happened. With Danny leaving town I was in no hurry to come back here. And I sure didn't want to be alone. So I went to Quentin's place."

"Seriously? You turned to that guy for comfort?"

"What do you know?" Connie asked, gesturing with her gun. "You never been a girl, alone, out on the street. At least he had no ties to these damned gangsters in MS-13. So I waited for him. But when he got home he was all freaking out. Said he had convinced Danny to take him with him wherever he was going. Says he got in the plane with Danny but they started arguing as soon as they took off. He's saying crazy shit like, he wanted me all to himself and Danny was in the way. Then he say he got so mad he…" Connie laid the gun down beside her and stared at the floor. After three deep breaths she added, "He said he pushed Danny out of the plane."

Hannibal snapped upright, and he felt a tightness around his chest. For a moment speech deserted him, but it didn't last.

"Are you saying that Quentin Sands killed Danny? And you knew this all along?"

"Well I couldn't hardly believe it," Connie said, leaning forward with her hand on the pistol. "He said he parachuted out of the plane and saw it crash and just ran off."

"And what did you say?" Hannibal asked, stepping closer.

"Why I told him he was crazy, that nobody does stuff like that, that I could never like a man who did something like that. I tried to leave but then he got real crazy and pulled a gun on me. It was like this one, not a revolver."

"My gun," Hannibal muttered. "Sands had my gun."

"I guess." Connie was looking more and more frantic. "He was waving it at me, talking all crazy and I didn't know what to do. I didn't think he'd shoot me right away if he really wanted me, so I begged him to put the gun down so we could talk. He put it down but then he grabbed me and he was being real rough, like he wanted it right then. I don't remember much then, but I know I pushed him off me and grabbed up the gun and…"

She stopped. Hannibal figured she wanted him to finish the sentence. He felt as though she had left him no choice. "You killed Quentin Sands."

"It was self-defense," she said in a high shriek.

"Yeah," Hannibal said in almost a whisper. "Maybe so. But he's no less dead. So you're here not just hiding out from MS-13 who might want revenge for your imagined part in the arrest of Pablo Rodriguez and his crew. And I guess you're also hiding from the police."

"Well, what the hell?" Connie asked through a sudden outbreak of tears. "Anywhere else I went somebody was going to come after me. After all I been through… doesn't a girl deserve a safe place to stay?"

Before Hannibal could respond, a new hysterical voice burst from the shadows behind Connie. "You fucking bitch! Perra sucia! Puta!"

Ozzie Hernandez stepped out of the shadows pointing a revolver that barely fit in his fist. Rage widened his eyes and stretched his mouth into a death's head grimace. "You knew! You knew all along how my brother died and you kept it to yourself? My heart was breaking. My papa's heart was breaking. And you smiled in our faces and said nothing. What kind of an evil creature are you?"

"No," Connie said, snatching up the automatic and swinging it toward Ozzie. "No! It wasn't me."

"But you knew. I went to your mother because I was worried. Then I came here to protect you in case you thought to come here. I was ready to go to war with MS-13 for killing Danny. But you knew. You probably know it all."

Hannibal stood with both hands raised, palms facing forward, as if he could push their emotions back to a safer place. But some part of him knew he could not. "Ozzie. Put that thing down."

It seemed inevitable. Ozzie's eyes rose to Hannibal. His right hand twitched, just the slightest bit. And Connie fired. Ozzie returned his attention to the girl but he could not make the pistol work. The hollowpoint round punched him in the chest and flared his shirt out the back. His face showcased more bewilderment than anger. He dropped his gun. He fell to his knees, hard. He canted forward but before his face could hit the hardwood Hannibal was crushing Connie's wrist in a vicious grip and her gun was falling toward the floor.

"He was pointing a gun at me," Connie shrieked. "A threat of lethal force. I was in fear for my life. I had to stop him."

"What you need to do now is shut the hell up," Hannibal said, wishing he carried handcuffs. "Unless you want to call a lawyer while I call the police."

Chapter 40

Monday

"Honestly, boys, Connie Babcock is a dream client," Cindy said. "If I was a criminal defense lawyer I'd take her on." She punctuated her comment by spearing a big forkful of her fried chicken salad.

"You're kidding, right?" Rissik set his burger down to stare at her. "At the very least she's a callous, casual killer. Even if neither of these deaths was premeditated. With all the questions swirling around her, I can't believe they only held her over the weekend. As soon as the courts were up and running, they cut her loose. And with such a low bail for a capital case."

Hannibal took another sip from his iced coffee drink and smirked. "She might be heartless, my friend, but she is also very sharp. Her story sounds weak to you and me, but it just about hangs together if you squint real hard."

"And a jury will," Cindy said. "They'll see those big brown eyes, that injured look and get behind this poor minority girl who lost her father so young and had to fend for herself. They'll vilify this long line of men who she will say all took advantage of her." Then she turned to Hannibal. "Was I right about the coffee drink?"

Hannibal nodded his approval. Coffee at a late lunch was not unusual for him. But Cindy had steered them to a Matchbox restaurant for him to try this cold brewed iced coffee billed as "Not your average Joe." He was sure it contained Irish Crème and maybe Crème de Cocoa but whatever was in there it was damned good.

"Right about the drink, babe, and probably about Connie Babcock. But I still have my doubts."

Rissik munched a handful of fries before speaking again. "Okay, Jones. I thought this meal was to celebrate closing a messy case. But at the risk of messing with my own closure record, what about her arrest bothers you?"

"Not the arrest," Hannibal said, "I mean, I'm a witness to one killing and I have no problem believing she'd kill for what she wants. But I also can't positively see her hand in the other two deaths. My real problem is Quentin Sand's part in all this. It just doesn't work for me that he'd kill a guy and jump out of a moving plane out of jealousy."

"Well, he was airborne," Rissik said. "Maybe jumping out of a plane was no big deal."

"That's just my point," Hannibal said. "I mean, this guy was a Ranger, but he got me involved with this case just because he didn't want to face Danny himself. Her story credits him with a lot more balls than that."

"I see," Rissik said. "And the whole thing about forcing him to drink poison? That bit does seems like a stretch."

"No, actually, I got no issue with that part." Hannibal said, wiping his mouth with a napkin. How did his woman manage to wolf down that messy salad and never spill a drop? She never even picked up her napkin until the end of a meal. "At least that fits in with my picture of Sands as gutless. But the timing still doesn't work for me. That's why I put in a call to Dr. Staub Friday night after they arrested Connie."

Rissik swallowed and washed it down with a long gulp of Ginger Ale. "Staub? You mean that babe you were chatting up down at the Norfolk medical examiner's office?"

Hannibal and Cindy both stared at Rissik, but the stares were different. Then Cindy turned her eyes to Hannibal, who turned his eyes to the remains of his lunch. "Yeah, seemed like there was an angle she hadn't looked at."

He clenched his eyes tight when his phone rang, then pulled it out and stated at the screen. "Speak of the devil." He took another long sip of his drink, then pushed a button. "Hannibal Jones. Hey, thanks for ringing me back, Dr. Staub. You got something?" He glanced up. Cindy's face said clearly that this was not a conversation she wanted to be left out of.

"Hey, I'm here with Detective Rissik, you know him, and my lady friend Cindy Santiago who is an attorney. Let me put you on speaker." Then he laid his phone in the middle of the table.

"Hello, Detective," Staub said through the phone. "And glad to meet you, Ms Santiago. Well, you probably already know that when we perform an autopsy, there are lots of things we'd never look for without a good reason. There are a number of tests one can do but they are expensive and we're using taxpayer dollars here. For example, each thing you screen for in a decedent's blood is a different test and they all cost money."

"Yes," Rissik said. "I'm sure you would not have screened for common poisons if this nosy P.I. hadn't made you think murder. The most obvious cause of death was the crash."

"Exactly so, detective," Staub said through the phone. "And I wouldn't have questioned the time of death either, but he made a good argument for wanting to be sure."

"Wait," Cindy said, now interested in the case. "I thought he was killed just before the crash. Wasn't he flying the plane?"

"Well that was the prevailing theory," Staub replied. "But this morning I looked at some other things. Like his stomach contents."

Only Hannibal was familiar with Stuab's tendency to stretch her story for dramatic effect. "All right. We already know his intestines were blistered, and I think you said that was some sort of alkaloids. I was thinking like antifreeze. But what was it about his stomach contents?"

"Well…" she paused again, causing all three listeners to lean in closer to the phone. "It's not what was there. It was the quantity. His stomach was pretty empty. Nothing weird there, except the whole alimentary tract was"

"Of course," Rissik said. "When you die you," he glanced at Cindy, "you void. But his pants were largely intact so you should have seen all the contents anyway,"

"Nope," Staub said. "I have to think someone cleaned him up a bit post mortem. And by the way, Jones, your guess about the poisoning would be wrong."

"Not antifreeze?" he asked. "Drain cleaner then?"

"No, tests showed this was from an organic source. It's in the Glycoside family. Glycosides are toxins found in plants. They all have at least one sugar molecule linked with oxygen to another compound, often nitrogen-based. They become harmful when the sugar molecule is stripped off in the process of digestion."

"That sounds like an ugly death," Rissik said. "Glad you did a full up autopsy, doctor. I guess all the useful info came from his stomach."

"Oh no," Staub said. "It got more interesting when I checked his eyeballs. You don't get that kind of damage in a crash."

At this point Cindy understood the game and joined in. "That's amazing Doctor. Where DOES a person get that kind of damage to the eyes?"

They could feel Staub's smile through the phone. "A freezer, I think. I believe the aqueous humor had been frozen."

"Well this changes everything," Rissik said. "All right, Doctor. Just how long was Danny Hernandez dead?"

Staub was pacing. Hannibal could hear her heels clicking across the floor. "I'd estimate the decedent was deceased three or four days before the crushing and fire damage of a plane crash. Of course it's hard to tell if the body was indeed frozen."

The three diners were speechless for a moment. Rissik broke the silence. "So it was all a setup."

"Danny was murdered," Cindy said, falling back against her seat, "and someone wanted us to think he died in the crash. But why would anyone…?"

Hannibal waved for the check. "I think we need to ask the person who lied to me so convincingly Friday. But I bet she's in the wind."

"Maybe," Rissik said. "But she thinks she's in the clear and she's not going to want to act like she's guilty of anything. She might be moving slowly, not wanting to draw attention to herself."

"Well, she'd be crazy to go back to the house where she killed a man," Cindy said. "Home to mama?"

"To say goodbye?" Hannibal asked. He reached for his phone, but stopped short of using it. "Her mother would surely deny seeing her, even if she was standing right in front of her. Orson, could you get the Maryland troopers to send a car?"

Rissik was already pushing buttons on his phone. "I'll put in the request, but I'm pretty sure you're wrong. This girl is too close to the end of her tether. So let me just check the airports, and the bus and train stations too."

The railway station in Burke Centre, an easy fifteen minute drive from Rissik's office, is a modest affair with two tracks and one daily Amtrak Northeast Regional train. When Hannibal reached the platform he found Connie leaning against the fence, facing the track, in the shadow of the quaint clock tower. It was the first time he had seen her dressed for comfort rather than to impress, in jeans, a plaid shirt, a denim jacket and sneakers. When she saw him her eyes flared wide for a moment. Then her calm demeanor returned.

"Come to make sure I leave town, sheriff?"

"Oh no, dear, I'm here to bring you back."

"Jumping the gun, aren't we?" Connie asked. "I haven't broken parole quite yet."

Hannibal put his hands in his pockets and turned toward the track. "I think train tickets landing you in Canada might be enough. If I was you, I'd spend the next few minutes finding, and hiring, a really good lawyer."

Connie stepped forward until they were side by side. "Now why would I need a lawyer, Mr. Jones," she asked. "I haven't done anything wrong. Besides, you're not an officer of the court, nor are you any kind of law enforcement person."

"And besides, you're smarter than me or any cop, right?" Hannibal asked.

Connie's smile vanished when Hannibal turned toward her. Her eyes bored into Hannibal. "I thought you were my friend. You don't sound like a friend right now. You're making me uncomfortable. I think I'll just take the next train."

Connie picked up her single small suitcase and headed toward the stairs to the parking garage. Hannibal followed at a comfortable distance. Connie stopped when Rissik appeared at the top of the stairs.

Behind her, Hannibal said "You know, I'm not Sherlock Holmes, and I'm not the gifted investigator that Detective Rissik here is. I generally get to the answer by following the same simple rules. But this time, you managed to throw so much smoke into the air that I forgot one of my most basic rules. I forgot to follow the money."

Connie spun to face him. "See, you lost me already. What money are we talking about?"

"Our boy Danny Hernandez did a pretty good-sized drug deal just before he disappeared. Whatever the details of his taking off in his brother's plane, I don't think he planned on travelling empty handed. I'm betting he planned to run off with all that money. Maybe a couple hundred grand in cash."

Connie's eyes went up and to the left as she listened to Hannibal's theory. "You think the money burned up in the crash? Oh, no, you think Quentin parachuted out of the plane with this big bag of money. That kind of makes sense."

"You are quick," Hannibal said, shaking his head. "But anyway, once I remembered the missing money I got to wondering about other stuff. For example, early on, when I was looking for you, I went to Ozzie's place. So all along I knew something nobody else did."

She couldn't resist. "And that was?"

"That someone had torn his place apart looking for something. Now what were they looking for? Seems the only thing in this whole case worth searching for was that big bag of money? But who, besides Danny and maybe Ozzie could have known about it? I could only think of one person. You."

Connie nodded. "Speculation."

"For sure," Hannibal said. "But then we met at the end of the trail: you, me and Ozzie. Now why was Ozzie looking for you? I mean, Sands was right about one thing. Evidently your milkshake DID bring all the boys to the yard, but I don't think Ozzie was following you with romantic intent. He wouldn't have needed a gun for that. And you genuinely did look like you were in fear for your life. So why was he really after you?"

Connie looked at Rissik, then turned back to face Hannibal. While she slowly paced backward down the platform, past Rissik, she fished her victim expression out of her kit bag and hung it on her face.

"Well, yeah, Danny had a big pile of money but that's all I know. Ozzie thought I knew where Danny hid the money, and he wanted it. He probably thought it was there in the rented house and you're welcome to look but I'm pretty sure Danny took the money with him like you said."

Again Hannibal smiled and shook his head, stepping slowly so as to maintain a constant distance between himself and the girl. "So you're saying you didn't know if the money was in the house or not, right? But you knew there was a gun hidden there though, didn't you? You had it in your hands when I arrived."

"Look, I'm really sorry I pointed that piece at you," Connie said. "I was so scared."

"Yes, I know," Hannibal said. "Scared Ozzie might say too much too soon. I think you killed him because he knew the story you told me was bullshit, and he figured you must have killed Danny."

In the distance Hannibal could hear the approaching train, rattling toward them. Connie took one more backward step and was now in the clock tower's long shadow. Behind her he saw the staircase leading down to the street. But her eyes were telling him she didn't want to run. She wanted his help.

"You don't believe that," Connie said.

Rissik called from the door, just loudly enough to be heard over the approaching train. "The trouble is, the autopsy told us that Danny was dead a couple days before the plane crash. There were also signs that his body had been exposed to some pretty low temperatures. That was enough for a warrant to search the Sands residence and his other property."

"Our forensics friend tells us there is no contact without transfer," Hannibal said. "I'm pretty confident they'll find skin in the freezer, and traces of something nobody wants where they keep their food. Human waste."

Connie's pulse was finally rising, her cool slipping away. "Why in the world would I want to kill Danny? He was good to me, and I didn't know anything about this money you're talking about."

"Sorry." Hannibal said, watching the train approach over Connie's shoulder. "Can't buy that. Greg Howard was still sniffing around you. You were his new plan, the real reason he was leaving his wife. She would have given him all the money he could want, but he wanted you. He wanted you to leave with him, and he knew you well enough to know you wasn't taking off with some broke guy. So it only makes sense that he told you all about the drug deal."

"That's crazy," Connie said. "Me and Greg were history since I got with Danny. I told you…"

"Actually, I'm thinking you were playing the long game with Greg," Hannibal said, getting louder as the train approached. "That would explain why you broke contact with your girlfriend Evelyn. I thought at first you stopped talking to her because you were in trouble. Now I'm pretty sure the real reason is that you were with Greg, not Danny, when you sent that birthday card to your mom that got this whole ball rolling. Danny was a good man, but Greg was making the real money, running dope out of the dojo."

Connie switched to sullen and injured, and slowed to let Hannibal get closer. "You don't understand. Danny was my love."

"No, I think money was your only love. And I think you were all prepped and ready to take off with Greg but you were having a little challenge prying him away from the woman he actually married. Then, before you could seal the deal, your in-between boy rips him off. That changed the whole picture, didn't it? All of a sudden, Greg is broke and on the outs with the bad boys. Danny was looking a little better since he had the drugs, but you knew Greg was the real catch, a man who could put some real money in your hand over time."

"Well if that was the plan it was a stupid one," Connie almost shouted. "Greg is in the wind."

"Quit playing stupid," Hannibal said. "I'm thinking that was the plan at first. But then you realized you could play all of them… all of US … and just take all the money and run. But you needed all the men to play their part to make your scheme work."

Rissik had walked up behind Hannibal. "Honestly, it's starting to sound like a little bit of a stretch, even to me. You think she worked all three of them?"

"They all wanted her," Hannibal said. "And they all wanted the money. So first she killed Danny…"

"I killed Danny?" Connie asked in a burst of righteous indignation.

Hydraulic brakes screamed as the nose of the locomotive pushed into the station. A handful of travelers moved around them to get through the doors Connie was eyeing.

"Danny was smart, tough, and careful," Hannibal said. "Who beside his girlfriend could have gotten close enough to poison him? And I saw the murder weapon, right there in plain sight."

Hannibal saw the first flash of fear in Connie's eyes. For an instant he thought she'd dive into the train but instead she dropped her bag, turned and sprinted down the open stairs. Her running shoes clattered down the steel steps with his leather soles slapping them in response. On the wide cement walk she broke to the right and darted through a cluster of people with the energy only desperation pumps into people. After several steps toward the parking lot she jogged right, moving toward the dense stand of trees that bounded the train station on that side.

The station was much like an island, tucked into a corner of the heavily forested Pohick Park. Hannibal darted in pursuit. He didn't know the area well, and did not want to risk losing sight of her. This girl had a gift for disappearing.

Hannibal was panting loudly when he broke through the tree line, working to keep Connie in sight. He dodged though the tall trees that were that odd mix of evergreens, elms and maples that ran rampant in Northern Virginia. About a hundred yards in he was neither gaining on her nor losing ground but he didn't want to turn an ankle trying to bring the girl down.

"Where do you think you can go?" he shouted. "There's nothing out here but…"

At that moment she stumbled onto a narrow paved path. Her palms hit the ground but she quickly regained her balance and moved forward as if running for her life, which perhaps she was. But now, despite his dress shoes and suit, Hannibal was gaining on her. Her breathing was more labored and soon she would grind to a halt.

Past Connie Hannibal could see they were approaching a street, a quiet cul-de-sac of what looked like townhouses. She staggered a bit, looked up, took in the view of civilization and turned to face him. Hannibal skidded to a halt on the path. It never occurred to him that she might be travelling armed until he was once more staring down the barrel of a shaking automatic.

"You know, it's a rare individual that gets to point a gun at me three times," he said, holding his hands out away from his body, palms toward her. "Think you can do it this time? Kill a man when he expects it?"

Even just a dozen feet into the woods it was unlikely anyone would hear a gunshot well enough to determine direction. Hannibal considered how it might go. She was still panting hard, her hand shaking with her breathing. He could dive to the side, off the path and draw his own pistol. She'd fire as soon as he moved. She'd hit him or she wouldn't. But while he prepared to move Connie surprised him with a question.

"What makes you so damned sure I poisoned Danny?"

"Seriously?" Hannibal asked. "Okay, the medical examiner told us it was an alkaloid, but something natural. But she said this stuff is nasty, causes blisters inside and out. It would be hard as hell to force someone to ingest it. So I figured it was something he ate, voluntarily, right?"

"Sure, but anybody could have…"

"Nope," Hannibal said, taking a step closer. "Only somebody who he'd trust to cook for him."

"His father?" she asked. "Or… I wasn't the only girl he was with."

Hannibal shook his head. "You're really reaching. And like I said, I saw them. Growing right in front of the rented house. Those pretty buttercups. People in rural areas grow them because deer eat most pretty flowers, but not these because they're so poisonous. You'd be hard put to find that stuff in the city. But I saw them there, with a patch that had been cut off. It was probably easy for you to just mix some into a salad for Danny. With a strong, sharp tasting salad dressing he would never suspect anything was wrong until way too late."

Hannibal watched her face darken, and the gun lowered a couple inches. He figured she was reliving that awful evening. She must have liked Danny at least a little bit.

"Yeah, that was the easy part. The hard part was watching the convulsions, hearing his screams. It's rarely fatal you know, because there's time for someone to call 9-1-1. It's a long, slow, painful death. And you watched it. You watched him die and kept him from leaving or calling anyone while he was too weak to resist you."

Then her face hardened and she raised her gun with both hands, her breathing steadier now. "You're a very smart man. But no one else will figure all that out."

Behind her, a voice said, "I got most of it." Her head snapped around to see Rissik, at the tree line, aiming his Glock at her. After one sharp breath she returned her focus to Hannibal.

"Drop your gun. I'll kill him." Connie turned to the side, so she could see both men. Hannibal was closer. Rissik was probably the better shot but if hammers dropped Hannibal was the more likely loser.

Rissik leaned against a tree, keeping Connie in his sights. "Look, Jones, I admit I get all you've said. But Danny was also a big guy. How does this little slip of a thing get his big, dead ass up off the floor and into the chest freezer?"

Hannibal's eyes narrowed, but Rissik responded with a soft smile. It struck Hannibal that Rissik was just playing devil's advocate, stalling for time and trying to relax the situation. Hannibal decided to make his case the way he might to a jury.

"Obviously she couldn't," Hannibal said. "That's why she needed the others. Greg thought he was getting the girl and getting his money back from the guy who got him stabbed. And he didn't have to kill anybody. He just had to help move his rival's corpse into the freezer."

"So except for him, everybody thought Danny was still alive," Rissik said.

"Yep, and she pulled me into it to cement the false timeline."

"You think I pulled you into this?" Connie asked, clinging to her innocent look even while holding a gun on him.

"This was probably your smartest play," Hannibal said. "You told Sands you knew a way to get Danny out of his way. He didn't know that was already a done deal, right? So you got him to play cop and convince your poor mother to call me. He might have thought it was a sneaky way to get someone else to give his rival some grief. In reality, it was a way of selling the idea that Danny was still around."

"She told you Danny was with her there?" Rissik said.

Hannibal nodded. "Actually, Sands told me Danny was there. Which, technically, was true I suppose. She wanted me to think Danny got the drop on me."

"Not Sands?" Rissik asked. "Or the brother, Ozzie. He was there with her too for a while, right?"

"Sands was too much of a wimp," Hannibal said. "And Ozzie wasn't a wrestler. And at this point I hadn't met Greg. In fact she had no reason to think I ever would. So when I found myself on the wrong side of a wrestling hold, I thought Danny."

Throughout this exchange, Connie's head whipped left and right, facing the speaker. Rissik drew her attention next when he said, "We've got you dead to rights, little girl. I should just shoot you right now."

Connie spun left, this time gun first. Her aim had just settled on Rissik when Hannibal dived forward. His shoulder crashed into her ribs as his right hand clamped on her right wrist. She hit the path hard, with Hannibal on top of her. Her gun skittered away from her. Lying on top of her, Hannibal could almost feel the fight flow out of her. He looked up to watch Rissik slide his own gun into the holster in his waistband. He walked toward down the trail, unhurried, while Hannibal wrestled Connie to her feet.

"Could you move with a little more urgency?" Hannibal asked, gripping Connie's upper arms. Rissik stopped for a moment to take in the picture, then pulled a pair of handcuffs from under his suit coat and pulled one of Connie's hands behind her to lock a cuff on. "I don't know if that little run constitutes a confession of guilt, but it certainly marks her as a flight risk. And of course, possession of a firearm is a parole violation."

"A senior detective like you still carries those things?" Hannibal asked as Rissik clicked the second cuff onto Connie's other wrist. She screamed over her shoulder at Rissik.

"Let me go! He's making all this up."

Hannibal ignored her. "So, you drove around to this end of the path while I chased this bitch on foot?"

Rissik nodded. "So, Greg Howard took your gun?" He was guiding Connie toward his car which was parked near the entrance to the cul-de-sac.

Hannibal, walking beside them, waved that comment away. "She kept Greg and Sands separate, remember? But the gun landed in Sands' apartment. Greg had no reason to go there. The only reasonable assumption is that Connie took my gun."

"Stop talking about me like I'm not here," Connie said through clenched teeth. "I didn't do any of that. And poor Danny was lost in that plane crash."

"You need to let that go," Rissik said. "We already know he was dead before the crash. Did you fly his body away?"

"I don't know how to fly a plane," Connie said.

"Right. You needed a pilot," Hannibal said. "Lucky for you, you had one. As I found out earlier, Sands had a private pilot's license too, and had done some sky diving. You probably promised him a big slice of the missing loot if he would help mislead the cops. So he went to the airport, took off in the Piper Cub and bailed out. He must have thought that the crashed plane alone would make people think Danny was on the run. What he didn't know was that you had stashed a dead body in the back."

"All that to cover up a murder," Rissik said, shaking his head. "So everybody would think Danny Hernandez died in a plane crash." Then he stared at Connie. "Too bad we can't question Quentin Sands about it."

"Yeah, he was kind of a loose end," Hannibal said.

"I liked Quentin," Connie said. To Hannibal it sounded less like a protest to him and more like practicing for a jury.

"Sure you did. But you were not about to share your newly found treasure with him. Besides, you knew he wasn't a killer. As soon as he heard that Danny's body was found in the plane wreckage he'd give you up. But no problem, right? You had my gun. And you had found out that killing a man wasn't so hard for you. So you went to his place and just gunned him down. Much cleaner than watching a man writhe on the floor while poison ate him up."

"How can you say that?" Connie asked. "You make me sound like some kind of a monster."

"No, just a psychopath," Hannibal said. "But not so crazy that you wanted to get caught. Leaving my gun in plain sight guaranteed that the police would waste time looking in the wrong direction. Problem is, I had no motive to kill Quentin.

In fact, knowing that Danny was already dead, nobody had a motive to kill Quentin except, well… you."

"That only works if somebody buys this whole crazy, convoluted story of yours." Connie stood rigid beside Rissik's car. Rissik opened the back door and stood behind her, ready to help her get in.

"Yeah, it is a little crazy," Hannibal said. "Even crazier that you would reach out to a gang boss like Rodriguez. But when I took a minute to think I had to wonder who at the Angel's Watch Shelter would know how to contact Rodriguez to let him know where you were. Of course, if my crazy story is right, you had good reason to want to make it look like you knew where Danny was hiding all that time. So you got yourself picked up by MS-13 so they could pull the story out of you. A story you wanted them to have."

"Seriously?" Connie said. "What kind of idiot would let themselves be taken by MS-13?"

Behind her, Rissik snorted. "Oh, wait, I know this one. The kind of idiot who knows Hannibal Jones will show up to rescue them. So you could look like the loyal girlfriend, and get the spotlight on anything and everything except you and the bag of money Danny had."

"Crazy, isn't it?" Hannibal asked Connie. "For most of this case I've believed, like your mother, that you were just constantly getting involved with the wrong kind of men. But the truth is, all these hustlers were just trying to make it in a tough world. The problem is you. You're the wrong kind of girl."

Connie's face dropped into a frozen mask. Her eyes were hooded and Hannibal thought that he was finally looking at her true face. Her voice dropped into a deeper register.

"All you've got is a big bag full of supposition, assumption, suspicion and innuendo." Connie said. "But there's no DNA, no eye witness, no solid proof. And your story is so convoluted that jurors won't be able to follow it.

Besides, look at me. No twenty-first century jury will convict me. And I think your friend here knows that."

Hannibal slipped his Oakley's off his face and his eyes bored into hers. "Did Ozzie know about the money? Did he know you had it? I don't think so. I think he went to the rental house because he also figured out you would hide out there. I think he was there to help you, to protect you. And yet, you killed him too."

"In self-defense," Connie cried. "You saw him. He was going to kill me."

"He had just heard you admit you knew how his brother died," Hannibal said. "I might have shot you under those circumstances, but I'm pretty sure he would not have, because he was under your spell too."

"Again, no proof," she said with a smirk.

"Except this time there is an eye witness," Hannibal said. "And I will have no trouble testifying in court that Ozzie Hernandez was putting his gun down when you killed him with no provocation, no cause."

"You can't," Connie said. "You already made a statement, didn't he?" That last was to Rissik.

"You did support her self-defense story," Rissik said.

"Yeah," Hannibal said, rubbing the back of his neck as if milking a memory out. "But you know, I was under her spell to, like all the other men in this case. No jury would have any trouble believing that." He raised a palm to Connie, as if explaining a simple mistake. "You see? I'll make it clear that you killed him in cold blood because he knew where the money was, and you didn't want to share it with him."

Connie lurched toward Hannibal but Rissik held her back "That's a lie!" she screamed.

"Really? Well good luck proving that."

Chapter 41

Sunday

The Royal in the LeDroit Park neighborhood serves a fine breakfast to Hannibal's way of thinking. He was partial to the flat, round unleavened bread patties called arepas. And after his last couple of weeks, the cuisine of Colombia seemed oddly appropriate. He knew Cindy also loved them, and she said so again when he opened his car door for her to get out.

"I do love the food here, honey, and appreciate you inviting me along today. I know you didn't have to."

"Yeah I did," Hannibal said, taking her hand. "I need you to control my behavior this morning. If I came alone, I might hurt somebody."

She giggled as they walked in the door. "You probably shouldn't have agreed to meet them, but since you did, let's just make the best of it."

Hannibal had a moment to consider how lovely his companion was in a simple, crème colored dress and matching pumps. He was not here for work, not really, so he had pulled off his gloves and abandoned his black suit for casual khaki slacks, a blue golf shirt and a brown corduroy blazer. His sunglasses stayed in place.

Tina Unser spotted them the second they walked in and waved them over. Cindy grabbed Hannibal's hand and pulled him across the floor to Tina's table. The two women beamed at each other like long lost schoolmates. Hannibal wasn't able to display quite as much enthusiasm. Nor was

Tina's seat mate. In fact he didn't look too sure if it was safe for him to be there. In that, he was probably right.

Tina stood and gave Cindy a hug before waving a hand to her partner. "Cindy Santiago, this is my husband. Vic Unser. Actually, he's Greg but I'm still getting used to that. Vic, you know Mr. Jones. This is his woman, Cindy. She's a doll."

Hannibal and Cindy settled into their chairs while the two women chatted. Coffee arrived, and the waitress offered them menus.

"Don't need them," Hannibal said. "The lady and I will both have the arepa rancheros."

He looked at Vic, but Tina spoke up.

"Yes, I'll just have one of the guava pastries, please. The big guy here wants your sausage, egg and cheese biscuit." She never looked at Greg for confirmation, and he never said a word.

The ladies fell into small talk, sticking to the weather, fashion and politics. The arrival of food forced a lull in the conversation. Hannibal was more than ready to tear into his arepa laden with cheese, beans, avocado and just a bit of cilantro. He was waiting for Cindy to begin when he saw Tina turn a sharp eye on her man. He seemed to take the hint although his mind seemed to blank for a second. Finally, he faced Hannibal and forced a smile.

"So. she poisoned him, eh?"

Hannibal recognized Vic's reaction to a kick under the table. Not sure he could have done much better he said, "Well, yes, that's what the evidence says. I imagine you heard it all when you testified."

"He had to tell them everything he knew," Tina said, "And everything he did. That's what my lawyers said. And that's the only reason he's able to sit here with us today."

After another uncomfortable moment Hannibal said, "So you're going with Vic now? For good?"

"Well, it is my middle name, and it's what Tina knows me as, so why not? I'm not hanging out with any of the people who knew me as Greg. In fact, to all intent and purposes, Greg is dead. No more messing with drugs, or the people who are involved in that stuff. I was lucky to not land in prison and I'm not going to chance ending up there ever again."

Was he trying to sell Hannibal or himself? Hannibal suspected both might be true.

"Yes, but he's Vic Howard, not Unser," Tina said over the rim of her mimosa. "You know, when this one won my heart we just ran off to Las Vegas to seal the deal. But of course he was using a false name, so that marriage wasn't really real, you know. So now we've got to do it all over again with his real name, to make it all official."

Cindy reached across the table to seize Tina's hands. "Well I certainly hope we can count on getting invitations."

"Oh of course," Tina said. "In fact, I hope I can count on you to help plan the affair."

Hannibal removed his glasses to lock eyes with Vic. "You won't be repeating any of your past mistakes, will you Vic? Tina is good people. And as you know, I'm pretty good at finding people."

Vic leaned in, his facial expression asking for mercy or at least a little understanding. "Look, if I had wanted to run I'd have done it the day you boys took Connie in. But I'm tired of making bad choices. I know what you said to me that day in my apartment but I had to see Tina again. She's my one shot at redemption, see? She'll take care of me. This is the right path for me. I'll just be content to be…"

"A kept man?" Hannibal asked, almost but not quite under his breath.

"A loyal, devoted husband," Vic shot back.

"Well, I expect you two to stay in touch and watch and see the kind of man Vic can be," Tina said with a bright smile. Hannibal nodded and shared his first sincere smile since entering the restaurant. When he first heard Vic had returned to Tina he bristled at the thought that this hustler, and Connie's accomplice, was getting away with it. Now he wondered if he was instead accepting an appropriate punishment.

Then she reached into her pearl covered clutch purse. "Now, you and I have a bit of unfinished business Mr. Jones." She pulled an envelope from her purse and slid it across the table to Hannibal. "I know this is kind of crass, but I wanted you to have your fee and it seemed even worse to drop it in the mail or something."

Hannibal looked down at the envelope, then up at Tina's beaming face. "Look, I appreciate the gesture but I didn't actually earn my fee…"

"Nonsense," Tina said, emptying her glass and waving for a refill. "You returned my car AND I have my husband back. For good. So this is what I owe you, plus a generous bonus. Now don't be rude. Just take the money. Maybe it will cover for some client who can't really afford you."

Hannibal was about to reply but Cindy dropped her hand on the envelope. "Thank you, Tina. I know just the client." She's recently lost her daughter in a way, and she could use some cheering up."

Standing on the front porch of the Angel's Watch Shelter on that sunny fall afternoon Hannibal mentally flipped the pages back to how this case had begun. It was here that Sophia Babcock had first gotten his attention and saw that he was a man who could help her find her runaway daughter. The paint on the railings was beginning to peel and he thought he might have to bring some white paint with him on his next volunteer visit.

Cindy squeezed his left hand as he knocked on the door with his right. Sophia opened the door and greeted her visitors with a big smile.

"I am so happy to see you Mr. Jones, Miss Santiago."

"Please," Cindy said, "can't I get you to call me Cindy? And it is so beautiful outside, why don't we sit on the porch for a while?"

The three of them relaxed on wicker chairs drawn into a loose circle. Hannibal caught the scent of the lilies someone had planted along the front of the porch. This was more than a safe place for its residents. It was home for as long as home was needed. He turned to Sophia but she held up a hand to forestall his speech.

"I think I know why you're here," she said. "But before you say anything I want you to know that I don't hold any bad feelings toward you, Mr. Jones. You are not the reason my Concepción is in prison. I love my daughter very much and always will, but I am not blind to the fact that she has done some very bad things. The Lord loves us all, Mr. Jones, but he makes us accept the consequences of our own actions. I will visit her whenever I can, but she and she alone is the reason she is in that terrible place."

For a moment Hannibal was lost for words. He finally managed to mutter, "That is very kind of you."

Cindy leaned forward and patted Sophia's hand. "You have a very kind heart, dear. And I know that Hannibal appreciates your sentiments. No matter what, no one wants to see their own child in prison. But we actually had another reason for coming to visit you."

Sophia looked bewildered as her eyes moved from one of them to the other. Cindy smiled and nodded to Hannibal, who pulled the envelope from an inside jacket pocket.

"We know that Connie being sent away is just one more blow on top of many others life has dealt you," Hannibal said. "I've had some good fortune, and thought it would be good to share it with you. Recently, another client paid me a nice bonus for work I did for them. I want you to have it."

Hannibal leaned to offer the envelope to Sophia, but her hand did not move. Instead, her smile became even broader.

"Oh, no, I couldn't. Please, if you have extra, make it a donation to the shelter. My heart may ache today, but as far as money, I'm doing fine."

It was Hannibal's turn to look bewildered. Sophia scooted to the edge of her chair and leaned forward to speak in a very low tone to her visitors.

"You see, my dear Concepción did one good thing. The day before she was arrested she left a big duffle bag here for safe keeping. I had no idea what was inside until she called for me to bail her out of jail. It is actually a big bag full of money. I had to take some out to bail her out of jail but of course that was returned to me when she went back to jail. I haven't quite counted it all, but it is quite a large amount. So I'll be moving out of the shelter next week. If I'm careful it will provide me with a nice, warm, safe place for quite a while."

AUTHOR BIO

Austin S. Camacho

Author ● Publisher ● Writing instructor

Austin S. Camacho is the author of seven novels about Washington DC-based private eye Hannibal Jones, five in the Stark and O'Brien international adventure-thriller series, and the detective novel, Beyond Blue. His short stories have been featured in several anthologies including Dying in a Winter Wonderland – an Independent Mystery Booksellers Association Top Ten Bestseller for 2008. He is featured in the Edgar nominated African American Mystery Writers: A Historical and Thematic Study by Frankie Y. Bailey. Camacho is also editorial director for Intrigue Publishing, a Maryland small press.

To My Readers…

First, THANK YOU for going on this Hannibal Jones journey with me. I hope you enjoyed the trip and will investigate Hannibal's previous adventures.

I love to hear from my readers! After you've read my novel please do send me some feedback. Your opinions and reactions will help me with shaping future novels. You can write to me at ascamacho@hotmail.com and I will always respond. You can also reach me through my website – www.ascamacho.com – see my latest news on Facebook
https://www.facebook.com/austin.camacho.author
and follow my random meanderings on my blog
https://ascamacho.blogspot.com

The only thing better than hearing from my readers is meeting them! So, if you're a member of a book club, I would love to see you. If your group decides to read one of my books I would be most happy to attend the meeting when you talk about it. That way I can answer any questions you have and fill you in on the background of how that particular book came to be (and bring along some special gifts.)

Thanks again for reading my work, and I hope I get the chance to meet you or hear from you in the future.

Ciao, for niao,

Austin

CPSIA information can be obtained
at www.ICGtesting.com
Printed in the USA
FSHW011321140719
60005FS